Where Colors Meet Codes

Unmatched Hearts, Volume 1

Luna Verne

Published by Luna Verne, 2025.

WHERE COLORS MEET CODES

First edition. March 11, 2025.

Written by Luna Verne.

Table of Contents

CHAPTER 1 1
CHAPTER 2 9
CHAPTER 3 19
CHAPTER 4 25
CHAPTER 5 31
CHAPTER 6 37
CHAPTER 7 45
CHAPTER 8 55
CHAPTER 9 69
CHAPTER 10 77
CHAPTER 11 83
CHAPTER 12 93
CHAPTER 13 105
CHAPTER 14 113
CHAPTER 15 125
CHAPTER 16 133
CHAPTER 17 143
CHAPTER 18 155
CHAPTER 19 165
CHAPTER 20 175
CHAPTER 21 183
CHAPTER 22 195
CHAPTER 23 205
CHAPTER 24 213
CHAPTER 25 219
CHAPTER 26 231
CHAPTER 27 237
CHAPTER 28 243
CHAPTER 29 253
CHAPTER 30 263
CHAPTER 31 275

CHAPTER 32..291
CHAPTER 33..299
CHAPTER 34..303
EPILOGUE 313

CHAPTER 1

He tore through my world like lightning splitting the midnight sky. Yet, unlike lightning, I heard him before I saw him. My soon-to-be mortal nemesis, in my most favorite place on Earth: the Renaissance Faire of Irwindeal. As an admirer of Gandhi, I abhorred violence, but on that warm spring afternoon, his words almost inspired blood on my knuckles.

I never expected to feel so emotionally charged that day. But it was the week I had finally ended things with Trent, my boyfriend, for whom I had moved to California. A boyfriend so self-involved he couldn't tell my favorite color or food, but could remember the exact time and date of his last haircut. That day, I was moving out of the apartment I had shared with him and called home for two long years.

The only sliver of real happiness during those bleak two years in Irwindeal was the bi-annual Renaissance Faire. Held once in spring and once in fall, it had been a respite for me, a home away from a home I'd never really had. When everything else in life demanded I be someone else, the Faire and its people embraced me without judgment. Best of all, for four weekends a year, I could forget I was going nowhere in life and be someone entirely different.

That sunny Sunday, I parked my car, underslept as usual, and walked through the Faire's entrance gate with a hot black coffee in hand. It was like stepping into an alternate universe. The Ren Faire was in full swing. As I passed through the wooden gates, the sounds of lute music and cheerful chatter greeted me, transporting me instantly to the 16th century. It was April, and the crisp spring air, along with the azure sky, set the perfect backdrop for the colorful banners fluttering in the breeze. Vendors lined the dirt pathways, their stalls brimming with handcrafted goods. Intricately designed leather journals, gleaming swords, and delicate jewelry sparkled under the morning sun.

It hurt, to observe people enjoying their creativity, and knowing I had lost my own spark.

I shook my head and breathed in the scent of roasted turkey legs and freshly baked bread as I made my way to the main area, scattered with stalls and tents. In a nice shaded corner of the park was my guild, chatting and laughing outside our tent. Our space was decked out with Jolly Roger flags, nautical maps, a big treasure chest, a cannon, and antique knickknacks. Tables were laden with muskets, trinkets, and pirate-themed books. My guild had essentially adopted me as one of their own. A family. We entertained visitors by dressing up as pirates and enacting skits.

I had finally started feeling comfortable in my own skin. Not happy, but accepting. I hadn't yet lost the weight I had rapidly gained over the past two years, and my acne hadn't completely cleared up. My eyes still looked like dark potholes, and my posture resembled a melting candle. Years of declining self-worth could do that. But I loved how my corset fit my imperfect curves and how the boots I wore under my skirt gave me a confident lift. The tricorn hat even flattered my limp hair. This year, thanks to a special budget I'd set aside for the Faire, I had even bought and worn Renaissance-era earrings made of faux rubies. All in all, I felt as confident and pretty as I could, given the circumstances.

It also helped that I was moving to an amazing new place, finally dusting Trent off me for good.

Mentally, I was planning my new life in San Diego, and arranging a table full of pirate trinkets and artifacts, when I heard him.

"This is what happens when people have nothing better to do with their lives," came a deep, resonant voice, dripping with disdain.

My head snapped toward the speaker. I saw his side profile first. A tall, striking man with chiseled features, dressed in navy blue chinos, a light grey shirt, and a sharp, well-fitted blazer. As furious as I was about his remark, I couldn't ignore his appearance. I had never seen clothes hang so perfectly on a body before. It was as if the body had been tailored first, and the clothes stitched around it. He was one of the few not dressed in Renaissance garb, standing close to our tent with two other people.

He swung his broad shoulders and surveyed the Faire through expensive sunglasses. "These people play pretend and call it culture," he added.

"Hey, be nice," scolded the woman beside him. She was dressed as a druid fairie, arranging wines on top of an impressive staff.

"Elena, you dragged me here on a Sunday morning. It's when I get most of my important work done. I should at least get to vent," the jerk responded. "But really, do these people actually believe they would've survived the Middle Ages? From the looks of it," he said, nodding toward a patron dressed as Bilbo Baggins, "they can barely survive in this world."

The guy standing between the jerk and fairie guffawed loudly. He wore shorts and a Nike t-shirt.

"You hear that, babe?" the Nike guy asked, still laughing.

"I do. Both him, and your laugh," the fairie replied.

"Oh... you mad about that, babe?" he asked, grabbing her and planting a patronizing kiss on her head. She looked furious as she untangled herself from his arms and rearranged the flower crown on her head.

"Elena, you're different," the jerk continued. "You're a respected, successful therapist. I doubt these people are making any real contributions to the world."

Now, before I tell you what I did next, it's important that you know the kind of person I am. I once ate dangerously salted pasta at a restaurant because I couldn't bring myself to send it back. In junior high, I sat through a two-hour class on a broken chair because I didn't want to raise my hand and ask to switch. In college, my best friend ghosted me for something I didn't do, and I couldn't even explain myself. I spent years with a self-serving man without telling him how much he hurt me. I was a nervous, anxious chicken in a human suit, and if I could avoid conflict, I would, at any cost.

But something about his voice, his remarks, and his overly coiffed hair stirred anger in me. His hands in his pockets, his overly shiny shoes...I wanted to punch him.

When I couldn't hold it in any longer, I dropped the spyglass I was holding, walked up behind him, and spoke in a quiet yet firm tone.

"Excuse me," I said.

He turned toward me, and the moment I saw his full face, I lost my voice. For a second, his piercing dark brown eyes seemed kind, as though they could only see me. But the very next moment, I saw them for what they were—a vessel of judgment and mockery.

"That's a pretty big talk from someone who isn't smart enough to realize he's insulting the very company he keeps." My voice trembled slightly but grew stronger with each word. "This isn't about survival in the Middle Ages. It's about celebrating art, history, and imagination. Things that enrich lives, unlike your narrow-minded judgments."

The air between us crackled with a strange mix of animosity and something else, something electric, undeniable. Despite his arrogance, I couldn't ignore the way my pulse quickened under his intense scrutiny or how his eyes softened for a moment as he took in my pirate garb and the fire in my eyes.

"Huzzah!" His druid-fairie friend responded to my outburst, raising her staff like a champagne glass.

"Ooooh," the Nike guy made a sound, "looks like someone just got schooled!" he laughed.

Everyone around us, including my guild, had stopped to watch.

My mortal enemy looked at the staring faces, then took a deliberate couple of seconds before responding.

"It might be the norm in your Middle Ages," he said, stepping closer, forcing me to crane my neck to meet his gaze. "But it's not 21st-century convention to eavesdrop and jump into conversations you're not a part of."

As he finished speaking, I realized how flustered he was. His tanned skin had grown warmer, his voice was on edge, and the veins in his neck were popping, even though his face remained composed. As much as I wanted to tell him off, I feared getting sliced.

I took a few steps back.

"Your voice was loud enough to be heard in the next tent," I replied. "Next time you don't want someone to eavesdrop, try keeping your contempt at a lower volume." I glanced at his attire and added, "Or maybe try blending in."

I wanted him to feel self-conscious about his clothes the same way he tried to insult us for ours.

He raised his chin to respond, but the fairie placed a calming hand on his arm. He glanced at her and shook his head.

"This is why I don't come to places like this," he muttered to her, though he knew I was within earshot. "These people think they're better just because they can't afford a suit." With that, he turned to his friends. "I'll see you guys tomorrow." Then, he walked away.

As soon as he was out of sight, the fairie approached me, her expression apologetic.

"I'm so sorry," she said. "I know it's not nice to hear those things, but please don't let his words spoil your day."

Her empathy struck a chord with me, and my anger melted away. I nodded. "Thank you."

"I'm Elena," she said, extending her hand.

"Ivy. You have a beautiful staff."

"Thank you! I love your earrings. And your corset! And that pin on your hat!"

I laughed. "Thanks." Her attempts to cheer me up, even though I was practically a stranger to her, didn't go unnoticed. My curiosity got the better of me. "You're really kind. Can I ask you something?"

"Sure."

"Why didn't you say something to your friend? In a way, he insulted you too, didn't he?"

She paused for a moment. "Long story," she said, her smile fading slightly. "But why don't you—"

"Babe," her boyfriend called out from a distance, impatience clear in his voice. "We gotta go!"

Elena's face fell, her fingers clutching the folds of her flowing green skirt. "Well, so much for spending a month perfecting this look." Her eyes trembled with a hint of disappointment, and for a moment, she seemed lost in her own thoughts as her energy dimmed. Then, she perked up again.

"Hey! But we'll have the fall Faire!"

"We do," I agreed. "I hope to see you then."

"See you then! Bye, and... I'm really sorry again."

I nodded, and she flew away.

The Faire continued to buzz around me, music and chatter filling the air. But my heart still raced. Not just from the confrontation, but from a confusing feeling I couldn't shake. I tried to focus on the present, to enjoy the event I'd looked forward to all year, but I couldn't.

Then the thought of a real problem hit me. Moving. I hated moving. I grew up in Sprigwing, Illinois, and stayed there my entire life until I finished my undergrad at UIS. That's where I met Trent. After we graduated, he wanted me to move with him to his hometown, Irwindeal, a city in L.A. county. We'd only been dating eleven months, on and off, but I didn't want to miss out on what I thought was a real relationship just because I was afraid of moving to a new state. Besides, the idea of leaving a place I didn't even like for sunny California was tempting. I wanted to be brave, to seize what I thought was my chance at the life I wanted. So, I said yes.

We were supposed to drive out together. I was packing everything I could because I knew how expensive California was, and I didn't want to waste money on things I already had. Moving back to Illinois wasn't part of my plan, anyway.

Then, two days before the move, Trent told me he had a high school reunion in Irwindeal and decided to fly instead. So, I packed the rental van and drove across the country by myself. I'm 5'3" and weighed 110 pounds at the time.

By the end of that miserable trip, my back was wrecked, and I had blisters everywhere. To make matters worse, Trent was too busy preparing for job interviews, because "apartment hunting took all his time". So I ended up unpacking alone as well. Ever since, even hearing the word "moving" triggered me.

But this move was worse. I wasn't just packing my things; I was packing up my dreams and the relationship I'd invested in for almost three years. The stress was nauseating. And don't get me started on the finances. Yesterday, I'd put down a huge deposit for the new apartment, leaving my bank account in the three-digit range.

As the sun began to set over the Faire, fear for my uncertain future gripped me again. Just like when I left Illinois, I wondered again if I'd ever find my way in life. But glancing back at the spot where I had stood up to a stranger earlier, I took a deep breath and smiled.

The tides were changing. This was just the beginning.

CHAPTER 2

I stood in the center of my old apartment, surrounded by boxes that held the remnants of a life I was desperate to leave behind. The walls, once suffocating with the weight of memories, were now bare, stripped of the art I had created but never dared to hang. The apartment was dark, muggy, and crammed with the energy of someone who had always taken more than he had given. I had asked Trent to give me a day free of him so I could do this. Yet his shadow still lingered in the corners, making me feel like I was doing something wrong.

But I had finally packed the last of my things.

"Are you sure you don't want to leave some of this behind?" Adrian asked, holding up an old Stars Hollow throw pillow whose edges were wearing out. Adrian was my best friend, and today, my lifeline.

"That pillow has seen more of me than anyone else in my life," I argued. "It deserves to go with me, not decay here." Stars Hollow, Gilmore Girls' quaint little town, and the pillow designed after it were the two places where I often took my tears and loneliness. "Its stink helps me fall asleep."

Adrian chuckled, tossing the pillow into a box labeled "Bedroom." He glanced around, his usually thoughtful face marred with concern. "Ivy, I'm really proud of you, you know. Getting out of this. Not everyone can do it. I know that more than anyone else. This move... it's a big deal."

"It is," I agreed, trying to steady my voice. Even now, every corner of the house reminded me of the last two years. The dining table where I'd spent countless nights sketching in silence, terrified Trent would mock my work if he saw it. The living room couch where he'd hogged every conversation, never letting me get a word in. The bedroom where I'd cried after he guilted me into canceling plans I'd looked forward to for weeks, just so we could do what he wanted. I took it all in, one last time.

"I've spent too long in this place, Adrian," I said, then. "Too long being a pillow myself. This move is how I'm going to take my life back and find out what I'm made of."

Adrian nodded, his expression serious yet kind. That was his superpower. "That's the Ivy I know," he said.

I'd met Adrian in eighth grade when he had just moved to Sprigwing to live with his grandparents. It amazed me how a new kid could walk into a school and town he barely knew, acting like he'd been part of it forever. Meanwhile, I had lived there my whole life and still felt like an outsider. I couldn't help but wonder how he did it. Almost like he read my mind, he sat next to me at lunch one day and asked what I was reading. I was deep into Anne of Green Gables and spent the entire lunch break raving about it.

Two months later, once we were close friends, he admitted he had already read the book but wanted to give me something to talk about. He was only thirteen! We'd been inseparable ever since. Until he left for college to study architecture in L.A. and be closer to his parents, and I stayed in town. Between classes and dating Trent, I lost touch with Adrian.

A year after I moved to California, when I started admitting the ugly side of Trent to myself, I felt lonelier than ever. That's when I thought of Adrian and emailed him, asking what he was reading. Just that one line. It was the first time we'd spoken in more than four years. He replied, 'can only rave about it at a lunch break.' So, we met for lunch the next day, and he became my rock again. Over the past year, we've rebuilt our friendship, leaning on each other and sharing everything. For months, he'd been trying to convince me that Trent wasn't the one. I finally accepted and broke up with him.

A wave of relief and sadness swept over me as I taped the final box. Trent was my first love, and as much as I had grown to hate him, I wasn't ready to let go of my feelings for him. The feelings that were more like a mourning for the death of our relationship. I forced myself to remember why I was leaving to keep the pain at bay. It wasn't hard. For almost three years, Trent had made me question my decisions, doubt my own worth, and feel inferior. He never gave me the space or time to be myself. He was a parasite that only took, took, and took, until I was nothing but a shell. This place… it was a tomb of who I used to be. Moving to San Diego, to the beautiful apartment I had found for myself, was a way of shedding my skin and finally living for me.

"I can't wait to be happy again," I mumbled as I placed my keys on the kitchen counter. Adrian crossed the room and pulled me into a tight hug.

"You will be," he said. "And what better place to do it than in a gorgeous apartment with an ocean view," Adrian said, smiling now. "I'm jealous you found that apartment first."

Adrian had just moved from L.A. to downtown San Diego for work when I first emailed him, and he often asked me to visit. Despite living in L.A. county, I had never been south. So when the time came to decide where to move after Trent, San Diego was the only place I could think of. Adrian lived in a studio, so we couldn't share the place, but this way, he'd at least be close.

Feeling lighter, I punched him in the shoulder.

"Dude, you live on the beach!" I said, mentioning his beachfront studio. "If your house was any closer to the ocean, you'd need a boat."

He grinned. "Yeah, okay. But it's no high-rise condo with a hot bachelor."

I laughed.

"I don't know if he's a bachelor, and I didn't say he was hot. I said he was nice."

After a terrible breakup, everyone makes at least one big, rash decision. Bangs, tattoos, a palette cleanser. Mine was signing a sublet agreement for an ocean-facing, expensive condo in a high-rise in America's Finest City. If I was giving myself a second chance, I'd rather do it looking at the Pacific.

I was leasing a bedroom in a two-bedroom apartment. That's all I could afford if I wanted to stay close to the beach in San Diego. Nolan, the guy, with whom I chatted on the Sublet app, said he owned the place and needed some extra cash for the summer. He sounded polished, no-nonsense, busy, and rich. Someone completely opposite of me. But when I cracked a silly joke, he laughed and told me he hadn't laughed in ages. That's why he was willing to let me move in by only paying a deposit and not a full month's rent in advance, as he had first expected.

He seemed like a sincere guy, and the app verified his profile with background checks and everything. So, I went for it.

"He better be nice," Adrian said.

I looked at him, feeling a sense of family, something I hadn't felt in forever.

"Thank you, Adrian," I said, my heart swelling with gratitude. "For everything."

Then I took one last look around the apartment. The walls no longer felt oppressive; they were just walls, plain and empty. The ghosts of my past were fading.

"Ready?" Adrian asked, placing the last box on the push cart.

"More than ready." I took a deep breath and followed him out the door, leaving behind the darkness of my old life and stepping into the light of what was to come.

ON OUR WAY TO THE NEW apartment, I stopped myself from expecting too much. I had seen pictures of both the building and the condo, and they were gorgeous, but I knew I didn't take to places easily. It always took me a while to fall in love with a space.

But I was wrong.

As soon as we stepped into the lobby of the forty-story building, Adrian and I froze, our mouths slightly open. It was grander than any five-star hotel lobby I'd ever seen. The vast space was framed by sleek marble walls, their cool gray tones complemented by warm golden accents shimmering in the soft glow of crystal chandeliers hanging from the ceiling like clusters of stars. Plush velvet seating in deep navy and emerald green was arranged around polished coffee tables, creating cozy enclaves for residents. The reception desk, a long, curved masterpiece of dark wood and glass, was manned by a sharply dressed gentleman who greeted us with a nod.

Adrian, taking it all in, whispered, "It's the usual modern aesthetic. Clean lines, open space, minimalist luxury. But they've nailed the execution. It feels like an art gallery and a lounge rolled into one."

It was hard for me not to be impressed, but when an architect with high standards gives his nod of approval, you know the place is special.

After picking up the apartment keys that Nolan had left at the reception, Adrian and I took the beautiful elevator up to the 31st floor. I still couldn't believe it. I was going to live on the 31st floor!

I opened the door to my new apartment, and my heart pounded in a rhythm that felt both thrilling and terrifying.

"Woah," Adrian exclaimed, stepping in behind me.

The space was a far cry from the cramped, shadowy place I'd left behind. The open-plan living room was sleek and modern, with floor-to-ceiling windows flooding the space with sunlight and offering a breathtaking view of the ocean. A glass door led to a spacious balcony, furnished with a small table and chairs, perfect for morning coffee while watching the waves. Everything about the apartment, the polished concrete floors, the minimalist furniture, the airy design, whispered of freedom and new beginnings.

My fingers tightened around the keys as I glanced at Adrian.

"You okay?" he asked, his voice gentle.

I nodded, though I wasn't sure. Moving into this place felt like stepping into a new life. One where I was free to be myself but also had to confront everything I'd buried. The smell of the last two years still clung to me. I couldn't embrace a better future without rinsing off the past, and for that, I wasn't ready. "I think so," I replied. "It just feels... surreal. I'm not sure if a place like this deserves me."

Adrian smiled, nudging me. "You're the only person I know who'd wonder if a home deserves you. This is exactly what you deserve, Ivy. And more."

I wanted to believe him. I really did. But there was still that gnawing fear in the back of my mind. The fear that maybe I wasn't ready for this, that I'd made a mistake. I shook off the thought and forced a smile.

"Although," Adrian continued, looking around, "I'm still not sure how you're going to afford this."

I explained again how this was only a six-month lease. My palate cleanser. Some people sleep with someone to cleanse their palate after a breakup. I needed a new, beautiful home to cleanse the relationship I had shared with Trent. After I was refreshed and ready, I'd move to something more affordable. This beachfront condo was my post-breakup makeover.

I set down the box I was carrying and hurried to my bedroom, my heart racing. When I opened the door, I teared up. My first bedroom. Just mine. Growing up, I had shared a room with my sister, lived in a dorm in college, and then, before I knew it, I was living with Trent. I'd never had my own space before, and only someone who hadn't would understand the significance of it.

"Adrian!" I yelled, marveling at the spacious, neatly organized room, with an open blue sky peeking through its big windows. Next to the window was a small work desk. The walls, though bare, were a soft gray tone that complemented the natural light, creating a calming atmosphere. The furniture in the room was mostly empty, just like the walls. I imagined how I'd fill the space with my art, with the things that reflected me. This time, I wouldn't have to worry about upsetting someone with my choice of bedsheets or night lamps.

"You're going to love it here," Adrian said, looking around.

"I already do," I whispered, almost to myself.

I was picturing where I'd put my easel, how I'd arrange the desk so I could look out at the city as I worked. I could already see myself waking up here, the first rays of the sun nudging me awake, ready to face a new day.

We explored my bathroom and the rest of the apartment, careful not to enter Nolan's private spaces. In his last email, he'd stated that his bedroom and the hallway around it were off-limits. I could use the kitchen, the living room, and the balcony. It was more than enough.

"So, when do you meet your new roommate?" Adrian asked as we started unpacking some boxes in the living room.

"Sometime today, probably," I replied, pulling out a stack of books. "We've only communicated through the app. He seems like a very busy man, which is great. I'll have the place to myself. He's a little... blunt, but nice enough."

Adrian raised an eyebrow. "Nice enough to sublet a room in a place like this? You sure he's not after something else?"

"And by something else, you mean sex?"

"Your hair locks."

I laughed, some of the tension easing. "If that's his thing, I'm in trouble. I've been shedding like crazy from stress."

"Ivy, seriously. You haven't even met him. Who moves in with someone without stalking them first?"

"I told you, the app vetted him. They were incredibly thorough when I applied, and look at this place. I had to pounce on it."

"Fine, but keep 911 on speed dial," Adrian said, only half-joking. I could see that behind the jokes, he was really worried.

I put the books aside and sat next to him on the floor. "I'll be fine. I can read people easily now after living with red flags all my life. You know me. If I went down that rabbit hole, I would have found one reason or another to back out of this. I wouldn't even have moved to San Diego. By not overthinking this, I am trying to do something different here."

"But what if he's a psychopath?"

"I've survived worse," I argued, talking not about Trent this time.

Adrian knew it wasn't a joke. He didn't laugh, just nodded. I tried to lighten the mood with a grin.

"There's nothing the universe can throw at me that I can't handle now."

Just then, we heard the front door open. My stomach churned. The reality of meeting my new roommate suddenly hit me. I took a deep breath and tried to steady my nerves.

The door closed, and firm footsteps echoed through the hallway. Adrian and I both turned toward the entrance, and that's when I saw him.

Again.

My breath caught in my throat as recognition slammed into me like a freight train.

It was him.

The arrogant jerk from the Renaissance Faire. The one who'd insulted everything I loved with a single, mean remark.

Nolan was the jerk.

My mortal nemesis.

My new roommate.

CHAPTER 3

For a moment, I couldn't move. All I could do was stare, my mind struggling to reconcile the coincidence. How could it be him? Of all the people in San Diego, how was this the person I was going to be living with? Why didn't I look him up or at least Google his picture?

His eyes narrowed as he recognized me, too, and I saw the same disbelief mirrored in his expression. Good, at least I wasn't catfished or conned.

But his expression changed as soon as he glanced at his phone and wore the same cold, calculating look I remembered from before.

"You," he said, his voice dripping with disdain.

"Me," I echoed, the shock still paralyzing my thoughts.

Adrian, sensing the sudden tension, stepped forward and asked me. "You've met this guy?"

Nolan's eyes flicked to Adrian, then back to me. "We've met," he said, his tone flat and uninviting.

"Oh," Adrian said, glancing between us, his hands in his jean pockets and shoulders hunched up to his ears. "Small world, huh?"

"Too small," I muttered, finally finding my voice. A surge of anger rose up, mingling with the embarrassment and disbelief. "*You* are Nolan?"

He crossed his arms over his chest, his stance as infuriatingly confident as ever. "Apparently."

My nemesis was wearing the same type of clothes as he had at the Faire. Only this time, it was black dress pants and a black tie knotted at the collar of his dark gray shirt. No blazer.

I could feel the blood rushing to my cheeks, my earlier determination to start fresh slipping away with each passing second. I was supposed to move in, settle down, and finally find some peace. Not get thrown back into another battle with this... arrogant, self-righteous jerk.

"Well," Adrian said, cutting through the thick silence, "you know each other. That's good, right?"

I wanted to laugh at the absurdity of the situation, but the sound got stuck in my throat.

Nolan's expression didn't change, but there was something in his eyes, something I couldn't quite place. It wasn't just annoyance or disdain. It was... curiosity? Amusement?

I felt a familiar sense of suffocation. This couldn't be happening. There had to be a way out, some loophole, some way to escape living with the last person on earth I wanted to see every day. Well, second to last. Trent would always hold the top spot.

I gazed around at the apartment, an almost perfect oasis, and it broke my heart to think of rejecting a place like this, but living with this person...

"Look," I said, forcing myself to sound calm. I couldn't let him see how much he was affecting me. "There's clearly been a mistake. We don't have to do this. I can find another place. Let's just cancel the arrangement. I'll pack up and go."

Nolan's expression remained cold and impenetrable, exuding the same infuriating arrogance I remembered all too well. "Cancel the arrangement?" he repeated, as if the very idea was preposterous. "That's not how it works... Ivy, is it?"

Where's a baseball bat when you need one?

He walked to the kitchen, grabbed an old-fashioned whiskey glass, and filled it at the fridge's water dispenser, all while maintaining steady eye contact with me. "I don't back out of contracts. That's," he took a sip, "unprofessional and ruins reputations."

The way he said "unprofessional" made my blood boil. It was a jab, a way of insinuating that I was somehow less competent or serious about life than he was.

"Besides," he continued, his voice calm but edged with superiority, "people who are serious about life keep their word and fulfill their commitments. This is a legally binding agreement," he raised his phone screen in my direction, "we both signed it, and I'm not in the habit of backing out of signed contracts."

My stomach gurgled as he spoke. I couldn't do this. Not with him.

"You and I both know this isn't as big of a deal as you're making it out to be," I retorted. "No one with better things to do cares this much about canceling a rental agreement. Get me out of this!" I tried to fold my arms over my chest, but my hand got stuck under my open hoodie.

For a moment, his dark eyes glimmered. Maybe with surprise, maybe amusement. But then it was gone again, replaced by a hardened look that sent a chill down my spine. He placed the glass on the kitchen island, walked closer, and lowered his voice as if to drive the knife in deeper.

"You're free to leave," he glanced at the agreement on his phone, "Ivy."

The bastard was pretending as if he had forgotten my name!

"No one's forcing you to stay," he added with a shrug, his tone almost mocking. "But don't expect to get your deposit back."

My heart dropped. "What?"

"That'd be okay though. At least you wouldn't have to say goodbye to the one month's rent that you should have paid, but didn't."

"You asked me not to pay it!"

"You're welcome. I saved you your entire month's paycheck."

I glanced at Adrian for a second, trying to steady my breath. Then I looked back at the jerk. "You can't keep my deposit."

"I can, and I will," he cut me off smoothly, his voice icy. "You walk away, you lose the money. It's in the contract."

My face flushed with hot anger and frustration, but his remained calm. He was doing this on purpose, I realized. He could let me go if he wanted to, but he was choosing not to, just to spite me.

"Hey," Adrian said, glancing between us. "I don't know what's going on." He turned to me. "You're explaining all of this later. But, man," he faced Nolan again, "come on. She clearly doesn't want to live here. Don't force her. Give her the deposit back. We can all be—"

"Who are you again?" Nolan cut him off, as if he hadn't listened to a word Adrian had said.

"You're doing this out of spite," I accused him, my voice trembling slightly as I struggled to keep my composure.

He didn't deny it. Instead, a small, almost imperceptible smirk tugged at the corner of his mouth. "I'm doing what's legally within my rights," he said simply, as if that was all the justification he needed.

The room seemed to close in around me, the walls pressing in tighter. I wanted to scream, to throw something. I could feel Adrian's eyes on me, full of concern, but I couldn't look at him now. Not when everything was falling apart around me.

And then it hit me. Nolan was doing this because of my reaction. Had I shown eagerness to live here, he probably would've terminated the contract right then. Somehow, he was insulted by my repulsion. I was starting to understand him.

I swallowed hard, fighting back the helplessness rising inside me. "I'll stay," I said, hoping to catch a brief shock on his face.

But he just nodded, as if the matter was already settled. Without another word, he turned and walked back to his room.

Six months until the lease ends. Six months of living with my mortal nemesis. Six months of adding another layer of stress to my already complicated life.

So much for wanting a second chance.

CHAPTER 4

It was Saturday. I stood in the middle of my new kitchen, staring at the row of meticulously labeled glass jars in the cabinets. Each one was filled with something—rice, quinoa, spices, and even some kind of fancy coconut sugar—that I knew I'd never touch. The sheer organization of it all was pretentious and infuriating.

All I wanted was a quiet moment to make my coffee, maybe even do my first sketch on the gorgeous balcony, before tackling the boxes still cluttering my room. But instead, I found myself in the kitchen, wrestling with the annoyance that came from seeing Nolan's hyper-organized, bland aesthetic.

For the first five days, I'd done my best to avoid seeing his face. He woke up at 5 a.m., went to the building gym for an hour, came back, showered, had breakfast at the kitchen island, and left for work by 7 (two whole hours just to get out of the house!). His return time was unpredictable, but four days out of five, he came back after 8 p.m., giving me the place to myself for more than twelve glorious hours, eight of which I spent working from my bedroom desk (I worked remotely as a copywriter for medical device industry) and four lazing around on the giant couch, watching Gilmore Girls for the hundredth time and avoiding unpacking. Lorelei's drama with running out on her fiancé was stressing me out, but I was well-rested, so no complaints.

Or so I thought, because I had no idea what the weekend would bring.

I was waiting for the French press (my rent also included using his kitchenware and furniture, and yes, the jerk only had a French press. I'd left my Keurig at Trent's) to brew my coffee when I heard the telltale sound of Nolan's house slippers approaching.

He walked in, exuding that same cool, collected energy that seemed to follow him everywhere, like he had a monopoly on it. His dark hair was slightly tousled, probably from some morning run or whatever people like him did on Saturday mornings. He was wearing a black t-shirt over fitted black joggers.

Nolan had, as they say, a swimmer's body. Muscular, but not bulky like some steroid-fueled gym rat. He was around six feet, lean, and toned. My sweet spot. I finally admitted to myself that my roommate, slash nemesis, slash the jerkiest jerk in the world, was hot.

That instantly made me aware of my own appearance. An oversized Lion King t-shirt, pajama shorts, and fox slippers weren't exactly helping my disheveled hair and puffy eyes.

He moved past me, barely glancing in my direction, and grabbed a bottle of water from the fridge.

"You're up early," he commented, his tone neutral but somehow still managing to sound like a judgment.

"It's only nine o'clock," I replied, trying to keep my voice steady. "Some people like to sleep in on weekends." And there I went again, reacting like I understood his sarcasm. That's exactly what he wanted. To insult me without outright insulting me.

He shrugged, taking a sip of water. "Just making an observation."

A silent minute passed before he grabbed a cutting board and started slicing an apple.

"Just so you know," he said, eyes focused on his perfect slices, "those tons of takeout containers go in the recycling bin."

I froze, my hand hovering over the French press plunger. "Excuse me?"

Nolan finally looked at me, raising an eyebrow. "Didn't know you were anti-recycling."

"That's not the part I had a problem with."

He made a face like that was news to him.

"Not everyone has the privilege of buying fresh groceries and spending hours making their own meals," I argued. "Besides, I've never seen you cook."

"That's because I meal prep on Saturday mornings. And privilege..." He opened the recycling bin and glanced at my Thai takeout container. "How much did that pad Thai cost you? Delivery, tax, and tip included?" He then opened the fridge and pointed his knife at a stack of neatly packed containers. "Weekday lunches. Six dollars each."

I hated this guy.

"It's not just about the money. You need time..."

"Didn't you spend four hours yesterday watching Netflix?"

"You're spying on me?"

"You were talking about it out loud to your boyfriend last night."

"Adrian is not—" I stopped myself, exasperated. "It's not exactly 21st-century convention to eavesdrop and butt into conversations you're not a part of." Hah!

If I wasn't mistaken, a hint of a smile shone at the corners of his mouth, but I didn't want to stick around to confirm. There wasn't a clever comeback left in me, so I turned to leave. But, of course, he wasn't done.

"I don't care what you do in your room, but I'd appreciate it if you kept the kitchen and living room clutter-free," he said, glancing at the throw blanket I had left on the couch last night. "It clutters my mind."

But now I had a better retort. A quote.

"Ever heard the saying," I asked, one hand in my shorts pocket and the other gripping my mug, 'If a cluttered desk is a sign of a cluttered mind, then what is an empty desk a sign of?'"

He smirked, his eyes narrowing slightly as he leaned against the kitchen counter.

"That's the kind of quote lazy people make up to justify their mess. I'm more of a 'clean space, clear thoughts' kind of guy," he said. "Maybe if you tried it, your mind wouldn't feel so cluttered all the time."

I reminded myself to keep my calm, because I knew it would bother him more.

"This clutter," I said, gesturing vaguely, "is called living in. It's what you do when you have an actual personality, instead of living in a sterile, soulless environment."

Nolan raised an eyebrow and leaned on the kitchen counter, clearly unfazed by my jab. "I prefer efficiency," he said, popping a thin slice of apple into his mouth and crossing his feet at the ankles.

Oh god. My breathing. I couldn't stop staring at his lips.

"There's nothing wrong with having things in order," he added. "It saves time."

"Sure," I said, exhaling sharply. "Life's all about saving time. Not about surrounding yourself with things and people that make you happy."

Nolan gave a short, humorless laugh. "Because fairy lights and hoarded junk are the key to happiness."

"They definitely bring more joy than your ergonomic furniture and noise canceling headphones."

Nolan didn't reply, but I could feel his gaze linger on me longer than necessary. Finally, he pushed off the counter and headed for his bedroom.

"You're not the only one who lives here," he said over his shoulder. "Try to keep that in mind."

As he disappeared, I let out a breath I hadn't realized I'd been holding. I had no energy for early-morning conversations, let alone fights. Yet I kept engaging, just to have the last word. Why?

This wasn't why I had moved to this new place I could barely afford. I was here for a reason. To make a fresh start, to do the things I never could because of Trent, to become a better version of myself.

I walked to the kitchen sink and emptied my coffee. It was time for something different. I'd never been a fan of tea, but in the spirit of change, I had bought a box of jasmine tea, the only one I could tolerate.

Once it was ready, I curled my fingers around my delicate ceramic cup, inhaling the soft, floral scent. The warmth seeped into my palms, grounding me. This would be my new ritual. Taking time to savor small moments, to truly inhabit this space.

The balcony door creaked as I stepped out, the humid breeze teasing the ends of my hair. From the 31st floor, everything below seemed tiny, like little elements of a live doll house. The only vast thing was the ocean that stretched out before me, sun-warmed and endless, reaching far beyond my self-imposed limitations. I set my sketchbook on my lap, flipped to a blank page, and willed inspiration to strike.

But my fingers hesitated. The pencil felt foreign in my grip.

I swallowed, trying to ignore the tightness in my throat. It had been so long since I'd drawn.

A breath. Another. Still nothing.

With a quiet sigh, I closed the sketchbook and set it aside. Maybe tomorrow.

Back inside, the apartment still felt unfamiliar. Too pristine, too much like a space that wasn't mine yet. I needed to change that. Grabbing my keys, I slipped out the door.

An hour later, I returned with a bundle of potted plants. Small, leafy symbols of defiance. Trent had always hated indoor plants, calling them a "pointless trend." So, of course, they were the first thing I bought for my new home.

I placed a potted palm by the balcony door, a pothos at the corner of the kitchen island, and the rest in my bedroom. The sight of them brought a semblance of satisfaction.

And yet, the weight in my chest remained. The adrenaline of moving to this gorgeous apartment had faded, and in its place, silence settled in. Too heavy, too sharp around the edges. I didn't regret leaving, but I hadn't figured out how to exist in this in-between space, where freedom felt just as terrifying as it did exhilarating.

I stared at the plants, the unopened boxes, the blank sketchbook.

It was going to take more than a few tangible comforts.

CHAPTER 5

Volunteers had gathered at a tent on the beach. Our building's tenants association had organized a beach cleanup, drawing a modest crowd. Waking up early on a Saturday to pick up trash wasn't exactly my thing, but I wanted to embrace all the parts of this city, this new life. It was painful, this struggle between wanting to relax and needing to get my act together, but I was trying.

It's why I bit the bullet and volunteered for the clean up. I even put on a cute yellow sundress I'd bought ages ago but never wore.

I arrived a little late, clutching my tote bag, and still trying to shake off the lingering frustration from living with the devil. The first person I noticed at the registration table was Nolan. Of course, the king of recycling had to volunteer for a beach cleanup. Standing tall in a forest green button-down and black pants, he was talking to the organizers. It looked like he was guiding them, not the other way around.

I waited for him to step away before registering myself. Armed with a pair of work gloves and a trash bag, I made my way toward the shoreline.

Oceans had always astounded me. Growing up in a landlocked state, I had never seen one. When I mentioned that to Adrian in school, his jaw practically hit the floor. As a kid who grew up in California, he couldn't imagine someone going their whole life without seeing the ocean. He spent the next few days talking about how great it felt to be on the beach. Since then, it had been a goal of mine to live near the ocean.

When Trent asked me to move to California with him, I was overjoyed. I told myself I'd visit the beach every weekend. That never happened. I was too caught up in the emotional mess of my relationship, barely visiting the beach three times in two years. It's funny how you can dream of the ocean all your life but hardly visit it when you live less than an hour away from it. I've been in a situationship with the Pacific Ocean ever since.

That's why I had wanted an ocean-view apartment. I wanted to live close to the beach, to fulfill the promises I had made to myself when I was a girl full of dreams.

With my flip-flops still on, I stepped into the water. The waves curled and crashed against the sand, their foamy edges stretching toward my feet before retreating, teasingly gentle. The salty breeze whipped through my hair, and I inhaled deeply, closing my eyes. The lull of the cool water offered me a strange comfort. This was the first time I was truly registering the ocean with all my senses. Before, I'd been too busy making sure Trent's needs were met to really notice.

The newfound comfort reminded me of a day long ago, back in Sprigwing, when my sister, Amber, and I had found our own little paradise. We didn't have beaches there. No sprawling ocean to lose ourselves in. But we had found a river, a spot just outside of town. It was far from perfect, but it was ours. I could still remember the sound of the wind brushing through the trees along the bank, the sticky heat of the summer sun, and the freedom that came with knowing that, for a few hours, we didn't have to be home.

Home. That word never really felt like it belonged to us. Not when Dad left before I could even remember his face, and not with Mom, who was always preoccupied with her own distant and detached life. We weren't her daughters; we were just afterthoughts.

Amber had done what she could to fill in the gaps. Being four years older, she took on the role of caretaker, even though she was a child herself. She microwaved frozen meals, told me it would be okay when Mom didn't come home until late, and on days when things felt too heavy, we'd head to the river. It became our little escape. We'd sit on the bank, skipping stones, watching the water ripple under the setting sun. Sometimes we talked about nothing; other times, we talked about everything like dreaming up futures that didn't involve Sprigwing or the empty house we lived in.

The breeze picked up, lifting my hair. I smiled at the ocean spread out before me, so different from the river I remembered. But somehow, it stirred the same feelings, a yearning for something bigger, something freer than the life I had known.

Amber left as soon as she could. After high school, she packed up and moved to Colorado, ready to start her own life, far away from our mother, and from me. I was left to figure things out on my own.

She had her own family now and we were estranged. I didn't blame her. Amber had done her best. But standing here, with the ocean stretching out before me, I couldn't help but feel the familiar weight of abandonment settling on my shoulders. First Dad, then Mom, then Amber. All of them gone in their own ways.

The waves crashed again, louder this time, pulling me back to the present. Maybe that was what I needed now. To stop trying to fill the empty spaces left by people who were never really there to begin with. Maybe it was time to stop looking back at rivers and start looking ahead to oceans.

"You're late," said a voice beside me.

I turned to find Nolan, holding an almost full trash bag.

The entire past couple of weeks, since our fight about clutter, had been a mix of bickering and reluctant adjustments with him. Our arguments ranged from trivial things, like the proper way to fold laundry, to more intense debates about art and AI. Yes, AI. That's what the jerk robot does. Creates AI models that will probably replace someone like me one day. Both the copywriter and artist in me. As if I needed more reasons to despise him. Each disagreement left me feeling like we were trapped in a cycle of irritation and loathing.

In my past, I had managed to distance myself from people who brought me so much stress. Well, except Trent, but that was a different case. Though, I did eventually distance myself from him too. With Nolan, I didn't understand why I couldn't just pretend he was invisible.

I registered his remark: You're late.

Before I could retort and tell him to mind his own business, he raised a hand.

"Just stating a fact, not accusing."

For some reason, the way he said it fizzled my irritation.

"I am busy," I said, slipping on my gloves. I wasn't in the mood for an argument, even though his calm demeanor always rattled me.

"Make sure to crush the plastic bottles and boxes before throwing them in the trash bag. They'll take up less space, and you'll end up using fewer plastic bags."

Not another lesson.

"Where do you find the energy?" I asked.

"Energy for what?"

"Telling people what to do all the time."

He laughed, and I forgot what we were arguing about. The sound of his laughter was sweeter than the waves. It almost made me chuckle, dissolving the tension between us into the salty air.

I bent down to pick up the nearest litter. Nolan came up behind me, this time closer than before. I knew if I turned, I'd bump into his chest, so I suppressed the urge to do that and decided to step away. But before I could move, he spoke, his voice close to my ear.

"There," he pointed to a section of the beach, "start over there. This patch has already been cleaned."

I had to make a conscious effort to breathe, which only made it worse because his scent swept over me. He smelled like a deep, dark, woody forest. My heart raced. I took a second to compose myself and stepped away from him.

"Looks like you didn't do a great job," I said, dropping trash into my bag.

"That's kelp. It's deliberately not picked up from the beach. Helps prevent erosion and supports the beach's natural regeneration process."

"Oh..." I muttered, staring at the slimy thing in my bag.

"That's exactly why I tell people what to do all the time." He shrugged, wearing his usual smirk.

I had to admit, I was impressed by his fun fact. But I was trying to decide how I should react.

"That's... actually cool. I didn't know that," I said, placing the kelp back where it belonged.

Maybe he hadn't expected that response from me, because he stood there for a second, his eyebrows scrunched up. Then, with a heavy breath, he walked away.

I moved to the area Nolan had sensually designated to me and started picking up rubbish. The sand was littered with remnants of visitors—a stray flip-flop, crumpled fast-food wrappers, empty water bottles, and soda cans. Humans really had a talent for turning paradise into a landfill. We were like overconfident artists, determined to leave our mark on every canvas, even if it meant ruining the painting.

The sun rose higher. The chatter of other volunteers filled the air, mingling with the sound of the surf. A child ran past, her laughter light and carefree. The silhouettes of surfers bobbed against the horizon. Seagulls squawked overhead, diving for scraps, while families dotted the shore, some sprawled out sun-tanning, others helping their kids build lopsided sandcastles.

I found myself momentarily lost in the rhythm, my frustration gradually giving way to a grudging sense of accomplishment. Believe it or not, successfully cleaning a small section of a San Diegan beach was my biggest win of the year. As much as I had wanted to sleep in, I was glad I had sacrificed my Saturday morning for this. Even if it meant getting another round of instructions from Nolan.

Every now and then, I had glanced over at Nolan. More than once, I caught him looking at me too. Probably checking if I was picking up the right trash.

I scanned the beach, half-expecting to spot him again, but he was gone.

CHAPTER 6

On my way home from the beach, I stopped for soft tacos at a taco truck. One of the great things about living in Southern California was the endless supply of delicious Mexican food. As I ate, I watched a very French-looking man staring at the sidewalk, trying to capture its chaotic beauty in his little sketchbook with a ballpoint pen. I observed him the same way he observed other people skating, riding bikes, and walking on that sidewalk. With curiosity and inspiration. He stirred something in me. Something painful yet hopeful.

I was already out and dressed; I might as well make the most of it. I opened my phone and Googled "Artists meet-ups in San Diego". One piece of advice the Internet gave me the other night to get back to art was to connect with fellow artists. My search today took me to the Meetup website where I created an account. Another great thing about living in a city like San Diego was that there was a Meetup group for basically everything under the sun. There were more than a dozen artist-focused meetup groups in the city. One of them was meeting up in the nearby area soon.

I went to the nearest Michael's and bought a new sketchbook, a set of sketching pencils, an eraser, some paintbrushes, and a box of acrylics. New city, new supplies. Then I drove to the venue.

It took me ten whole minutes to find parking, triggering annoyance even before I got there.

As I stepped into the small café on Mission Boulevard, the air smelled of vanilla and roasted coffee beans. The sound of the ocean was faint, muffled by the hum of traffic and the chatter spilling out of the coffee shop. A faded surfboard mounted on the wall and strings of fairy lights hanging from the ceiling gave the place a laid-back vibe. Despite it being tourist season, most of the customers were locals, sipping lattes, typing on laptops, or lounging with dogs at their feet.

I adjusted the strap of my tote bag and scanned the room. The meetup group I'd RSVP'd to was easy to spot. A cluster of people gathered at a corner table, sketchbooks open, pens and pencils scattered like a chaotic still life.

I almost turned around and left. This wasn't my thing, being a part of a big group. Not that I didn't want to, but I always stuck out like a sore thumb. But the new Ivy couldn't back off. She had already spent too much time wallowing and romanticizing doing things instead of actually doing them. Too much time telling herself that she just needed one more night of binge-watching Gilmore Girls. It had to stop.

I sighed and ordered my coffee before hesitantly joining the group. Not at the table, though. That felt too intimate, too vulnerable. Instead, I slid into a chair near the corner of the room, close enough to observe but far enough to feel inconspicuous.

My chair overlooked the street from the glass doors, where beachgoers in flip-flops and board shorts wandered past with surfboards under their arms. Across the road, the sand gleamed like powdered gold under the afternoon sun, dotted with colorful umbrellas. A couple of pelicans swooped low over the water, their wings cutting clean arcs through the sky.

It was beautiful, sure. But I wasn't in the mood to appreciate it. My thoughts kept circling back to my inability to create again. So, I focused on the group. They were a mixed bunch. Some clearly seasoned artists with fancy tools and confident strokes, others fumbling with flimsy paper and hesitant lines. A girl with arm tattoos was sketching a digital portrait of a child, her tablet propped up against her latte. A guy with a thick beard worked meticulously on a pencil sketch of an anime character.

They all seemed so... absorbed. Like they belonged here. I, on the other hand, couldn't even muster the energy to open my sketchbook.

"Hi! Is this seat taken?" I looked up to see a woman with a bright smile, purple hair, and a necklace jangling with mismatched trinkets—a compass, a fabric flower, and a cowbell. She didn't wait for an answer before plopping down beside me, her sketchbook and a big box of paints spilling onto the table.

"I'm Cleo," she said, extending a paint-stained hand.

"Ivy," I replied, shaking it.

"Wait, you look familiar." As she said that, I couldn't help but find familiarity in her face as well.

"Pirate guild? Irwindeal?" I asked, placing her.

"Fuck yes!" She jumped. "I have seen you there. Too bad we never got to chat. It's a rad group."

"I agree."

"So, you're new here, right?"

"Yeah. First time."

She beamed, her energy almost overwhelming. "You're gonna love it. These guys are awesome. Super chill, no pressure, just a bunch of art nerds geeking out together."

I nodded politely, already regretting sitting here.

"So, what kind of stuff do you like to draw?"

"Uh..." I hesitated, trying to think of something that didn't sound like I had no idea what I was doing. "I guess I like everything... mainly vibrant art and portraits. I'm really inspired by artists like Van Gogh and Frida Kahlo."

Cleo's eyes lit up. "Oh, yes! Frida is my girl too. The raw emotion in her work is just... incredible."

"Yeah, totally," I said, forcing a smile. The truth was, I hadn't thought about art. Really thought about it. In months. Not since Trent had convinced me it was a waste of time. But Cleo's enthusiasm was contagious, and for a moment, I wanted to feel that spark again.

"Okay, let's do this!" Cleo said, flipping open her sketchbook. Her pages were filled with colorful, messy, dynamic paintings. Abstract swirls, pop art, and what looked like a fantastical cityscape.

I hesitated, then slowly opened my own new sketchbook. My hands hovered over the pencils in my bag. What should I draw? The beach? An animal? A random face? Nothing came to mind.

The other artists were already immersed in their work, their pens and pencils moving with confidence. Cleo hummed softly as she sketched, her lines fluid and effortless.

I stared at my blank page, feeling a familiar weight settle in my chest. Just draw something, I told myself. Anything. But my hand wouldn't move.

Minutes passed, and the page remained empty.

I glanced at Cleo's sketchbook again. She'd already filled half a page with a whimsical scene of sea creatures playing instruments underwater.

"Need help getting started?" she asked, noticing my still-pristine page.

"No, I'm good," I said quickly, avoiding her gaze.

She didn't push, thankfully, and returned to her drawing.

I picked up a pencil and made a single mark. A tentative, shaky line. It felt wrong immediately, and I erased it, leaving a faint smudge.

My chest tightened. This was a mistake. I wasn't ready for this.

"Hey," Cleo said softly, breaking the silence. "Are you okay?"

I froze, then snapped my sketchbook shut.

"Sorry, I just remembered I have to go," I said, grabbing my bag.

Cleo blinked, taken aback. "Aah...ha. Well, it was nice meeting you here, Ivy."

"You too," I mumbled, already halfway to the door.

As I stepped back into the street, I felt a mix of relief and shame. I had tried, hadn't I? At least I'd left the house, met new people. But as I walked, the faint echoes of pencil strokes and quiet laughter lingered in my mind, a nagging reminder that I had failed.

Again.

WHEN I GOT HOME, I made the mistake of lying down "just for a sec." I woke up to the sound of faint traffic, darkness creeping through the windows. My stomach growled for more tacos and chilled soda, but I ignored it, heading straight to the bathroom to wash off the beach, the café, and the sting of failure.

Still groggy, I stepped out of the shower, only to realize I'd forgotten my towel. Water dripped down my body and soaked my thin tank top and cotton shorts as I put them on. Both clung to my wet skin in ways that left me feeling like I was in an erotic photo shoot. I figured Nolan was either holed up in his room or out because the house was eerily quiet, and the thought of drying and dressing up seemed like too time consuming. I badly needed a cold glass of water after the abnormally hot shower.

Getting out of the bathroom, I headed towards the kitchen. As I rounded the corner, my heart stopped.

Nolan was on the couch. Shirtless. In a pair of joggers that camouflaged well with the furniture around.

The dim lighting cast sharp shadows over his chest and arms, the ridges of muscle flexing as he scrolled through his phone. He looked like he'd walked straight off a Men's Health cover, all effortless dominance and maddening self-assurance.

His gaze snapped to me. A slow smirk tugged at his mouth.

"Well, aren't you a sight for sore eyes?" His voice was lazy, laced with amusement, but his eyes said something else. Something that made my breath hitch.

Heat crawled up my neck as I crossed my arms over my chest. "What are you doing here?" My voice came out sharper than intended.

He cocked an eyebrow. "I live here."

"I meant half-naked."

For a second, I thought he might actually grab a shirt. Like maybe, even he wasn't immune to this situation. But then, he seemed to make a choice. If you've got it, flaunt it.

And flaunt he did.

I swallowed hard, my gaze helplessly tracing the sculpted edges of his abs, the sharp cut of his obliques, and the V-shaped grooves that disappeared beneath the waistband of his joggers—dangerously low, tauntingly hot. It took me a beat too long to realize I hadn't heard a single word he'd said.

"What?" I murmured.

His lips twitched. "I assumed you were out. Your room was dead quiet. Got distracted by an email while changing and ended up here." He leaned back against the couch, completely at ease. "Which, by the way, is very unusual. Unlike you, apparently, I don't make a habit of parading around like I just lost a wet T-shirt contest."

I scoffed, shifting on my feet. "Impressive knowledge of such contests, Nolan. That a hobby of yours? Watching girls get wet?"

"I know because I take note of wasted water when I see it." His gaze flickered down, and only then did I realize I was standing in a small puddle.

Before I could respond, he gestured toward the kitchen island. "Speaking of water wastage, those plants of yours are begging for a funeral."

I huffed. "They're doing their best to keep this place from turning into a lifeless dystopia."

His expression was unimpressed. "Then maybe try watering them. Unlike me, they don't thrive on sheer willpower."

I rolled my eyes. "You could empty a glass of water in them, you know. They say gardening is therapy. You definitely need some."

His eyes dropped to my chest, lingered, and suddenly, I realized my hands had slipped away from covering myself. Under the wet fabric of my tight, cream tank top, my breasts were oozing and pointing in all the wrong ways.

Nolan exhaled sharply, shaking his head. "You should really get dressed before discussing watering. Hard to concentrate with all these...visual distractions."

I blinked. Visual distractions?

"Oh, you're one to talk," I shot back, gesturing toward his bare chest, but my elbows stayed firmly glued to my breasts. "You think I'm the only one causing distractions here?"

He dipped his chin. Slow. Calculated. Dangerous. "Are you saying my body distracts you?"

Then he stood.

Walked toward me.

My stomach flipped as my brain scrambled, firing off frantic signals while he closed the space between us, every inch of him radiating something lethal.

"I...you..." My words tangled. "I was merely discussing plant mortality."

"Right. Plant mortality." His voice was silk-lined metal.

Another step.

My pulse hammered.

I tried to back up, but my foot slipped in the puddle, and suddenly, the floor was gone.

Nolan caught me without hesitation, one hand gripping my wrist, the other pressing against my lower back.

His electric touch burned against my wet, cool skin. His raw natural scent wrapped around me, and for a second, all I could do was breathe him in. My chest rose and fell against his, the heat of his bare skin bleeding through the damp fabric of my top.

His fingers curled slightly against my back, steadying me, but he didn't move away. His grip was firm, possessive, like he was testing how I fit in his arms. And damn it, I hated how perfectly I did.

I looked up to find his gaze already on me. His jaw flexed, his lips parting slightly like he had something to say, but the words never came. Instead, his eyes flicked down. To my lips, to the beads of water still clinging to my collarbone, to the thin strap of my tank top that had slid to reveal more than it should.

And then, before I short-circuited or did something catastrophic, like lean into him, I tore myself away and bolted for my room, aware of his gaze on my back.

CHAPTER 7

Following yesterday's scandal, I toweled off extra thoroughly after my shower and threw on the bulkiest bathrobe I owned. Wrapping my wet hair in a towel, I headed to the kitchen to heat up a frozen meal.

I knew Nolan was home, so I had no intention of eating anywhere but my room. Just as I was finishing heating up the frozen lasagna, the doorbell rang. I glanced toward the door, knowing Nolan would answer it. That was just his thing. He *had* to be the one to get the door, even when it was something I was expecting. I never argued; I hated answering the door anyway.

Besides, I had no desire to be seen in what was arguably my most unflattering look. Quickly shutting off the microwave, I rushed to grab a soda before heading to my room. I saw Nolan emerging from his room, looking as put-together as ever, dressed in a suit and ready to go.

"Elena," Nolan greeted as he opened the door. His tone was kinder than usual. "You're early."

"Only by a little," a woman's voice responded, cheerful and light. She stepped inside, her eyes immediately landing on me. "Hey, Pirate Girl!"

It was Nolan's friend from the Ren Faire. From her tone, I could tell she was in on the drama between her friend and me.

Nolan excused himself and disappeared back into his room.

"Hey, Druid fairie," I replied, adjusting my robe and shifting the bundled towel on my head for no reason. She was wearing a solid peach cocktail dress with strappy sandals, her hair cascading in waves over her shoulders, just like the other day.

I wasn't sure what the social protocol was when encountering the close friend of your nemesis slash roommate whom you'd once briefly met. Out of nervousness, I put my meal back into the microwave and waited for her to react.

"So," she walked up to me in the kitchen, "how's it living with Nolan? I heard you're giving him a hard time."

I gave a goofy smile, looking for words to refute that statement.

"No, no. It's good," Elena explained. "He finally found someone who can keep up with him." She sniggered, glancing toward Nolan's closed door, clearly quoting something Nolan had said about our situation. It surprised me.

"You know how the higher taxes in California are called the 'sunshine tax'?" I said. "Our drama is my 'oceanfront apartment tax.'"

Elena let out a hearty laugh. It made me envious. I wished I could laugh like that. I'd never laughed with sound.

"Well, don't judge the book by its cover. I know you don't want to hear this from his friend, but he's really not that bad."

"He'll have to earn that opinion," I said, debating whether to ask the same question I'd been curious about since the Renaissance Faire. "Hey, that day at the Faire, when I asked why you weren't insulted by his remarks, you said it was a long story. Is it too long to share today?" I finally asked, not knowing what else to talk about with her.

Elena seemed to reflect, as though trying to remember our conversation.

"Sorry," I added quickly, reading her hesitation. "It's just been bugging me. You don't seem like the type to let anyone talk about you that way."

She glanced at me the same way she had at the Faire. I felt like an idiot and reminded myself that awkward silences were better than asking something dumb.

"I'm not sure if Nolan told you, but I'm a therapist," she started. "Seeing situations objectively is my bread and butter. You know how people like us feel at home at places like the Renaissance Faire?"

"I do."

"That's because we always feel out of place in the regular world. Like outsiders, like everyone's out there judging us, telling us we don't belong."

I nodded, understanding exactly what she meant.

"Well, that's how Nolan was feeling at the Faire. Out of place. Judged. He didn't tell me that, of course, but I know. It's why I had forced him to come, so that he could get used to socializing outside his circles. More people stared at him that day than I got stares in my fairie costume at the grocery store."

"So you are saying, people like me intimidate him?"

"Oversimplification, but yes. Very likely."

"But that doesn't give him the right to react that way," I argued.

"I know," she said, calmly. "But none of us are perfect, right? When we're forced into roles and spaces not meant for us, we either suffer inwardly or lash out."

Elena's empathetic wisdom struck me again. I shook my head.

"That's very profound," I said. "I've experienced both reactions myself."

"It's human nature."

Something flickered in her eyes as she spoke, reminding me of how she'd looked at the Faire, right before she'd apologized for Nolan. There was warmth between us, but also distance, like she was holding something back. Was that a therapist thing, the distance? Or was she hiding something?

"But I'm glad someone finally stood up to him," she said, smiling. "I let it slide because I see him like a harmless little brother."

I couldn't imagine Nolan as harmless or little if I tried. I was about to say as much when Elena said probably the most beautiful thing I've ever heard.

"Nolan is my wind chime in this noisy, screaming city."

It only took that one sentence for me to think of Nolan in a completely different manner.

"You don't like San Diego?" I asked her.

She hesitated before answering. "Never been a city girl. I'm from Idyllview. Ever heard of it?"

"I don't think so."

"It's a little town up in the mountains, about an hour and a half east of here. San Diegans know it for its apple pies. I know it as the place where people give directions using family names instead of street signs."

"So, you grew up there?"

"I did. Two doors down from the Palmers." She grinned, waiting for me to get the joke. I didn't grow up in a small town, but as someone from Illinois now living in California, it cracked me up.

"See? Small town girls can be fun too," she teased.

It was clear she identified more with that part of her life.

"Miss it?" I asked.

"Always. I wish I could live there forever."

"Then why'd you move here?"

"Jay, my boyfriend. The one laughing like a maniac at the Faire." The Nike guy. "He's from here and doesn't want to live like a hermit in a log cabin, his words. So here I am with him, for the past five and a half years."

"Wow, five and a half years. That's great."

"Ehhh…" She trailed off, then quickly changed course. "We all have our ups and downs, right?"

I nodded, thinking how it had only been downs here for me.

"Elena, let's go," Nolan had reappeared, now with shiny shoes and styled hair. He looked like a celebrity, but when I noticed his face, the familiarity hit me harder than I expected. He felt personal, not someone distant I'd watch on TV.

I tightened the belt on my robe and played with the ends of the towel wrapped around my hair, feeling foolish.

I wanted to ask what kind of party had them dressing up like that, but Elena answered before I could.

"It's a surprise cruise party for Jay," she said, her smile faltering for a split second before she brightened up again, as if she was wearing the mask. "It was really nice seeing you again, Ivy. We should hang out sometime. I like you."

I cackled, feeling silly for not being able to say the same, even though I liked her too.

"We should."

"Elena!" Nolan called, more insistent this time.

She gave Nolan a playful slap on the arm as they headed out the door.

I couldn't shake the feeling that something was off with Elena. There was a heaviness in her eyes, like she'd just cried and covered it up with makeup. I knew that mask. I'd worn it myself. Whatever it was, it lingered in my mind long after they were gone.

I LAY ON THE COUCH, crunching on kale chips. I hated to admit it, but Nolan had almost convinced me to cut back on junk food. The TV cast flickering shadows around the dark room as Lorelei chased her dreams of opening an inn, despite her struggles. It amazed me how people, especially women, just went after what they wanted and achieved their goals.

When I left Sprigwing, I promised myself I'd take up a job and focus on my art on the side until that passion became my full-time job. I wanted to be a professional artist. To see my work displayed in a gallery someday, even if no one bought it. That vision had been with me since childhood, and for a while, I worked towards it. When I first moved to California, I stayed in touch with my art buddy from UIS, and we painted together over Zoom. I was improving.

But slowly, a shadow crept into every aspect of my life, and I didn't even notice when I dropped my paintbrush. That's one of the side effects of living with a narcissist. You start doubting everything, even something as simple as choosing the right brand of paint. I hadn't painted or sketched anything in the last eleven months.

That's why I was so desperate to get back to art.

I didn't hate my copywriting job. The steady pattern of deadlines and client requests was a welcome contrast to the chaos in my head and at home. But writing about how great medical devices were sucked any remaining joy out of me and left no room for anything else creative.

I'd accepted it was a necessary evil. The work paid the bills and afforded me this beautiful house. I still, however, couldn't accept that I didn't work hard enough to fulfill my actual dreams.

With Lorelei and Sookie bickering in the background, I responded to Adrian's text. He was my only solace in this chaos, though my heart broke for him. His parents were going through an ugly divorce after three decades of a terrible marriage. As if growing up in a verbally abusive household wasn't bad enough, Adrian was now being used as a pawn in their separation. His struggles with his toxic parents were draining him, when he had so much more to offer the world. I tried to support him as best I could, but telling someone how sick their own parents were wasn't my strong suit. I wished I could tell him to cut the cord and walk away, like Amber did. But I couldn't.

I'd texted him about my day at the beach, my talk with Elena, the artist meet-up, and this unexpected side of Nolan's personality.

The one that his friend disclosed to me, not the semi-naked one I saw yesterday.

"Looks like someone's falling for their roommate," he replied.

"Falling for Nolan? I'd rather dive into the Pacific and clean up the entire ocean's plastic with my bare hands," I texted back.

He sent a laughing emoji, followed by another message.

"Don't let him provoke you. Set clear boundaries and live your best life. You don't need that kind of stress right now."

"Yes, sir. Sleep now. Good night." I hit send.

It was past midnight, but sleep felt far off.

The door clicked open, and I jumped at the sound. Nolan walked in, and even in the dim light, I could see the tension in his jaw and the rigid set of his broad shoulders. He was still in the suit he'd worn to the party, the dark fabric clinging to his toned body in a way that made my breath catch. Although, his jacket was unbuttoned, and the tie around his collar hung loose. I hated how my body reacted to him.

He didn't say a word as he closed the door behind him, his eyes locking onto me with an intensity that sent a shiver through my spine. For a moment, I was frozen, watching him cross the room like he was stalking prey. He grabbed a barstool from the kitchen island and dragged it over, the sound of wood scraping against marble loud in the silence. He sat down close to the couch, legs spread, his posture authoritative, almost predatory.

Flashes of his bare upper body slideshowed in my head, which I tried hard to shake off.

He glanced at the TV. Lorelei and Rory were whining about the beautiful spread Emily had arranged on their dining table. I touched the couch in inappropriate ways trying to find the remote. Once I did, I paused the show.

"Do you enjoy discussing my personal life with people you barely know?" His voice was calm. Too calm. But there was an edge that made my stomach twist.

"What are you talking about?" I asked, feigning ignorance. But I already knew where this was headed.

"Elena told me about your little conversation," he said, his eyes never leaving mine. "That's crossing a line, Ivy."

I stared at him, trying to ignore how he said my name. As though we'd known each other for ages. Once I pushed past that, my temper flared. "I was just making conversation. Keeping *your* guest company while you gelled your hair. I wasn't prying."

"That's not the point," he said, leaning forward slightly, his presence overwhelming. "You don't get to intrude on my personal life and discuss intimate details with my friends. We're roommates, not friends. Elena is *my* friend, not yours."

My hands clenched into fists. "You forced me to stay here, remember? You wouldn't let me cancel the contract, and now you're accusing me of crossing boundaries? That's rich, Nolan."

He leaned back, his expression darkening. "That's a separate issue. We're discussing this right now."

"I've had enough of this," I snapped, standing up. The sudden movement made him raise an eyebrow. "You think I want to be here, dealing with your self-righteous, arrogant attitude? Talking to your friends after you insulted me in front of them? I'm here because I didn't have a choice. I talked to her because I didn't have a choice. Yes, I asked her why she wasn't offended by your comments at the Ren Faire, but that's it. But you're right. We're not friends. Adrian was right. I need to set boundaries with you."

His face went cold at the mention of Adrian. I saw the anger simmering beneath the surface. As if to calm himself, he turned his gaze away from me, staring at the TV.

"What's with them always talking at a million words per hour?" he muttered, still staring at the screen.

"What?"

"That show you're always watching. Don't they ever stop talking? Every time I'm around, they're just... yapping. It's infuriating!"

This man was insane.

"Boundaries, Nolan. That's what we're talking about. You're not supposed to be observing what I'm doing."

"Right." He stood, his frustration resurfacing. "Let's set some strict ones so we never have to cross paths again. I don't want you meddling in my life, and I'll stay out of yours."

"Fine," I bit out, stepping closer. "But don't think for a second that I'm going to tiptoe around you. This is my space too. I pay rent for my room and the common areas. I'll live here however I damn well please."

"As if you were being considerate before," he shot back, clearly alluding to our soaked and awkward encounter.

"Oh, please. As if you don't strut around half-naked like you're in a damn cologne commercial," I snapped.

He exhaled. "Fine. Then let's make a schedule for using the common spaces."

"Why don't you let your AI make it?" I mocked. The last time I'd suggested something, he bragged about using AI for trivial tasks. I'd shot back with, *Oh, THAT'S why you're heartless.*

He must have remembered that argument too, because he stayed silent, probably thinking it over. For half a minute, we stood there, the tension thick between us, neither willing to back down. Then he stepped closer, towering over me, his eyes blazing with animosity. I saw his fingers twitch.

"Stay out of my way," he whispered.

I held his gaze and replied, "So do you."

Then he turned and walked to his room, leaving me standing there, trembling with a mix of anger and something else I couldn't quite name. But I was glad the lines had been drawn.

I stormed into my room and angrily snacked on a packet of potato chips.

CHAPTER 8

NOLAN

I had long learned to ignore the calling of my heart. Shove it aside, bury it beneath layers of logic and ambition. Yet there I was, listening to the solid drumming of my heart as she stood there, nose in the air, voice laced with fire and a stubborn glare, mocking me for my use of AI and reminding me how she once called me heartless.

"Then let's create a schedule for using the public spaces," I had suggested.

"Why don't you let your AI make it?" was her response.

Despite her attack, I felt like I was losing my grip over my hatred for her. Something was shifting.

It's why I was glad the boundaries were set. It was a relief being able to tell her off for talking to Elena. But now, this email that I received this morning, that's not what I had expected. I would have to beg the very person I loathed.

But I'm getting ahead of myself. Let me tell you how Ivy Delaney, the little-nothing, completely disrupted my life, and why I loathe her. It all started on one of the worst days of my career.

On that godforsaken day, I found myself at the epicenter of chaos; a medieval circus for grown-ups that they call Renaissance Faire in this country. An overpriced costume party for escapists, masquerading as culture. For a society obsessed with progress, people sure loved pretending they lived centuries behind.

Another thing I had learned to ignore was the noise of the world, yet there I was amidst the racket of music, laughter, and fake accents that arose like a taunt against my time-starved existence. When I stepped into the madness of Irwindeal Faire, it smelled like wood smoke, sweat, and roasted turkey legs.

Repulsive and sickening.

Everything looked alien and absurd.

I didn't belong here. I had bigger things to do, better places to be. My mind was trapped on a single track: my start-up.

It was a terrible day. I had just been celebrating finding an investor after months of pursuit when he backed out without warning that morning. Gone. Just like that. Everything I'd built, everything I'd sacrificed, was slipping through my fingers. And here I was, surrounded by grown adults dressed as jesters and pirates, celebrating while my world burned.

I glanced at my watch, minutes bleeding out like casualties in a war I couldn't afford to lose. Every tick reminded me that time was currency, and I was broke. Yet instead of chasing a solution, I was paying my dues to friendship.

Elena had insisted. "Everyone needs a little fun now and then."

But she should've known better. I don't do fun. Not like this.

Jay had been relentless too, calling every hour with lame threats if I bailed. Between him and Elena's generous home-cooked dinners over the last few weeks, I had no choice but to be there.

So there I was, glaring at the fools around me and narrating the absurdity to Elena and Jay to entertain myself. "I doubt these people are making any real contributions to the world."

And then I heard her.

"Excuse me."

Two simple words, cutting clean through the noise like a blade.

I turned, and there she was. Braided hair draped over her shoulders, a corset cinched tight, elevating her breasts, and a tattered brown skirt skimming her boots. A pirate. Of course. A tankard hung from her belt, a pouch rested on her hip. Her entire look practically shouted "overcommitted".

But it wasn't the costume that stopped me. It was her face. I knew her. Or at least, I'd seen her before. Somewhere.

She didn't give me a chance to figure it out.

"That's a pretty big talk from someone who isn't smart enough to realize he's insulting the very company he keeps."

The words hit their mark, leaving the silence around us heavy.

I stared, stunned. Did she just…?

Her voice had that sharp edge of defiance, like she was ready to challenge the world on principle alone. I'd never seen eyes like hers: blazing with indignation, hiding something deeper I couldn't yet name. Pain? Sadness? Whatever it was, it made me pause.

Until I remembered she was berating me.

The shock wore off quickly, replaced by an irritation that curled deep in my gut. First, she eavesdropped on a private conversation. Then she had the audacity to challenge me in front of my friends and whatever ragtag crew had been cheering her on.

Jay laughed, the traitor. So did Elena. Everyone within earshot turned to watch. I, Nolan Sterling, was being lectured by a pretend pirate. In the last place on Earth I wanted to be.

I straightened, letting the tension settle into a calm, cold resolve. My eyes dropped to the little-nothing, her face barely reaching my shoulder.

"It might be the norm in your Middle Ages, but it's not 21st-century convention to eavesdrop and jump into conversations you're not part of."

I met her stare, willing her to back down. She didn't.

Instead, she glared harder, like she had something to prove, like she was trying to convince herself of something while taking it out on me. And it clicked.

I remembered where I'd seen her.

The Sublet app.

She was the woman who had applied for the room in my condo last week.

This little-nothing, dressed up as a pirate for pleasure, wants to live in a high-rise, ocean-view, luxury condo?

What a joke.

I replayed her first message in my head, that sarcastic reply she'd sent to my perfectly reasonable lease terms: 'Six-month lease. No pets, no smoking, no disruptions, and no interfering in my space, work, or life. First month's rent and deposit upfront. Rent paid on time. Keep the place clean. If you can handle that, we'll move forward.'

"Efficient," she had replied. "But do I also have to offer you my first born, or just a rental agreement will do?"

She had made me laugh. For half a second, I'd been charmed by her wit, until I reminded myself that charm wasn't worth a damn in my world.

Looking at her now, I wondered how I could've thought she was funny or... something else. She was insufferable. Arrogant. Self-righteous.

I would reject her application as soon as I got home. Tell her off on the app, the place where she would be a vulnerable little rabbit looking for a hole. Feeling better about how I had a way to get back at her, I stood tall and peered into her eyes.

For a second, she faltered. Just the slightest step back. Good. Victory felt sweet.

But then she spoke again, casually critiquing my clothes, as though a $1500 suit tailored to perfection deserved ridicule from someone in thrift-store pirate garb. I almost told her off. Almost reminded her that she couldn't even afford the cufflinks I was wearing.

Elena's hand on my arm stopped me.

It's the curse of having a therapist for a best friend. She knows exactly how to pull me back from the edge. Just her gentle and knowing touch was enough to tell me this was not worth it.

I let the pirate have her last word, spun on my heel, and stalked off.

But when I reached the edge of the grounds, something made me look back.

She was still there, talking to Elena, her defiance practically radiating off her. Cute, a traitorous voice in my head muttered. I ignored it.

The day had already been a disaster, and she'd somehow made it worse. Even though I hated it at the Faire, I would have at least spent some quality time with my friends, but she took that as well.

She needed to be punished for wasting my time.

She deserved to be punished.

And lucky for me, I held all the cards.

WHEN SHE WALKED IN with her boxes and that pathetic boyfriend, I knew exactly who she was.

I'd vetted her thoroughly before agreeing to sublet the room. I wasn't stupid. Her social media, references, credit report, I'd combed through it all. By the time she set foot in my apartment, I knew everything about her the Internet could tell me. So when I saw her at the Renaissance Faire, it wasn't hard to connect the dots.

That feisty woman in the pirate costume, the one who had the audacity to challenge me, was the same woman who would be living under my roof.

The fact that she didn't recognize me at the Faire? It said even more about her. She hadn't even bothered to research the man she'd be sharing a house with. Naive. Reckless.

At the Faire, I decided my revenge would take the form of a rejection letter for the sublet. But that felt too easy. Too clean. I wanted her to feel the weight of her choices. Letting her live in a house I owned? That was the real punishment. A daily reminder that she could only afford to lease a sliver of the life I was living.

It was satisfying to think about.

But the ultimate pleasure had been watching her face when she realized who I was. She was at the mercy of the man she'd insulted a few days ago.

Her audacity, again, though. She tried to back out of the contract, as if I'd let her off that easily. No. She had to stay. She had to pay the price for crossing the wrong guy.

Convincing her wasn't hard. I made her think she had no other choice. That's my specialty, after all. Trapping the rabbit in the cage. Now she was here, living under my roof, and I decided to remind her every day just how insignificant she was compared to me.

What I hadn't anticipated was how living with her was also going to be a punishment for me.

It's maddening. Her clutter is everywhere, the TV blares late at night, takeout containers pile up in the trash, and for some reason, the spoons always end up in the fork section. It's infuriating.

But what really drives me insane is how she moves through life. No urgency. No plan. It's like watching someone fall off the roof of a high-rise in agonizing slow motion.

She floats through life as if it won't chew her up and spit her out. Carefree. Unbothered. And it makes me want to scream.

If I lived like her, I'd have nothing. No respect. No success. No place in this world. I don't have the luxury of "living in" or "having a personality," as she'd mentioned. I've already lost too much to risk losing anything more.

She can't just waltz into my life and act like I've been living it all wrong. I made up my mind: I'd teach her a lesson and find new ways to make her life harder.

Then I saw her at the beach.

The tenant association had "organized" a beach cleanup. Sure, they got the credit, but it was my work. People half-ass everything unless I step in. So, I did what I always do. Took control and directed the volunteers.

She stood by the seashore, her yellow sundress fluttering in the breeze, damp hair wild and untamed around her shoulders. The sunlight hit her just right, making her look like the only thing in color on the beach while everything else faded to grayscale.

For a moment, I forgot to hate her. She looked... peaceful. Cute, even. The chaos I associated with her didn't exist in that moment.

For one insane second, I wondered what it would be like to just... talk to her. No sharp words. No tension. Just listen to her. Hear what she had to say.

And then, before I could stop it, my mind wandered further. What would it feel like to kiss her?

I shut it down. Hard.

This was utterly unproductive. My job was to remind her of her place, not waste time imagining what her lips would feel like. Wouldn't that just be an irresponsible way to spend the important minutes of my life?

I walked up to her, ready to pull her back to reality. She was late. She wasn't doing her job. But when she turned to face me, something was different.

She was in a weird mood. Her voice was softer and the usual fire in her eyes was muted.

I started to lecture her, falling back into the role I knew best. But then she did it again.

She made me laugh.

How dare she.

If she knows I can laugh, she'll think I can cry. That's how enemies get you.

I stepped closer, using my size to intimidate her. A tried-and-true tactic.

But she didn't flinch. Didn't even turn to face me. I was standing so close, my mouth right above her ear. I could see the curve of her neck giving way to the curves of her chest, her skin gleaming under the sunlight. She was irresistible. I wanted to grab her and kiss her shoulder where the yellow strap of her dress grazed her skin.

The feeling was unnerving. Upsetting. I'd never lost control over my breathing before. Ever.

I caught myself leaning in, breathing in the soft floral scent of her shampoo.

My brain screamed at me to stop.

Damage control.

I whispered something about her cleaning the wrong spot and pointed out her mistake—putting kelp in the trash. Anything to break the tension. She accepted the criticism without complaint.

Too easily.

Was she playing me? Letting me think I was in control only to strike when my guard was down? Was she trying to be cute on purpose?

I couldn't take the risk. I moved away before she could twist me in knots again and cost me this war.

But before I left the beach, my eyes found her more than once. I told myself it was to check her progress.

But really?

I just wanted to look at her.

And as if some universal power was out there to get me, it took my subconscious in a twist up way, and showed me more of her than I was ready to see.

She was standing there, water pooling at her feet, her clothes clinging to her every damn curve. The thin tank top had turned nearly translucent as it hugged her waist, her stomach, the faint outline of her boobs. Her shorts weren't any better. Wet cotton plastered against legs much longer for her height. A drop of water slid down her throat, disappearing in her cleavage, and for one ridiculous, fleeting second, I wanted to chase it with my tongue.

I should have looked away. I tried to look away. But my traitorous gaze dragged over her, cataloging every inch before she moved, before she stepped back, before her foot slipped, before I caught her.

My hands locked around her without hesitation. I hated how perfectly and easily she fit against my palm, and how I felt everything. Her rapid pulse under my fingertips, the curve of her waist, the unmistakable warmth and firmness of her nipples against my bare skin, the way she was frozen in my arms. I wanted to do unspeakable things to her.

For seconds, I just stood there, taking in the way she felt, the way she smelled of flowers and sea salt, the way my body reacted like it had a mind of its own.

And I despised it.

She was a distraction I didn't need. A waste of my time, of my focus. I had more important things to do than get caught up in this, whatever the hell this was. So I shoved the feeling down, locked it away, and let her go like she burned me.

Only an ice-cold shower could douse what she left behind.

I HAD DECIDED TO COMPLETELY ignore the little-nothing, but last night, just as I was having a great time at Jay's birthday party, Elena dropped the Ivy bomb.

She told me how they'd talked about me, my insecurities, my friendship with Elena. Well, not in those exact words, but I got the gist.

That made my blood boil.

Why did I even care if Ivy talked to Elena? It wasn't like Elena needed my protection. She's stronger than most people I know. But I couldn't shake the feeling that Ivy was meddling in something she had no business touching. My friendship with Elena was sacred. The only non-mechanical thing in my life.

She's been my rock for years. I met her in college, not long after my mother died. My father had checked out on me by then, hollowed by grief and disinterest. I was barely surviving. Broke, hungry, aimless, drowning under the weight of my own life. Elena had been the one to pull me back up. She treated me like family when I had none, feeding me her homecooked meals at lunch, listening when I couldn't even put my thoughts into words.

Despite being my polar opposite, she's the only person who's ever gotten me. Maybe it's because she's a therapist, but I never had to explain myself to her.

When she met Jay, I was jealous at first. Not romantically, of course. Just... knowing I would lose the one person I cared about. But she loved him, and I was happy for her. The three of us became our own little unit. For the first time in years, I didn't feel alone.

Now Ivy was wedging herself into that dynamic, and I hated it. Elena isn't the type to gossip. I know her better than anyone. So why the hell was the little-nothing getting into her head? The thought of the two of them discussing me, dissecting me like some unsolvable problem, made my skin crawl.

What if she filled Elena's ears with all the things she throws at me to my face? What if she told Elena about our forced living arrangement or her theories about me being "heartless"? Worse, what if they concluded that I was broken and all of this is a sham?

No. I refused to let Ivy unravel it.

It's why I confronted her. Told her straight-up she couldn't talk to Elena. She, of course, had the audacity to mock me and ask *me* to stay out of her way.

I decided I'd had enough. I had sublet the room in my apartment to collect a little extra fund for my start-up, but she wasn't worth the rent. It was a wrong move, sharing my house with a stranger, especially with her. I'd tell her to pack her things and leave. Even give her deposit back if that's what she demands. I'll get my life back in order.

That was the plan when I stormed back to my room last night after our fight. That was the plan this morning.

And then I got the email.

The guy I hired to handle the content and marketing for my start-up, after weeks of vetting and interviewing, quit before his first day. Took another job, the bastard.

I paced the room, tension buzzing under my skin like an alarm. Normally, I thrive on problems. New obstacles give me something to conquer. But this? This felt personal. First, the investor backed out at the last minute, now the employee. It was as if the universe was working against me.

Heat radiated in my chest making me nauseous.

This was my dream, my life, the culmination of years of sacrifice and focus. I can't let this happen.

I scanned through my inbox, looking for the list of backup candidates. Between dozens of those emails, I found the links I'd emailed myself weeks ago. Links to Ivy's portfolio.

Out of frustration, or maybe desperation, I clicked through. I'd skimmed her work before. But this time, I actually read.

And damn it, she was good.

One article she wrote about a portable ECG monitor was so convincing that even I, someone who is skeptical and hard to impress, felt compelled to give it a try.

Even her website was impressive. It was visually aesthetic and perfectly aligned with her brand and work.

The solution to my problem stared back at me from my screen.

Am I really thinking about hiring her?

No. No. That's absurd.

I sat back, rubbing my jaw. Pros and cons, Nolan.

Pros:

She's talented. Perfect for the job. She knows the health-care industry inside and out.

She's already vetted, more than I would have vetted an employee. Hell, she's living in my apartment.

She's accessible. Right in the house.

And surprisingly, despite how much I hate her, I trust her. She's principled. She'd never leak my work or compromise my start-up.

She'd be easy to boss around.

Cons:

I hate her.

I slammed my fist against the desk, the realization hitting me like a punch. I was obviously going to favor my rational side over my emotional one. I needed her.

Ridiculous.

She was about to get kicked out of the house this morning, and now I had to ask her to work for me.

But this is who I am. I'm a man of control. I plan, I execute, I do what's necessary to win.

The AI I'm building is going to be revolutionary, and nothing, not an arrogant, chaotic woman or my own pride, is going to stand in my way.

I was wrong. Subletting my apartment was a strategic move. This would be, too.

I was going to hire the little-nothing.

Now I just had to figure out how to convince her to work for someone whom she equally hated.

CHAPTER 9

It was the weekend, something I never thought I'd dread. But now, it had become the days I might stumble into my nemesis, with whom I shared a house.

I tiptoed into the kitchen, hoping to grab a quick breakfast without running into Nolan. Ever since our fight about his friend two nights ago, we'd done an excellent job of staying out of each other's way. It was like we were living in two different worlds, and I was perfectly fine with that.

I opened the fridge, reaching for the milk, when I heard a door creak open. Please, not now.

Sure enough, Nolan walked in from his bedroom, wearing dark brown joggers and a white t-shirt that fit snugly around his arms and chest but was relaxed at the waist. Again, my sweet spot.

I had never seen him in light colors before, and, no doubt, he looked gorgeous. Even without all that product in his hair. In fact, the fluidity of his dark, soft wavy hair made him more charming.

What the hell was I doing, dissecting why my enemy looked gorgeous on a lazy morning!

I took my eyes away from him, just as he glanced at me for a split second and made a beeline for the kettle. His Highness drank only tea because, apparently, "coffee overstimulates the brain." What kind of person who doesn't drink coffee even owns a French press?

I'll give him one thing, though. His French press was giving me life. I loved how it brought out the essential oils in the coffee, something that paper filters and Keurig pods killed. It also saved me a ton of money.

We both froze, each of us clearly hoping the other would leave the kitchen. Neither of us moved.

Fine, I thought. If he's staying, I'm staying. Leaving first would feel like surrendering. I grabbed the milk and poured it into my cereal bowl, trying to act casual, like his presence didn't bother me at all.

Nolan fumbled with the kettle, clearly trying to keep his distance, but our kitchen wasn't exactly spacious. We ended up performing this ridiculous dance, avoiding each other as much as possible. He reached for a mug just as I leaned to grab a spoon, and we both jerked back, narrowly avoiding a collision.

I bit my lip, trying to hold back a laugh. This was so stupid. Here we were, two grown adults, acting like we were in some kind of silent movie, all because we couldn't stand being in the same room together.

Nolan muttered something under his breath. Something that sounded suspiciously like a curse, and I couldn't help but smirk. He was so intent on his thoughts or ignoring me that he spilled tea leaves all over the counter. I stifled a giggle as he frantically tried to clean it up without looking at me. Forget Gilmore Girls. Watching Mr. Neat make a mess might be my new favorite show.

I turned back to my cereal, determined to stay cool, but the tension in the room was too much. I ended up dropping the entire box of cereal on the floor, sending frosted flakes flying everywhere.

"Oh, for crying out loud," I groaned, bending down to pick up the mess.

Nolan snorted, and I shot him a glare. "Something funny?"

"Nothing," he said, a smirk tugging at the corner of his lips. "Just impressed by your coordination skills."

I rolled my eyes, tossing the cereal back into the box as best as I could. "Like you're doing any better," I shot back, nodding to the freshly wiped counter.

He opened his mouth to retort, but then we both just stared at each other, the absurdity of the situation hitting us at the same time. It almost felt like we were going to laugh together.

But then, just as quickly, the moment passed. He grabbed his tea and headed for the door without another word.

As he walked out, I couldn't resist one last jab, referring to his bragging from a while ago. "Next time, maybe stick to a tea bag. Clean counter for your clear thoughts."

He paused in the doorway, glancing back at me with that same smirk. "And maybe next time, try not to create a cereal avalanche in this sterile, soulless environment."

I rolled my eyes again, but I couldn't help but smile as he disappeared down the hallway.

AS IF THE STRESSFUL morning wasn't annoying enough, I had to work on Saturday to keep up with my deadlines. I was at my bedroom desk, writing an article about the latest advancements in surgical robotics, trying to make phrases like *precision-guided instruments* sound interesting, when I heard a hesitant knock on my bedroom door. Odd. Nolan usually kept his distance. In the two and a half months I'd lived here, he'd never ventured to my side of the apartment. I had to give him credit for that.

So, I was surprised when I saw his face emerge from the partially open door.

"Hey," he said, his expression tight. "Can I talk to you for a second?" His face looked as if he had been prepping for a really difficult exam for the past few hours.

I pretended to look bothered, though my curiosity was piqued. "Sup?"

Goddammit!

He stepped into the room, hands shoved deep into his jogger's pockets. He looked... uncomfortable, like he was about to do something he really didn't want to do. I couldn't help but feel a small surge of satisfaction at the sight. What could possibly be making Mr. Unflappable so uneasy?

"I have a situation," he began, his voice clipped. "The person who was supposed to write the material for my start-up bailed on me last minute. Took another job."

"Oh," I said, unsure where this was going.

"I have a presentation with a potential investor in less than a month," he continued. "I need someone who can write. Someone with a medical writing background."

The way he said it, I knew he didn't want to ask me. But he was desperate, and it showed. I raised an eyebrow, crossing my arms. "And you're asking me?"

He nodded, clearly forcing himself to swallow his pride. "Yes. For three months. I know you're a copywriter, and since you live here, you'll always be around when I need edits or changes."

"Oh, *that's* why you want me."

"Not just that. I've read your work. You have talent when you're actually working."

"Please stop flattering me," I said, turning back to my computer. "I'm busy."

He stood there for a moment, calculating so hard I could practically hear it. The audacity of this guy.

"I'll pay you double what you're making right now," he blurted out, desperation creeping into his voice. "Of course, I won't be able to give you that many hours."

I leaned back in my chair, still facing the computer. It wasn't a bad offer. I did need the money, but the idea of working for Nolan made my stomach churn. If he could be that bossy about how I dried the dish sponge, imagine *working* under him. "I'm not interested," I said, trying to keep my tone neutral. I would never work for a jerk like that.

"I'll cover your rent," he added.

I turned around. "If you want to know one thing about me, or any woman for that matter, don't try to buy them when you need their help."

"What's your condition, then?"

I stared at him, wondering just how much he was willing to do to hire me. He didn't strike me as the type to throw money around just for the sake of it. "Why me?" I asked, genuinely curious now. "You can hire anyone."

Nolan sighed, rubbing the back of his neck. "I mean it. You're... good."

I wanted to be offended again by the borderline stalking, but in this day and age, there wasn't much you could do about it. My website wasn't hard to find on the Internet.

"And more importantly, I need someone I can trust," he added. "This is very important to me, and I don't have time to find and vet someone else."

There was a vulnerability in his voice that caught me off guard. It wasn't something I associated with Nolan, who always seemed so sure of himself. For a moment, I considered saying no again, just to watch him squirm. But the thought of not paying rent for the next three months was insanely tempting. I could do a lot with that money.

"Alright," I said finally. "But on two conditions."

He looked at me warily. "What's that?"

"First tell me how many number of ways did you think of to trick me into working for you. I am confident asking me straight away wasn't your first choice."

A soft smile escaped from one corner of his lips.

"Many."

"I knew it. What made you go this route?"

"It was least time-consuming. I don't have much time."

I knew he was being honest, because that wasn't exactly a nice thing to say.

"You tried something this morning, didn't you?" All that charm and joking after a really ugly fight? From Nolan? No way.

Nolan nodded, this time without the smile. It was a "I am an idiot" kind of nod.

"Thank you for your honesty. Now second condition. Ask me nicely."

He blinked, clearly not expecting that. But then he sighed, resigned. "Ivy, will you help me with this?"

"The magic word."

He took a deep breath, his chest rising and jaw tightening. "Will you *please* help me with this?"

I bit back a smile. "Fine. I'll do it for you. And three months' rent."

His shoulders visibly relaxed. "Thank you."

I was getting back to my screen, but got caught off-guard.

Nolan walked toward me, his steps deliberate, his gaze locked on mine. From my chair at the desk, I tried to look indifferent, but my stomach betrayed me. It fluttered so violently, I wanted to punch it.

I watched him, too closely, maybe, as the light from the window highlighted the sharp cut of his jaw, the determined line of his mouth, and the focused intensity in his eyes. His broad shoulders moved with that same quiet power he always carried, like every step he took had a purpose. My pulse quickened.

He stopped in front of me and extended his hand. "Welcome to my start-up, Ivy Delaney" he said, his voice steady, almost gentle. There was no arrogance there, no smugness or sarcasm, just something unfamiliar. Relief. He actually looked happy.

I could only stare at him. His face was open, unguarded, like he'd taken off a mask I didn't even know he was wearing. I couldn't help but meet him halfway. I slid my hand into his and offered a firm shake. "Pleasure, Nolan Sterling," I said, surprising myself with how soft my voice came out.

He nodded, as if satisfied, and let my hand go. "We will go to my office so I can show you what the project's about. You'll need to sign my work contract first, and then get going on the problem and solution statement. I need it for the website today."

I blinked. "What? Now?"

"Yes, now," he said, already halfway out the door. "Take your laptop."

I sat there for a second, stunned, my decision already thick with instant regret.

CHAPTER 10

As I reached for my car keys, Nolan's voice cut through the air. "Why waste energy on two cars? Just come with me." His tone left little room for argument, and before I could protest, he was already heading toward the underground parking. I hesitated, feeling the weight of his unspoken command, then reluctantly followed.

Nolan's electric car was sleek and intimidating, much like him. I slid into the pristine passenger seat and we drove out of our building. The silence between us wasn't as hostile as last night, but it wasn't exactly comfortable, either. I pretended to check my Instagram on my phone and glanced at him from the corner of my eye. He drove with the same controlled precision that seemed to define him. Focused, decisive, and fully in command. Even behind the wheel, he radiated a quiet dominance that made the car feel smaller than it actually was.

The trolley-tracks-lined streets of Downtown San Diego stretched ahead, the sounds of the city filling the silence between us. I watched his fingers tighten around the steering wheel, his jaw set with familiar tension. For a moment, I wondered what it would be like to break the quiet. But instead, I turned my gaze out the window.

When we arrived, I was surprised by the modest size of his workspace. A rented conference-style office in a shared building, just fifteen minutes from where we lived. It wasn't the flashy, high-tech setup I'd imagined.

He must have caught my expression because he explained, "I have enough bling at my day job."

I snorted, then realized why he was out twelve to fourteen hours a day. He was basically doing two full-time jobs. One for someone else, one for himself.

"No, seriously," he continued. "They gave me a private champagne fridge in my office. Just for me."

"Fine. I get it. You have all the luxury there, and this office is your humble Zuckerberg hoodie."

Nolan ignored my fantastic jab and led me to a huge desk cluttered with papers, diagrams, and several monitors flashing complex code. The room was empty, save for the two of us.

First he brought me a steaming cup of tea. Jasmine tea. Did he take note of the only tea in my kitchen cabinet, or was it just a fluke?

Then as I nursed the hot beverage, he made me sign a novel-length contract. I took my sweet time and pretended to read every word of it. That impressed him more than it annoyed him, which annoyed me.

"This contract was already drafted with my name on it," I said, narrowing my brows. "You haven't left my sight since I agreed to work for you. Were you being proactive or just overconfident?"

"Whatever makes you feel better." He pursed his lips and escorted me to what looked like his personal desk.

He pulled out an ergonomic chair for me and leaned over the desk next to me, pointing at the screens.

I was back in the dark woody forest, lost and overpowered. Right next to my eye, his shirt collar revealed a sliver of his neck, the faint line of a vein visible under the office light. This time, it was I who felt like a predator, because I wanted to sink my teeth in that neck.

Nolan cleared his throat, snapping me out of my wayward thoughts. Had he caught me staring? Be professional Ivy, I told myself, and straightened up on the incredibly comfortable chair.

"This," he began, gesturing at the monitors without wasting time on the small talks, "is what I'm working on. AI-powered predictive analytics for mental health. The goal is to use data and build a model that identifies early signs of mental disorders, mainly dementia, through eye scans. People could scan their eyes using their phones, and the model would predict potential risks. This could help them get treatment before things spiral out of control."

I stared at the screens, his words slowly sinking in. Mental health. My chest tightened. "You're working on a mental health product?"

"More like technology," he corrected. "But yeah. It's something I've always wanted to do." His voice softened, as if he were treading on vulnerable ground.

My throat clogged up. This wasn't just another boring tech start-up or the villainous AI I'd made it out to be. It was something meaningful, something that could save lives.

"I didn't know that..." I began, my voice trailing off as I tried to find the right words.

"That not everything made with AI is evil?" he finished for me.

"That you were human," I admitted, feeling strangely touched. "It's... impressive."

He smirked. "Don't get carried away. I'm still planning to sell it for millions to some loaded venture capital firm or big pharma."

And there it was.

Still, it didn't bother me. For the first time, I felt invested in something I was getting paid to write about.

"That's where I'm focusing all my energy right now. Finding an investor and, eventually, a buyer," Nolan said, his tone steady with determination. "I need additional funding to further develop this technology, which I'll secure in exchange for a stake in my company. Once it's fully realized, I plan to sell the model to an acquirer. I just wish I were as good with words as I am with numbers." His gaze shifted to me, a faint twinkle in his eyes. "That's where you come in. Your job is to help me create an irresistible package for this product. With your words."

I nodded, the weight of the task settling over me. "Okay. Let's do this. Where do we start?"

As we brainstormed and discussed about what to write first, I suggested we start with the societal and financial toll of untreated mental illnesses. "We could include data about how mental health crises cost billions annually in lost productivity. I have to look for the exact number, but I know it's in billions. If we highlight that angle, it'll resonate with your potential investor. The big guys hate losing productivity. Trust me."

Nolan blinked, stunned. "That's actually really good. How do you know all this?"

I didn't know if I was insulted or satisfied by his surprise.

I shrugged. "Research is part of my day job."

Although, all these "fun facts" about mental health? That's the result of random episodes when I succumb to the dark side and go down various rabbit holes on the Internet. Of course, I didn't admit that to my new employer.

We spent the next hour hashing out ideas. To my surprise, Nolan listened intently, occasionally nodding or adding his input. He was genuinely impressed. It was stimulating.

When we wrapped up, Nolan asked if I'd mind waiting while he finished some urgent work. I agreed and grabbed a coffee at the café downstairs, using the time to text Adrian.

"You WHAT?!" Adrian replied after I told him about my new gig. "Last time we talked, you were talking about setting boundaries with him, and now, what, you're setting up his meetings for him?"

"I'll be his copywriter, Adrian, not his secretary. I'll explain when we meet."

"He doesn't seem like someone who could differentiate."

"Stop it, Adrian. It's been so long since I've felt this good, this confident about my work, about my mind. Let me enjoy it."

"Fine. Enjoy the glory."

"How did things go at your mom's?"

"The usual. She and Dad screamed at each other, then she kicked him out. Again. I helped Dad move more furniture to his new place. Again. Same toxic cycle, same badmouthing. No concern for their only child or how it affects him. No interest in his work or personal life. Like I said, the usual."

"Ugh. I'm so sorry. You deserve so much more than this." On many days, I'd wished I could grab his parents by the shoulders, shake them violently, tell them how lucky they are to have a son like Adrian, and demand they treat him that way.

"Yeah? And what do I deserve?" he texted.

"How about some Ivy-style therapy? Hot coffee, junk food, sugary pastries, discussions on dark, existential topics that we don't want to have but end up having anyway, and our favorite Gilmore Girls episodes? Next weekend?"

"I'm in."

I took a breath and sipped the last of my coffee. For a moment, I thought he was acting weird.

"That is, if your new boss lets you take a weekend break," he texted back.

There it was. He sounded mad. Not in a protective way, but in some other manner.

"Hilarious :|," I replied.

It wasn't, though. Judging by Nolan's work ethic, I doubted he'd let me have a free weekend.

The drive home was quieter, but the silence felt comfortable this time. I found myself stealing glances at Nolan, seeing him in a new light. He wasn't just a smug tech guy; he was someone who cared. Sure, he cared for millions of dollars too, but he was investing his time and talent into something that matters.

Maybe, this job wouldn't be so bad after all.

CHAPTER 11

I had been at it for hours, the words on the screen blurring together as I tried to piece something coherent for one of Nolan's articles. My stomach growled, a loud reminder that I hadn't eaten anything substantial in what felt like ages. Leaning back on the couch, I glanced at Nolan, who was standing at the kitchen island. His intense focus fixed on his laptop and his fingers moved furiously across the keyboard.

"Hey," I called out to his back. "I'm starving. I'm thinking of ordering something. You want anything?"

Nolan turned his head slightly. "Another takeout?"

I shrugged. "Yeah, why not?"

He shut his laptop and turned around. "Let's eat out."

I blinked at him, startled. "What? Together?"

"I refuse to be your delivery guy."

"That's not what—"

Before I could finish, he had already disappeared into his room to grab his car keys.

I HESITATED WHEN I found myself sliding into the passenger seat of his car. This time, I had offered to take mine. Not that I loved driving or had any pride in my dingy, second hand MINI Cooper. I just didn't want to follow whatever he said. My gas tank, however, had other plans. So here I was, back in Nolan's Batmobile.

Going out to eat with him was not something I'd envisioned when I started working for him. It had taken me fifteen minutes to pull myself together. Put on a halfway decent dress, brush my hair, and slap on some lip gloss.

"There's an Indian restaurant I like," he said, pulling out of the underground parking.

"Indian?" I echoed, surprised. "You like Indian food?" I was a bit mad that he didn't ask my preference. I had never had Indian food before and have always been intimidated by it.

He glanced at me briefly. "Why the surprise?"

"I don't know. You don't strike me as the adventurous foodie type."

He smirked but didn't respond.

THE RESTAURANT WAS a hidden gem, tucked away on a quiet, unassuming street. It wasn't the cliché Indian spot often portrayed in movies. No vibrant decor or ornate traditional accents. Instead, it was cozy and exuded a simple, understated charm, with the rich aroma of spices filling the air. Instead of traditional sitar music, the speakers played 70s Bollywood songs—a detail I only learned when Nolan casually pointed it out.

At the counter, Nolan greeted the man behind it like an old friend, exchanging a few words in a language I couldn't place. The host responded with a hearty laugh before leading us to our table.

I had barely skimmed the first few items on the menu when Nolan waved the server over and began ordering with a confidence that left me staring. He didn't even glance at the menu, rattling off dish names in perfect pronunciation, even ordering an appetizer and entrée for me.

"You know your way around this place," I commented.

"My mother's Indian," he said casually, leaning back in his chair. "Grew up there. She is the one who taught me how to cook and showed me the importance of healthy, homemade meals. When she was too tired to go into the kitchen, this is where she brought me. So I always come here when I miss her food."

"I didn't know you were part Indian?" I said, surprised. That explained his deep features and olive skin.

Nolan shrugged. "It's not something I advertise."

"Do you see her often? Your mom?" I asked.

His expression softened for a moment before he looked away, his jaw tightening. "How's the article coming along?"

The deflection was clumsy, but I let it slide. "Can we not talk about work?" I asked, my tone firm. "I don't like thinking about it when I am eating."

Instead of giving me another lecture on how that's inefficient, he simply nodded.

While we waited, I took in the restaurant. The warm lighting, the soft, complex rhythms of the music in the background, an assortment of packaged snacks shelved in the corner, and a steady stream of employees from nearby companies coming for their lunch breaks. It was a welcome change from the tense atmosphere we usually shared at home.

When the food arrived, I was greeted with an explosion of colors and intoxicating aromas. Nolan's stern demeanor melted away as he introduced each dish with genuine enthusiasm.

"These are Pakoras—savory fritters," he said, pointing to a plate of fried snacks. "This is Veg Kadai, a mix of stir-fried vegetables in spiced sauce. Chana Masala—chickpea curry. That's Dal Tadka and Jeera rice," he added, gesturing toward a bowl of thick tempered soup and fragrant cumin rice. "That's Indian-style salad for the side and some papad for the crunch factor."

"Nolan, that's a lot of food!"

"Don't worry. I'll help you." I am sure he went for a wink, but then stopped himself.

His charm and friendliness was irresistible. Sitting across the table, was another version of Nolan that I knew.

"And this," he continued, holding up a piece of flatbread, "is Roti. Everyone in America raves about Naan, but there's nothing more comforting and homely than a simple Roti. You scoop up the food with it, like this."

I mimicked his movements, trying the Veg Kadai first. The flavors were bold and overwhelming, but in the best possible way. The dishes were spicier than I was used to, but they kept me wanting more.

"This is amazing," I said, genuinely impressed.

Nolan smiled. A rare, genuine smile that made him look like an entirely different person.

We ate heartily as he explained the spices and ingredients. It was clear he had a deep appreciation for his food, and I found myself drawn in by his passion.

"I need to learn more about the things outside my bubble," I admitted, taking a wonderful crispy bite of Pakora.

"You could accomplish so much more if you were more organized," Nolan said and took a sip of water. "You're so talented, but you're all over the place."

My eyes narrowed with a mix of frustration and surprise. I set my fork on the plate and took a moment before responding.

"You're working on mental health, right? Then you should know not everyone is wired the same way," I said, my voice sharpening. "Accomplishments don't automatically mean happiness. Just because you thrive on structure doesn't mean I'm lost without it." I exhaled, steadying myself. "Maybe I'm not as fast as you, and maybe I won't build something groundbreaking, but that doesn't mean I won't get where I want to go. I'd rather move at my own pace than force myself into a system that drains me."

For some reason, he simply looked at me without saying a word, as if he was urging me to go on. That dampened my temper. But before I could continue, my gaze shifted outside. A car just spilled into the restaurant's parking lot in the roughest, loudest manner.

And then, coming out of the car, I saw the last face I wanted to see on Earth.

Trent.

My stomach twisted into a tight knot.

I barely managed to mumble his name before instinct kicked in, and I turned my face away, shielding it with my hand.

What was he doing here? In San Diego? Of all places, why this restaurant? He hated Indian food.

My pulse drummed in my ears as I peeked through my fingers, watching him stroll inside like he owned the place. He leaned an elbow on the counter while waiting for his pick-up order, tapping away on his phone with that same cocky smirk he always wore. He hadn't changed a bit.

Countless memories, good and ugly, rushed towards me along with some contradicting feelings. I felt hurt, but relived. Angry, yet calm. I wanted to confront him, but also wanted to get buried in the earth, if that was the only way to avoid seeing him.

I held my breath as he spoke to the busboy at the counter. My fingers curled into my palm.

I hated that he could still make me feel small.

I hated that I cared if he saw me.

Across from me, Nolan hadn't moved. He didn't say anything, but I could feel the shift in him, his entire presence sharpening. His jaw ticked, his hand tightening around his glass. I could tell he was watching Trent, dissecting him the way he did with new problems.

The restaurant door chimed.

Trent walked out, never noticing me.

Only when his car pulled away did I exhale. I dropped my hand and reached for my water, as if that would somehow wash away the tension still clinging to my ribs.

I glanced at Nolan, forcing a smile. "So... where were we?"

His gaze was still on the door, like he wasn't quite ready to let it go. But then he turned back to me, studying my face for a long moment before leaning forward. His voice was steady, firm.

"Ex boyfriend?"

I nodded.

"Why were you hiding?"

I didn't know what to say. It wasn't like I had done anything wrong.

I took another sip of water.

"You were talking about me being all over the place, right?" I said, keeping my gaze on the plate. "That wasn't always me. Of course, I've always been... erratic, but I've been better at life. I used to have plans, routines. Big dreams and ambitions even. But when you've been in a relationship where every little thing you do is criticized, where you're constantly made to feel like nothing you do is good enough... you lose faith in all structures. You doubt every thought, every decision, every dream. Even yourself. It was..."

I stopped, feeling Nolan's gaze burning into me.

"It was?" he prompted, his voice low.

I picked up my fork and played with the rice on my plate, the grains sliding into chaotic patterns.

"For three years, I was with him." I looked outside the window at the spot where Trent had parked his car. "He made me feel worthless. Unless I did things his way. It was easier to just... stop trying. I lost touch with everything I wanted to do. And be."

Nolan's brow furrowed slightly, his lips parting as though to speak, but he hesitated. His fingers twitched on the edge of the table, betraying some internal struggle.

"How did someone like you end up in that kind of spot?" he finally asked.

"Are you blaming me?" I asked, raising my eyes to meet his.

"No." He straightened, his voice softening, almost thoughtful. "You're like... time itself. Nothing can budge you. You move at your own pace."

I blinked at him, unsure where he was going with this.

"I mean, you're so stubborn," he added, glancing away briefly before continuing. "Like a... hermit crab."

I picked up his water glass, sniffing it as I shot him a skeptical look. "Are you on something? Hermit crab? What are you even talking about?"

"Hermit crab," Nolan repeated and cleared his throat. He looked as if he'd been forced to go on stage naked. "They only leave their shell for a new one when they deem the time is right."

I tilted my head, still not following. "Right..."

Nolan shifted in his chair, running a hand through his hair and exhaling sharply. His jaw tightened as though frustrated with himself. He sat straighter, his eyes flicking away briefly before returning to me with renewed focus.

"Look," he said, his voice firmer now. "You're a headstrong woman. As far as I know you, no one can make you do anything. You'd only budge on your own accord. That's why I'm curious how you ended up in a spot where someone had that kind of power over you."

A wonderful warmth rose in my chest. I hadn't realized how badly I needed to hear those words. But coming from Nolan, I couldn't tell if it was a compliment or criticism.

"You make me do things I don't want to all the time," I said, half-teasing but also testing him.

"Oh, really?" He folded his arms and leaned back slightly, his dark eyes forcing me to deep-dive into my head to ask myself the same question. Did I always wanted to do the things he asked me to?

"Well, maybe not," I admitted after a pause, still sorting through my thoughts. "I don't know. But maybe that was the issue with my ex. My stubbornness. I didn't want to accept that my judgment was flawed, that I'd chosen the wrong person. That I went for him only because I was too lonely and he was the next available person. And then it was like finishing a movie you didn't like. You don't want to give up because you've spent so much time on it. You hope things will turn around. Sunk-cost fallacy. Maybe I was also bitten by that efficiency bug. It felt inefficient to let go of someone I'd invested years in."

For a moment, we both stayed silent. Nolan's features softened slightly, his earlier frustration melting into something that looked like understanding. Or was it judgment? Whatever it was, I was left feeling both lighter and heavier all at once.

"You finish movies you don't like?" he asked, looking genuinely surprised.

It cracked me up, and I admitted guilt with a shrug.

The server arrived and asked if we wanted desserts.

"I'm so full," I said looking at Nolan, responding to his silent question.

"We'll have the check," he told the server.

I insisted on splitting the bill, but Nolan said it was a work meal and that he was going to write it off. I rubbed my belly again, feeling content for the first time in years, and I was certain it wasn't just the food. I was filled with gratitude for Nolan, for bringing me to this restaurant, sharing about his mother and his culture, and even listening patiently to the most honest words I'd spoken in three years.

"As a thank-you," I said to him, "can I take you to one of my favorite places next time?"

I was sure I'd hear a no and that would be the end of it. I could go back to disliking him after showing kindness he would reject.

"Sure," he replied.

Dammit!

WHEN WE GOT HOME, NOLAN lingered at the kitchen island while I poured myself a glass of water to take to my room, where I planned to work the rest of the day.

"What's his name?" he asked suddenly.

"Whose?"

"The ex."

"Trent," I said, smiling faintly.

"Big loss. His." Nolan deadpanned, his eyes on the laptop screen.

And then, my heart was full too.

CHAPTER 12

The Gliderport stretched out before me, the wind catching the sails of paragliders as they soared off the cliff's edge. I gazed out at the vast expanse of ocean far below, the sheer drop a reminder that this wasn't just any seaside view. It was a perch hundreds of feet above the Pacific. This was my favorite spot in San Diego, maybe even in the whole world. A place that felt timeless and enchanting, where everything seemed to slow down.

I wondered if Nolan would be impressed by it or if he'd just scoff, dismissing it as another "frivolous escape" from real life. The reason I came here today was to see this place through his perspective, to check if a spot like this could move someone as practical and rigid as him.

I'd made the mistake of promising to repay him for taking me to the Indian restaurant. The past few days, I had agonized over where to take him. My actual favorite place or somewhere he'd like. But as the sun began to drift into the ocean, blanketing the cliffs in a golden glow, I realized I didn't care what Nolan thought. If he wanted to see my favorite place, this was it.

I went back to my car and turned the key in the ignition. All I got was the dull click of a dead battery.

"Perfect," I muttered, dropping my head. I pulled out my phone and called Adrian. Of course, it went straight to voicemail. He was out in L.A. visiting his mom. I had deleted Uber from my phone because my outdated model had no storage space left.

I needed to get out and make more friends, because there was no one else in the city I could call. Well, except...I sighed. What other choice did I have? It's not like I had a tree full of money in my backyard and could afford a tow truck or a mechanic. I stared at Nolan's name for what felt like ages, hesitating before finally pressing "Call."

He answered on the second ring.

"Ivy?"

For a moment, I regretted calling him. I didn't need a lecture on car maintenance. "Hey... I need a favor."

There was a pause, and I could practically hear him thinking, probably weighing whether or not to help me.

"My car won't start," I explained, trying not to sound too defeated. "I'm at Gliderport. Torrey Pines. Are you nearby?"

Another pause. "Give me seventeen minutes."

Wow. I've never not rounded minutes to the nearest ten.

"Thanks." I hung up, feeling a mix of relief and irritation. The last person I wanted to owe anything to was Nolan. I was already worried about how to repay his last good deed; I didn't need another.

As I sat there, waiting in the fading light, the beauty of the sunset seemed less important. My thoughts drifted back to the past five days. Ever since the lunch at the Indian restaurant, things had been... different between us. He was still Nolan, but I was starting to understand him a little. He was tolerable.

We'd made real progress on his website content. I'd even surprised him with an infographic, something not in my job description, instead of the lengthy pieces he'd asked for. His reaction still stuck with me.

"Perfect!" he'd said, looking awed and genuinely happy.

That rare smile of his had lingered in my mind for days. He'd been in such a good mood all week. Less critical, even a little warmer.

It felt like the tension between us had softened in a way I didn't expect.

While things between us had been going great, it was Adrian who had me worried. He had been acting strange lately, different, asking questions about my future and even about Nolan. I acted clueless in front of him, but I was not. It was obvious what was on his mind. What I didn't understand was why, and why now?

We had cleared the air about romance twice before. The first time was the week before he moved to California for college, back when I hadn't even met Trent. We were both drunk, sprawled out on my couch watching some ridiculous movie when, out of nowhere, he asked if I believed in marrying my best friend if I didn't find anyone else.

Naturally, as a rebellious, drunk seventeen-year-old, I had blurted out,

"Shut up! I wouldn't even marry for love."

Adrian had always been the hopeless romantic, a dreamer on an endless quest to find the one. Not that his dating history reflected that goal. He had a revolving door of girlfriends since he moved to L.A. But he yearned for it, for the One. I had always believed his obsession stemmed from his parents' toxic marriage. The trauma he endured living with them before moving in with his grandparents had left its mark. For Adrian, the thought of spending his life alone, or worse, with the wrong person, was his biggest nightmare.

The second time we had addressed the whole marrying-the-best-friend thing was when we met in L.A. By then, I had decided, whether or not I broke up with Trent, I would never marry him. Adrian had joked again about him and me getting together, but this time, I was more mature than my teenage self. We had an honest talk about why he kept bringing it up and why I didn't believe in it. Especially not with him.

I had told him he was my one true constant, my anchor in human form. Love had brought me wounds. His friendship was the balm, and I needed it to stay that way. Besides, even if I had wanted to, I couldn't see him romantically. I had been upfront about it, and he had seemed to understand. We had ended the conversation on a positive note, with him talking about the girl he had been into at the time.

Since then, things had been great. We had never needed to revisit the topic of romance, and it had never been an issue. Until now. Why was he acting up all of a sudden? Was it because of...

Headlights cut through the darkness, pulling me from my thoughts. Nolan's shiny black car rolled up beside mine, and he stepped out, looking annoyingly composed for someone dragged out on a rescue mission. From his clothes, it looked like he was at a meeting.

He didn't say a word, just popped open his trunk and pulled out a portable charger. I crossed my arms and watched silently as he slipped off his suit jacket. The sharp cut of his shirt clung just enough to hint at his lean, athletic build. When he undid the top button of his shirt and rolled up his sleeves, the sight of his neck and his veiny forearms caught me off guard. I glanced at his eyes to make sure he didn't see me breathe like a person out of oxygen.

A light stubble shadowed his jawline, giving him a rugged edge that contrasted with the clean lines of his attire. His hair was slightly tousled, probably from a long day at work, but it only made him more attractive.

Get a grip, Ivy.

"Always prepared, huh?" I said, breaking the quiet.

Nolan flashed a half smile but didn't look at me. "I hate being stuck somewhere."

It sounded like he wasn't just talking about the car.

Within minutes, my engine roared back to life.

"There," he said, slamming the hood shut.

I shifted, feeling a little sheepish. "Thanks for coming all the way out here."

"You're welcome," he said, placing his supplies back in his trunk and slipping on his jacket. "What are you doing here?"

"Meeting a…" I stopped. He drove here to help me. He deserved honesty. "Actually, this is the place I wanted to bring you to. As a thank you for that lunch."

He looked around the parking lot.

"Not this," I clarified. "I'll show you when…"

"Show me." He grabbed his keys to lock his car.

I hated how queasy my stomach felt. It wasn't anxiety, but butterflies. I was taking a man to a place so personal to me. A man like Nolan, the guy who hadn't even used his ocean-facing balcony for pleasure once.

Instead of the green patch of the Gliderport, I led him to the rocky terrain on the left.

"Well, it's not this dreary," I said as the darkness began to envelope the cliffs. "I wanted to bring you here at sunset. It's otherworldly at that time."

He didn't say anything and continued walking. We trudged over the uneven surface to get to the edge of the cliff.

"And the best part about this place," I continued, "is that tourists don't know about it. You'll always find parking, and it's never too crowded."

Again, silence.

I had to stop impressing him. He was not better than me. I took a deep breath and decided to just be myself.

"Let's sit here," I said, pointing to a smooth rock as we reached the edge.

"Sit there?" he asked. "One wrong move, and you could fall to your death."

I looked down at my lap, embarrassed and disappointed. This is insane. What the hell was I doing? Bringing people to my stupid little world and desires. No one was going to get it.

I was pressing my hands to the rock to get up when Nolan sat next to me. Before I could stop it, a goofy smile spread across my face.

Why am I such a dorky idiot.

The rock was big enough to accommodate both of us, but small enough that we were less than a foot apart. Our knees nearly touched, and every slight movement sent a whisper of warmth between us. His proximity was overwhelming. His scent, his presence, and it took effort to focus.

"You know how some people believe the Earth is flat?"

Nolan gave me a look of ridicule.

"I know, but if it was," I said, "this is what I imagine the edge of the world would look like."

He followed my gaze to the vast, dark ocean sprawling 350 feet below.

"When I first moved here from Illinois," I went on, "I wanted to see the ocean. It was summer, and the LA beaches were packed with tourists. So, following a Redditor's advice, I drove down to San Diego, and decided to hike Torrey Pines instead. Somehow, I mixed up the address and ended up here. Imagine seeing this for the first time, never having seen an ocean before. Ever."

He actually tried imagining it. I could see it on his face.

"It's hard to explain to someone who's seen the ocean their whole life," I said. "But that day, I decided I'd never leave this place."

I realized I was oversharing. I'd never told anyone about that moment, not even Trent. Well, I had planned to bring him here once and share that, but he'd been too busy recording a video for his YouTube channel to join me.

"You found the beaches crowded, so you decided to climb up a mountain to watch the ocean?" Nolan asked, his tone dry but laced with faint amusement.

"*That's* what you got out of this?" I frowned.

He let out his half smile again, his eyes glinting in the fading light. His gaze lingered just a fraction longer than necessary before he looked away. "Look, there's a ship," he muttered out of the blue, pointing toward the horizon.

I squinted into the twilight but saw nothing. "Where?"

He leaned in closer, his shoulder brushing mine as he pointed again. "Right there, in the center, under where the sun just set."

Finally, I saw it. A tiny speck beneath the purple-streaked sky, just visible against the velvety waves.

"So..." I ventured, my voice softer now.

"So?" he echoed, turning to look at me.

For a second, neither of us spoke. His eyes held mine, the wind teasing the loose strands of my hair. I saw his fingers twitching, as if he wanted to do something about my hair. I pressed at them, doing the work for him.

"Did you like this place?" I asked.

As usual, he took his time to think, his gaze steady and unreadable.

"I've been here before," he said at last.

I blinked, stunned. "How?" It was hard to imagine someone like Nolan, a man who radiated efficiency and purpose, spending time in an "unproductive" place like this, where the only activity was simply being.

"I paraglide. Over there." He gestured toward the green patch on the side. "Almost every other week. I've missed it the last couple of months."

"What?" My voice rose in disbelief.

"But I never thought of coming to this side of the cliff, let alone to this very risky rock."

"You paraglide by yourself?"

"No," he replied, deadpan. "I take the gliders."

I let out an audible chuckle. "I meant without a trainer."

As I spoke, a shiver ran through me. The ocean breeze had turned cold, and my thin Van Gogh T-shirt and jean shorts offered little protection. I knew temperatures drop pretty quickly by the ocean at this height, but I hadn't planned on staying here this long. I rubbed my bare arms, wishing I'd brought a sweater.

Without a word, Nolan shrugged off his suit jacket and draped it over my shoulders. The weight of it settled around me, the fabric still warm from his body. His hands lingered at my shoulders for half a second before he pulled away.

"Yes," he said, answering my earlier question. "Without a trainer. I started learning it when I was nineteen."

"Thank you," I murmured, pulling his suit's lapels close. It smelled of him—clean, foresty, something distinctly Nolan.

"Of course."

Trying to ignore how unfairly good he looked in just that white shirt—how the crisp fabric stretched over his broad shoulders—I quickly redirected the conversation. "What made you take up paragliding?"

"I envied the birds," he said, matter-of-factly.

The sentence hit me. Only Nolan could say something so poetic and make it sound like he was discussing stock prices.

I sensed there was more to the story, so I waited, letting the waves fill the silence.

"That was the year my mother died," he finally said, his gaze locked on the horizon, now darkening into night.

"I didn't know. I'm so sorry."

He nodded, his expression steely. "I was nineteen and stuck." He said the word "stuck" the same way he had said it a while back in the parking lot. With contempt. "She was the one person who lifted me, and losing her felt like losing my foundation. I hated what I'd become. Isolated, stagnant. The world kept moving forward, and I was left behind, flailing. It was pathetic, and I couldn't stand myself. I was—"

"It's called grief," I interrupted gently.

"What?" He turned to me, his sharp gaze almost challenging.

"What you were experiencing. You weren't pathetic, Nolan. You were grieving."

He tilted his head, as though weighing the truth of my words, before finally giving a small nod. "Maybe. But grief or not, I couldn't let it define me. I needed a way out, something to shake off the weight."

"What about your father? Was he in the picture?"

"Nope."

This time, I didn't wait. I knew that was a full sentence.

"So, you were talking about a way out..." I urged him to continue.

"My mother didn't have a happy childhood," he said, his voice lowering. "She grew up near the ocean in India and used to dream about being a fish. She thought if she were a fish, she could swim away from it all. Her pain, her struggles. She'd be free."

I wasn't prepared for this. In my best-case scenario, I had imagined Nolan saying something like, "It's nice," about this spot and then leaving. Instead, he was here, sitting close to me, sharing this deeply personal story.

I stayed quiet, giving him the space to continue.

"That idea, of swimming away, brought her comfort," he said, his tone still and firm. "But she never learned to swim. She was terrified of drowning. And somehow, she passed that fear down to me. So when I hit the same wall she did, I thought, if I can't swim, I'll fly.

That's how I found paragliding. Every time I'm up there, I imagine her below me, swimming in the ocean, free at last."

I was a writer, and I'd read enough beautiful prose to fill a library, but this was possibly the most profound and heart-wrenching thing I'd ever heard. It broke my heart.

"Wow," I whispered, my throat tight as I watched a distant bird soaring. "That's... beautiful." I looked back at him, fumbling for the right words. "I mean, I'm sorry. I didn't mean to romanticize your pain. It's just—"

Nolan raised a hand, cutting me off. "I know what you meant," he said. I couldn't tell if he regretted sharing something so vulnerable or if he was completely at ease with his own honesty.

After a while, I spoke again, needing to lighten the moment.

"I come here for the opposite reason," I said. "I love this place because it feels like it anchors me. All my life, I've been drifting...like some stray plastic bag in the wind, and I got tired of it. The first time I came here, this place felt like a semicolon; not an end, but a pause. A chance to rest until I'm ready to cross the ocean and find new ground."

"You should try flying, too," Nolan said, a look of reassurance on his face.

I didn't know what to say, so I took a moment, just like him. The moment turned into a second, and the second turned into a minute. The world went quiet and the waves got louder, and we just stayed, being.

"I'll follow you home," Nolan said suddenly, shifting as if to stand. "Just to make sure your car doesn't break down again."

I nodded, but neither of us moved. The rock beneath us seemed to hold us there, as if the night itself didn't want us to leave.

We sat there long after the sky completely darkened and stars and a moon popped in the sky.

He shifted closer, his thigh brushing mine. The heat of his body radiated through his clothes. My pulse quickened as I became hyper-aware of every detail. The faint scrape of his shoes on the ground, the soft rustle of his shirt as he moved, the sound of his breath.

I turned toward him, and our eyes met. The moonlight caught the angles of his face, softening the sharp lines that usually seemed so intimidating. He held my gaze, his expression unreadable yet impossibly magnetic.

Neither of us spoke, but the space between us seemed to hum with something unspoken. His hand moved slightly, brushing against my thigh, and it sent a jolt through me.

"We...should go," I managed, my voice barely above a whisper.

He stood first, offering me a hand. I hesitated, then slipped my fingers into his. The warmth of his touch grounded me as he pulled me to my feet. For a second, we stood there, closer than we'd been all night, as if we were the last two remaining humans standing at the edge of the world.

Nolan moved away first.

I followed him down the trail, glancing back at the rock we sat on. My most special place on earth became more special. I looked at Nolan's back and wrapped his suit jacket tighter around me.

With the sounds of the waves fading behind us, I felt the tides turning inside me. I realized, I was falling hard for this man. My roommate, my nemesis, the one I hated.

CHAPTER 13

Adrian was slouched on my bed, his elbow resting on his knee, fingers threading through his hair. He'd been like this since he walked through the door, barely saying a word before collapsing into the cushions. He hadn't accepted any of the things I'd offered him as Ivy-style therapy—coffee, junk food, pastries, or even our favorite Gilmore Girls episodes. But I could see a discussion on dark, existential topics brewing in the silence.

I sat beside him, rubbing his arm, my head resting on his shoulder. By now, we'd both learned that when our stress peaked, silent comfort worked better than an avalanche of assurances.

"They didn't just ruin each other's lives," he muttered finally. "They robbed me of a healthy one too."

I followed his gaze to the ceiling, catching the familiar flicker of pain in his eyes. The kind only family could inflict.

Squeezing his arm gently, I tried to steer the conversation elsewhere. He needed a break from his parents' drama. "How's that new project going?" I asked. "It's a hotel, right?"

He straightened, running his hands over his face. "Do you realize how insane it is? Two people who were supposedly madly in love at one point now can't stand to breathe the same air." I'd failed to change the subject. "It makes you wonder if we've been handed the wrong map."

"What map?"

"The whole layout of 'love at first sight' and falling madly in love and soulmates nonsense. Maybe love isn't supposed to be this dramatic, all-consuming thing, with complicated directions that we are supposed to follow one after the other. Maybe it's supposed to be simpler, like following the stars to find your way home."

"Adrian..." I tilted my head. "I know you're going through something, but please start making sense."

He stared at me for a moment, as if weighing a decision, then spoke again. "Maybe it isn't supposed to be this hard. It's supposed to be easy, like being able to sit calmly next to someone, even when you are burning inside."

"Adrian..." I said cautiously.

"Just hear me out, Ivy." He turned slightly toward me, my arm still curled around his. "Ever since I understood what love was, I promised myself I'd never be like my parents. I'd find someone I not only love but trust and respect. I've been searching for that my entire adult life. There are girls who are great, but they barely move me. Then there are the ones I connect with, but they end up losing my respect or trust.

I know what you're thinking," he said, reading my expression. "Believe me, I've tried to let go of this hopeless search. To stop chasing 'the one' and just take life as it comes. But on days like today, I wish for nothing more than a companion. A teammate. Someone to just sit beside me and make everything feel right.

A warning siren went off in my chest.

He took a moment before speaking again. "We've known each other since we were kids. The universe has worked its vicious ways to separate us, putting thousands of miles and an asshole between us, but we found our way back to each other. When life has hit me the hardest, you've always been there, and I'd like to think I was there for you too. Ivy." He retracted his arm from mine and held my hands. "What if...*you* are my home? The one where the stars have been guiding me to all along. What if you are the person I've been searching for...God knows how many years."

I stared at him, my mind scrambling to process his words.

"What the hell are you talking about, Adrian?" I finally said, less firmly than I intended.

"I'm talking about us," he said, his voice cracking. "Maybe this is how it's supposed to be. Maybe the best foundation for love isn't sparks or butterflies. It's trust. It's friendship. You're my best friend, Ivy, and I..." He hesitated, his hand gripping mine so tightly my thumb ring pressed into my skin. "I think I have feelings for you."

My throat closed up. This couldn't be happening. I opened my mouth to respond, but nothing came out.

"Adrian..."

A soft knock interrupted me. Nolan poked his head in.

"How's the revision—" He didn't bother finishing his sentence when he noticed Adrian. Nolan's gaze lingered on him for a moment longer. Then his eyes flicked over the both of us. We were half-lying on my bed, close under a blanket and holding hands.

"Hey," I said, snatching my hands from Adrian's. "Give me an hour. I'll email you the revised draft."

"Right," Nolan said, stepping back from the doorway.

Before I could say anything more, he was gone, and I heard his footsteps retreating down the hall. I dropped back on the bed, feeling a pang of guilt. Nolan had clearly needed something work-related, but Adrian, our friendship, needed me more right now.

"He hates me, doesn't he?" Adrian asked.

It threw me off, his question, but I tried to act casual. "Probably. But if it helps you feel better, he hates everyone."

"It's different with me. Every time we cross paths, he looks at me like I've sucked all the happiness out of his life."

"Hey, I'm the writer. Only I'm allowed to use hyperbole. You're fine."

"I think he likes you."

"What?"

"What about you?" he asked. "Do you like him?"

"Adrian, we were talking about us. I don't want to talk about Nolan."

He didn't look convinced but let it drop.

"I need to head out." He flipped the blanket and straightened his t-shirt.

"I think we should talk about...what you said. You have to rethink..."

"Ivy, I've thought about this a lot. Trust me. It's you who has to do the thinking now."

Without another word, he put on his shoes, grabbed his phone and keys, and left.

I was taken aback by what Adrian had said, but what hit me harder were my own thoughts. As much as I wanted to knock the air out of Adrian's lungs for ruining our friendship, I found myself wondering.

What if he was right?

I mean, I tried the whole all-consuming love with Trent. It didn't work out. In fact, it nearly killed me. What finally gave me comfort was Adrian's friendship.

I remember the night I told Adrian I was breaking up with Trent. It was late, and the rain outside was relentless. Trent had said cruel things before, twisting words that burrowed deep into my insecurities, but that day he crossed a line I couldn't ignore.

He called me from work, asking me to email him a file from his laptop. As I searched through a couple of folders, I stumbled upon a sub-folder labeled "Project Ivy." Confused, I clicked on it. Inside, there was a document full of notes and a video file titled "Handling Insecure Partners: The Psychology of Weakness."

It was a video he had uploaded to his YouTube channel for paid members. Trent, the self-proclaimed "confidence guru," ran a channel offering self-help, social dynamics, and lifestyle advice rooted in pseudo-psychology. For a whole month, he had used me as a subject for some sort of experiment, compiling daily observations into this video.

The attached notes made my stomach turn:

Day 6: Told Ivy that her goal should be to call herself an artist once she makes money from it. Got the expected reaction—defensiveness, followed by two days of silent treatment. Conclusion: struggles with constructive criticism.

Day 13: Praised her for standing up to her boss. Increased self-esteem levels observed. Conclusion: Positive reinforcement works.

Day 27: Set her old college pictures as the wallpaper on my laptop and phone to gauge her reaction. Conclusion: She didn't seem as rattled or interpret it as a hint to regain her previous body shape or style.

I couldn't believe my eyes. All my pain, insecurities, and vulnerabilities, reduced to data points and shared with strangers online.

When I confronted him, he gave me that chuckle I'd grown to despise. "I know it looks insane," he chuckled again. "But I was going to share my conclusions with you. It's psychology, Ivy. You're overreacting. I was only trying to know my girlfriend better. Is that a crime now?"

I left the house in silence, unable to even cry. The only thought echoing in my mind was of the Gliderport. It had always been my place of solace, but that night, the thought of the drop held a dark allure. A whisper that promised an end to the ache.

Soaked from the rain, I showed up at Adrian's door. Without saying a word, he took one look at me, pulled me inside, and grabbed a towel.

We sat on his couch in silence for what felt like hours. I clutched the towel like a lifeline while the storm rattled the windows. When

I finally told him, through sobs, that I couldn't do it anymore with Trent, that I wanted to die, Adrian didn't ask questions. He didn't offer empty platitudes or even say "I told you so," though he had warned me. Instead, he disappeared into his room and returned with a Rubik's Cube-sized architectural model of a house.

"Remember when we were growing up, you didn't dream about money or success or guys. All you wanted was a house of your own, somewhere you could live the way you liked and felt safe. Imagine a house like this," he said, lifting my palm and placing the tiny model in it. "Just yours. You, living alone by your own rules, painting, doing the things you love, with no one to tell you otherwise or stop you or judge you. You'll be the architect of your life. Think about how good that will feel, Ivy. That's a life you haven't lived yet, not with your family, not at the dorm, not with Trent, but it's there, waiting for you. I promise." He shook my palm, holding the model house. "Give yourself a chance."

He made me tea and sat back down beside me. We didn't talk about the Gliderport or why I went there, or Trent, or anything else that night. He just stayed there, his presence as solid and comforting as the tiny house in my palm.

It was his faith in me that helped me see myself waking up the next day.

Now, sitting on my bed, I opened my bedside drawer and grabbed the model house. A symbol. A promise. What if Adrian was right? Maybe love didn't have to be all-consuming or dramatic. Maybe it could be as simple as someone who kept you calm, even when you were burning inside.

For a moment, the fog in my head began to clear.

Then I heard the same soft knock.

Nolan appeared in the doorway of my bedroom, leaning against the frame with his arms crossed. His jaw was set tight, and though he didn't say anything, the energy he radiated was unmistakable. Controlled. But charged with something darker beneath the surface.

He glanced at me, then toward the bed where Adrian had been sitting earlier. The tension in his body was impossible to miss. The way his shoulders stiffened, his gaze unwavering.

He stood there like a sentinel, silent, his presence looming larger than usual, as though he was claiming the space in a way that left no room for anyone else.

"Adrian just left," I said, feeling the need to cut through the wordless intensity in the room.

"I noticed," Nolan replied, his voice even, though I could hear the undertone. He didn't ask why Adrian was here or why we were holding hands. He didn't need to. The unspoken claim in his posture said enough.

"You need something?" I asked.

"I am cooking you a dinner tonight. Don't order takeout." And with that he left the room.

I grabbed my knees, trying to shake off what just happened. My brain fogged again as I recalled the feelings I've been experiencing for Nolan. Our moment together at the cliff yesterday was anything but normal. I felt something, and I know he did too. Why else would someone like him share such intimate details about his life with me? Why else would he be so jealous of Adrian?

I placed the model house on my nightstand, its tiny windows catching the glint from the sun outside. Adrian's words echoed in my mind again, colliding with the tension Nolan had brought in. My emotions churned, tangled in a way that left me no closer to clarity than I had been before.

CHAPTER 14

Nothing recharges me like a good nap. Despite everything, the soul-satisfying siesta I had after the stressful afternoon left me feeling light and refreshed. I decided to leave my worries for the next day, freshened up, and changed into my most conventional looking loungewear—dark green shorts and a plain white T-shirt.

When I walked into the living room, Nolan was unloading ingredients from the fridge and grocery bags, lining them up on the kitchen counter with the precision of a chemist preparing some alchemical masterpiece. He was wearing a blue linen button-down shirt over black linen pants, the shirt untucked. It was the most casual I had ever seen him.

I knew he cooked, but I usually holed up in the bedroom when he was in the kitchen. I'd never seen him in action before. Trent was a decent cook too, but he only ever stepped into the kitchen when we had friends over. Always the showman, wanting to score as many compliments he could out of one meal.

"Sit," Nolan said, nodding toward the stool by the kitchen island. "Dinner will be ready in an hour."

The thought of a homemade meal, something other than greasy takeout, was tempting. But an hour? I grabbed my laptop and settled at the counter, deciding I might as well get some work done.

Nolan moved through the kitchen with a perfect balance of command and ease. His face was calm, his movements efficient. It wasn't rushed or frantic, just... deliberate. Watching him felt almost voyeuristic, like I was seeing a private ritual he never shared.

There was something oddly captivating about the way he handled a knife, slicing vegetables with measured precision. His hands were steady, his forearms flexing with every stroke. It was mesmerizing. From the corner of my eye, I saw him peeling ribbons of zucchini and rolling them up like fruits roll-ups. Then he tossed cherry tomatoes into a hot cast iron pan. The sound of the sizzle rung through the quiet apartment.

I wanted to comment on it, but Nolan's silence felt like an unspoken rule I shouldn't break.

One of my paradoxes is that I love silence and people who can comfortably savor it, yet my anxiety insists on filling the quiet with words, as though my own silence might be mistaken for rudeness.

So I opened my mouth. "How was your day?" I asked, completely forgetting the chaos of our afternoon.

"Productive," he said, not as a statement, but with a tone of self-assurance.

He turned his attention back to the risotto, stirring it with a patience I could only envy. There was something undeniably attractive about how he didn't feel the need to keep the conversation going.

My mind began to wander down dangerous paths I wasn't sure I wanted to explore.

But it was impossible not to notice the raw physicality of him. It was almost primal, the subtle shift of his chest under the fabric of his shirt, the steady rhythm of his body as he moved between tasks. My gaze lingered on his tanned neck, and I felt like a predator again wanting to bite at his jugular.

I bit my lip, annoyed at my own spiraling thoughts. This was Nolan, the same Nolan I had argued with, fought with. The same Nolan who had somehow managed to be both my nemesis and my employer. I could accept having a tiny crush on him, but why did

I suddenly want to prop myself up on the counter, wrap my legs around his waist, and lick the corner of his lips?

And then it hit me. I did the math.

It had been over four months since I'd last had sex. Weeks before Trent and I broke up, we'd stopped being intimate, and even before that, it had been… mechanical, like I was doing it more for his benefit. I hadn't had a truly satisfying orgasm in years.

I shook my head, trying to shove those thoughts into a couple of boxes in my closet that I still hadn't unpacked three months later.

"Need any help?" I asked, desperate for a distraction.

Nolan glanced at me, pausing mid-stir. "You want to help?"

I shrugged. "Yeah, sure. What can I do?"

He considered for a moment before saying, "You can make the dressing for the salad."

I frowned. "Can I make something I'm actually good at?"

He paused, studying me. "Fine. What are you good at?"

"Gratin Dauphinois," I said, pronouncing it like how my French grandmother taught me.

Nolan scanned me, caught off guard. "Dauphinoise potatoes? You know how to make *that*?"

"You know what that *is*?" I asked, surprised. What doesn't this guy know?

"Of course. We have potatoes," he said.

"Do *we* have cream?" I emphasized on the 'we', teasingly.

"I eat plant-based. Make it without dairy."

"But the cream is the best part! That's like making snow cones without syrup."

He shot me a look that he often gives me when I crack silly jokes while working.

"Fine," I said, rolling my eyes. "I'll improvise. Do you have flour? Butter? Oh, wait, you won't eat butter either, right?"

"Flour's in the pantry," he said, pointing with his knife. "Plant-based butter in the fridge. And go easy on the butter."

Raising an eyebrow, I gathered the ingredients.

As I peeled the potatoes, I wondered how I'd slice them thin by hand when Nolan opened a cabinet, pulled out a mandoline slicer, and placed it on the counter.

"Of course," I said. "Of course, you have a mandoline slicer casually lying around in your kitchen cabinet."

And then, he smiled. A full, unguarded smile with teeth and everything. My heart fluttered, and the butterflies in my stomach went wild.

As I started preparing the dish, I could feel Nolan's eyes on me, like he was secretly judging my every move. I created white sauce out of plant-based butter, flour, and oat milk to substitute for cream, then started slicing the potatoes.

We fell into an odd rhythm. Me slicing the potatoes in a messy frenzy, spilling slices outside the bowl, while Nolan, ever the perfectionist, kept his side of the counter pristine. The mishaps didn't stop there.

I was putting away the butter when the lid of Nolan's glass butter dish slipped from my hand and fell to the floor.

Nolan grabbed my arm and pulled me into him, as if to shield me from the broken glass. My back slammed into his body, and I felt the light scrape of his stubble against my temple. For a moment, we stood frozen, his hand firm on my arm, his body a wall of heat behind me.

"I'm okay. It didn't break," I said, glancing at the lid on the floor. I picked it up and waved it in front of Nolan. "It's my hidden talent, smashing glass without breaking it."

"Sure," Nolan said, shaking his head with a faint smile of amusement.

I rubbed a halved garlic clove around a buttered baking dish, its sharp scent filling the kitchen. Layer by layer, I arranged the potatoes, pouring the white sauce over them and adding small chunks of garlic. My grandmother's signature touch. She had taught me how to make this dish when I was eleven because it was my favorite, and my mother refused to make it. Or anything else for that matter.

"If you want to eat it every week, you'll have to learn it yourself," she had said in her thick French accent.

When I placed the dish in the oven to bake, I realized it wasn't the act of cooking I hated. I actually enjoyed the process, even though it took me thirty minutes to finish. So why had I stopped?

Was it the exhaustion from Trent's constant criticisms? Or just life grinding me down?

Nolan broke my train of thought.

"Go have a seat. I'll set the table while it bakes."

"I can help," I offered.

"It's my dinner. You've done enough."

I nodded and turned to leave the kitchen but paused at the doorway to ask what had been on my mind for a while.

"Do you mind if we eat on the balcony? It's really nice outside tonight."

I braced for his response, expecting something along the lines of, 'Civilized people eat inside,' or 'We already have a space specifically designed for eating.'

But instead...

"Okay," he said simply. "I'll call you when it's ready."

I went to my room and pulled on my favorite rust-colored cardigan, worn soft over six years. Digging through a drawer, I fished out a pair of cozy socks. It might get chilly outside.

I hesitated in front of the mirror, then decided to undo my messy bun, letting my hair fall over my shoulders. A quick spritz of mist on my neck and a dab of lip gloss later, I felt... more presentable.

When Nolan called me, I stepped onto the balcony and froze.

The space was transformed. A small, square dinner table sat near the railing, set with two perfectly plated dishes and two glasses of red wine glimmering beside a single lit candle.

As I took my seat, I couldn't help but admire the plate before me. A gorgeous looking pesto risotto, topped with roasted tomatoes, baked zucchini roll-ups, and my golden-crusted gratin dauphinois. Nolan disappeared briefly, returning with two small salad plates, which he placed beside our wine glasses.

Then, instead of sitting across from me, he dragged his chair adjacent to my left and sat down.

I straightened up, nerves kicking in, and instead of obsessing over how close he was, I forced myself to focus on the moment.

The food looked amazing, but it wasn't just the meal. Nolan had put so much effort in serving me this dinner. For a brief, heart-stopping moment, it felt like... a date, the way Nolan had set everything up. But I couldn't say that, after all, it was I who had requested to sit outside, and sitting outside in the dark required a candle.

I looked to my right toward the Pacific in the distance, the water glimmering under the moonlight.

"Very good," Nolan said with a small nod of approval as he tasted the gratin.

I grinned and took a bite myself, praying my dish wasn't a disaster.

"Hmm... Interesting," I said, savoring the creaminess and the subtle garlicky hint. "I thought the flour and oat milk would ruin it, but this... isn't bad at all."

His expression told me everything: I told you so.

I worked my way through the plate, tasting everything. The simple arugula, date, and walnut salad, which tasted better than than all the salads I had in my life, because of how fresh and perfectly dressed the ingredients were; the tender zucchini roll-ups stuffed with cashew ricotta over a bed of marinara; and finally, the risotto, warm and utterly comforting. That risotto would rule my palate for years to come.

Nolan gave me one of his rare, genuine smiles, his expression softening as he watched me devour everything.

"You're a magician," I said, shaking my head in disbelief, my mouth still full.

"It's my hidden talent," he replied, his tone playful, echoing my earlier joke.

We talked and ate, the warmth of the food mingling with the crisp summer evening of San Diego. Nolan talked about his journey of designing the AI model for his start-up, while I shared how I stumbled into copywriting after struggling to find a job in my media studies field. We were more open with each other than ever before, yet we remained cautiously tethered to safe topics. Work, ambitions, and career paths, steering clear of the minefields of family or deeper personal matters. For that, I think we were both grateful.

For the first time since I'd moved in, there was something in the air besides tension.

Hoping the remaining three months passes just as smoothly, I took a big sip of wine and leaned into the cool ocean breeze. When I glanced at Nolan, I found him already looking at me.

Under the candlelight, his serious face glowed with a faint trace of tenderness.

He reached out, catching a strand of my hair fluttering in the breeze, and tucked it gently behind my ear. The brush of his fingers against my ear sent a shiver down my spine.

"Thanks," I murmured, unsure what else to say.

When he looked into my eyes again, holding the gaze a few seconds longer than usual, I couldn't ignore the question forming in my mind. The candle might have been necessary, and the balcony was my idea, but... the fancy dinner? The wine? The way he tucked my hair behind my ear?

"Can I ask you something?"

"Shoot," he said, scooping up another bite of risotto.

"Why did you offer to make me dinner?"

He set his fork down, tightening his jaw briefly. "Because I felt like it," he answered, his tone even, his gaze unwavering.

"But..."

"Don't overthink it," he interrupted gently. "I just felt you deserved a good home-cooked meal. I am not great with words, and acts of service is how I express my... gratitude."

It was surprising that he knew about different love languages, but that wasn't what struck me. It was the way he said it. Intimate, sincere, and the warmth of his words spread through my chest. If I wasn't so happy, I might have cried. No one had ever taken the time to cook for me or show me real gratitude. Ever. I've spent most of my life hungry, starving, not just for food but for care, and thankless, doing for others without so much as a nod in return. Just being seen as someone deserving of a good meal and a little kindness felt like the world to me.

"Thank you," I said softly.

"Thank *you*," he replied. "I went over the revised draft. Barring a couple of changes," I cringed, but his generous smile, uncreased my nose, "it looks great. You sure have a way with words."

To my utter disbelief, I felt my cheeks flush. "It's your project that brought it out of me," I said. "Usually, I'm writing about overpriced machines sold and bought by soulless corporations. That kind of work feels like just putting one word after another to pay the bills. But knowing how much of a difference your start-up could make, it made me want to expect more from myself. I've never written seven drafts of a single article before."

"Perfectionism is beautiful," he said simply.

"Umm... I'd call it pressure."

"I'd call it the need to give your best," he argued, a hint of playfulness dancing in his tone.

"Dauphinoise potahtoh, Dauphinoise pohtaata."

I quipped and glanced up from my plate to find Nolan staring at me. A brief silence hung between us, and then he laughed. A rich, musical sound that I'd first heard during the beach cleanup. It was heavy yet light, strong yet tender, rhythmic yet wild. I wanted to grab his face and plant a kiss on that mouth.

As I sat there by Nolan, laughing and savoring each moment, it all became clear to me. Adrian was wrong. The all-consuming, dramatic love is overrated, yes. But there's another kind. The kind that isn't rooted in friendship yet grows steadily toward it.

I wasn't sure if that was what I was building with Nolan. I wasn't even sure if love was something I wanted right now. Not after everything I'd been through with Trent. But one thing I knew for certain: I didn't deserve a relationship built on calculations or a fear of being alone. Love shouldn't be the product of overthinking or careful analysis; it should simply happen, natural and unforced.

I deserved that. And Adrian did too, his one true companion, the one he'd been searching for. Letting him believe I was "the one" or that our love and concern for each other had some ulterior motive, would betray everything our friendship stood for.

The realization brought a wonderful lightness to my chest.

I took a second helping of the risotto, and then Nolan brought out dessert from the freezer. A mango coconut sorbet he had made from scratch.

"You made this at home?" I exclaimed, savoring the sweet, tangy dessert on my tongue.

"It's not as difficult as you think."

"Still…" I argued. "Who knew that behind all the brooding and computer coding, there's a Michelin-starred chef just waiting to break free?"

Nolan laughed again, and my heart seemed to hum in response.

WE CARRIED OUR PLATES back inside.

"I'll take it from here," Nolan said, reaching for the dish in my hand.

"No, I'll help. The dishes…" I glanced at the mountain by the sink, remembering one of the reasons I'd stopped cooking, "are a lot."

"I've got this," he said again, his voice firm, leaving no room for argument.

I nodded and turned to grab some water from the fridge. When I turned back around, I walked straight into his chest.

"Sorry," I murmured, inhaling his scent. This time he smelled like red wine and cool ocean breeze.

Instead of stepping aside, he stayed rooted in place. I wanted to get away, knowing well I was with the person I was supposed to hate. He was my land lord *and* my employer, for god's sake. But I didn't move either, caught in the gravitational pull of his presence. It felt right.

He took a step closer. I placed the water jug on the counter, suddenly conscious of how erratic my breathing had become. I couldn't bring myself to meet his eyes, afraid I'd give away too much.

He reached out and grazed his hand through my hair, before sliding the tip of his fingers to my nape. Each nerve of my body ignited in response. With his other hand, he held the side of my waist, pressing the elastic of my shorts into my skin.

My hand instinctively found his arm, and I was struck by how solid he felt beneath my finger.

With his thumb, he nudged my chin upward, his other fingers still pressed on the back of my neck. When I finally met his gaze, his expression was raw, intense. Hunger burned in his eyes, but behind it, I saw something else. A battle, a hesitation.

The king of efficiency and perfectionism was weighing pros and cons of kissing me, wondering if he wasn't making a mistake. It was written all over his face, bright as day.

The realization jolted me. I pulled back.

His eyes narrowed, a hint of something—disappointment? frustration?—crossing his face.

"It's late," I said, my voice soft but firm. "I have an early meeting tomorrow." It wasn't a lie; I did have an in-person copywriters' conference to attend.

I turned and walked away, closing my bedroom door behind me.

I couldn't do intimacy born of calculations again. The first time Trent and I kissed, I let it happen. Not because I wanted to, but because we'd been on four dates, and it felt wrong, unfair even, to deny him a kiss on the fifth.

No more math. No more logic. If I was going to risk this again, it had to be all heart. From both sides.

I couldn't be a compromise, not even for Nolan.

CHAPTER 15

The drive back home from the copywriters' meeting, which could easily have been a video conference, was just as draining as the meeting itself. I had completely fallen out of touch with the ability to socialize in groups larger than two people.

Since moving to California, I'd been working from home. Sure, I tried my hand at a few odd jobs during the first couple of months, but I was searching for something stable, something aligned with my academic background. At one of Trent's friend's parties, I met a woman hiring copywriters for my current employer. She asked me to email her my résumé after Trent joked, "Only Ivy can turn an anecdote about being stuck in traffic into a three-act screenplay."

Adrian often questioned how someone as perceptive as me could stay with someone like Trent for so long, especially when he treated me so terribly. One reason was the sunk-cost fallacy. The other? Between his dozen critical remarks about everything I did, wore, or said, he'd give one or two compliments so genuine and profound they could lift me above the world and feel better about myself. That remark about my storytelling, it wasn't just flattery; I knew he truly meant it.

The job wasn't what I was looking for, and the pay wasn't great, but it let me work from home. I thought that would leave me enough time and energy to focus on my art.

It didn't.

If not for the renewed excitement I'd discovered writing for Nolan's start-up, I probably would've quit the copywriting gig within the next few months.

I lowered my chin and used one hand to brush the hardened icing from my cinnamon bun off my shirt while unlocking the apartment door with the other.

As the door swung open, I was greeted by a vaguely familiar face.

"Ivy! Hey," Elena said with a bright smile.

My automatic response, a polite "Hey" accompanied by an equally polite smile, kicked in before I could think. Then the memory of my argument with Nolan flooded back, the fight we had because I talked to his friend. I wasn't going to let him accuse me anymore of crossing the boundary.

I turned my head, catching sight of Nolan in the kitchen filling the tea kettle. Without acknowledging either of them further, I walked past, pretending I had something pressing to attend to.

"Nolan!" Elena's voice was low, laced with reprimand, and just sharp enough to make me turn back.

Nolan was shooting warning looks at Elena before his expression shifted and sagged into something that resembled defeat.

"Wait, Ivy." He looked down at his empty tea cup, his voice measured.

I stopped and glanced between the two of them.

"I'm sorry for the way I got angry about you talking to Elena," he began, the words sounding rehearsed. "It wasn't my place to dictate who either of you should or shouldn't talk to. Moving forward, I have no issue if you both choose to communicate." He paused, raising a brow slightly at Elena.

Elena gave him an assuring nod and then smiled at me.

"That's very mature of you, Nolan," she almost bowed to him with her hands clasped together, a mischievous grin on her face. Then she turned to me. "Tea, Ivy?"

"Sorry," I stammered, scrambling for an excuse. "I have—"

"Ivy." Nolan said my name differently this time, with a tone layered with unspoken frustration or questions, likely stemming from last night when we almost made out. "I was leaving, anyway." He filled the mugs with hot water. "Please feel free to hang around."

He grabbed tea bags from the cabinet, dropped them into mugs, and set two steaming teas on the kitchen island before disappearing into his room.

I stood there, frozen, unsure of what to say.

"Care for some chat?" Elena's calm voice pulled me back to the present as she offered me a mug.

It felt impolite to refuse tea from someone who was as warm and tranquil as tea itself.

"Thanks," I murmured, accepting the cup.

I smelled jasmine under my nose. The only tea I drank. This was the second time Nolan gave me the right tea. Did he make note of my taste?

Elena headed for the couch, glancing over her shoulder to indicate I should join her. She wore a cream-colored blouse layered under a sand-colored cardigan, paired with high-waisted, sage green trousers and stylish brown ankle boots.

All my life, I had been terrible at making friends. Partly because people weren't that interested in being friends with me. I was the one standing in the corner at a party, lost in my own head. Adrian had been my first true friend after my sister, and he was the one who had approached me. After he left, I met Trent, and since then, my only friends had been his friends. That's why I didn't have anyone now. They all disappeared when I broke up with Trent.

So, it surprised me that someone like Elena was so interested in talking to me, enough that she schooled her close friend for it.

"Are you sure Nolan won't be upset that we're talking?" I asked.

"Ivy, we're approaching the end of the first quarter of the 21st century. Women don't need men telling them who they can talk to."

When she put it like that, I couldn't help but light up.

"Good point," I said. "But I'd really appreciate it if we didn't talk about Nolan."

"I agree," she replied easily. "But before we don't talk about Nolan, I'd like to apologize. The other night, I didn't mean to relay our conversation to him. He was doubting himself and I had to say a few things about our talk to make a point."

"It's okay," I said. "I don't blame you."

"Thanks." Elena took a sip of her tea, then leaned back. "So, tell me something about you, Ivy." Her tone was curious but casual, like she actually wanted to know, not just filling silence.

I raised a brow. "I'm sure he-who-must-not-be-named has already told you everything."

She made her big-sister face again. "You think his limited opinion, based on three months of knowing you, tells me everything I need to know about you?"

Damn. Clever.

I exhaled a soft laugh despite myself. "Okay, fair." I hesitated before asking, "Why are you so interested in talking to someone like me?"

"What do you mean, 'someone like you'?"

I glanced down at myself, making a vague gesture as if to say, this dull, messy, broken piece of work right here. "I'm not exactly the easiest person to befriend. I didn't even try to talk to you."

Elena shrugged, unfazed. "Honesty. I like it." She set her cup down. "If we're being real, I'm doing this for me as much as for you. I don't really have any close girlfriends, and I want one. There's something about having that kind of connection... it just makes life better."

I studied her. That feeling, that longing, I understood it.

"I get that," I admitted. "My best friend is a guy. We'd take a bullet for each other, but... some things, he just wouldn't get."

Elena nodded knowingly. "So why didn't you make more friends?"

I tapped my fingers against my cup, thinking. "It's a long story. You got a week?" I said, only half-joking.

"I do." She tucked her legs underneath her and swept her hair back. "Shoot."

The way she said "shoot", it reminded me of Nolan.

I let out a breath. "I was in a relationship for almost three years. We broke up right before I moved here. And during that time... I made his world mine. His favorite food became my favorite. His travel destinations, my dream trips. His friends were my friends."

Elena listened. Not just waiting for her turn to speak, but actually listening. No glancing at her phone, no distractions. It was oddly... comforting.

"I never really built my own life," I admitted. "Didn't even notice it happening. One day, I woke up, and it was all his. And when it ended, I didn't know what was left of me."

She was quiet for a moment, eyes flickering with something unreadable. Then, almost absently, she said, "I'm you."

I frowned. "What?"

"I mean... I'm the past you."

I tilted my head. "Meaning?"

Elena exhaled, shifting slightly. "I've been doing the same thing. For the past five and a half years. With Jay." She swallowed, then continued, "Unlike you, I did have my own friends. But the moment I got into a relationship, I stopped hanging out with them. And the ones I did see? They started bringing their partners, because I always brought mine. Even Nolan, my closest friend, became a shared friend. After Jay and I got together, he bonded with Jay, and they became just as close. I can't even remember the last time Nolan and I hung out, just the two of us."

I hesitated. "That's... normal, right? That's what happens in relationships?"

"Not for Jay." She let out a short laugh, but there was no humor in it. "He has his own life. His own friends, hobbies. Meanwhile, I'm the one who automatically thinks of him first, the one who turns girls' nights into couples' nights, the one who won't do anything unless he's part of it." Her voice grew quieter, heavier.

The room felt... still. Not awkward, just heavy with unspoken things.

I shifted slightly. "Sorry if I—"

"No, Ivy." Elena reached out, giving my hand a quick squeeze. "Don't apologize. We were talking about you, and I completely hijacked the conversation."

"That was...more than okay," I said honestly. A part of me didn't want to dwell on my past, but another part wanted to know more about Elena. "I just didn't want to upset you."

"You didn't," she assured me. "If anything... this actually helped."

She stood abruptly, looking for a place to set her mug. I took it from her.

"You okay?" I asked.

She nodded, but her mind was somewhere else. "Yeah. I just need some time to think." Then, softer, "But I really like talking to you and want to know more about what you were saying."

I smiled. "I liked talking to you too."

As she reached the door, she glanced back. "Message me a time and place. Let's go out next time."

I nodded.

She grinned. "Bye, Pirate Girl."

A laugh bubbled up. "Bye, Druid Fairie."

The door shut behind her, and I stood there for a second, holding my tea.

Did I just make a new friend?

CHAPTER 16

I sat on my bed, wrapped in two blankets, as the golden hour light spilled across the wall behind me. My fingers hovered over my laptop keys, but my mind resisted focus, craving rest instead. Ever since Elena left four days ago, I'd felt feverish and drained. I probably picked up something at the copywriters' meet-up, where, like an idiot, I forgot to sanitize after shaking hands with someone visibly battling the flu. The thought nagged at me, especially the worry that I might have passed it to Elena. But when I checked in on her, she seemed fine.

After that night in the kitchen, when I'd pulled away right before the kiss, I thought Nolan would either resent me or avoid me completely. He'd certainly looked offended at the time, and Elena had only made things worse by siding with me and urging him to apologize. I was convinced we'd never be cordial again.

But he surprised me.

He hadn't just been pleasant. He'd been uncharacteristically kind during my illness. For someone who valued deadlines so much, I'd expected him to be frustrated that I couldn't work on his website. Instead, he'd been patient. No pressure, no sharp words.

Every single evening, he brought me soup, despite my resistance. He checked in on me regularly and even ran out for medicine the first night when my fever spiked. Last night, when he delivered yet another bowl of his homemade soup, he placed the spoon inside and stirred it for me before handing it over, knowing I'd burned my tongue the night before.

That small, thoughtful gesture broke me. It was one thing to cook a fancy dinner for someone, but caring for someone who was sick, gross, and cranky felt like a selfless act of love, romantic or otherwise.

I was still a little upset with him for hesitating before kissing me, but I couldn't deny how much his kindness meant. I'd never forget this side of Nolan, even if, or when, things went downhill between us.

I tried to shake the thought of him away as I shifted my focus back to my work. The fever was gone, the cold and cough had subsided, and my mind was finally clear. I had a lot of catching up to do.

Just as I scrolled through my draft, Nolan walked in, holding a large bowl of soup. He set it down on the nightstand with that same quiet composure that always seemed so effortless for him.

"I increased the portion size," he said. "I think you can stomach more food now. It's red lentil soup with whole wheat croutons. How are you feeling?"

"Much, much better," I replied. "You didn't have to bring me soup in bed anymore."

"Eat it." He pointed his chin firmly toward the bowl.

"Thanks." I picked it up, noticing the spoon already inside and the soup stirred to perfect temperature. The familiar knot formed in my throat, and I quickly changed the subject to distract myself.

"You know, I feel like a grandma having dinner this early, with the outside still so bright," I said, glancing out the window at the clear blue summer sky.

"You *do* sound better," he commented, his eyes briefly meeting mine before returning to his phone.

"I'm actually doing great. There's still a little weakness, but I can breathe now without sounding like a broken kettle. Sorry I couldn't do anything these past four days, but I've been working on the final draft of my last article. We can start brainstorming the next one after I am done eating." I slurped a big spoonful of warm, comforting soup. Unlike Nolan's usual bold flavors, this wasn't heavily seasoned, but the garlic and lemon hit just the right spot. It felt like life returning to my veins. "This soup is amazing! Thank you so much."

I looked up to find Nolan staring at me, a confused expression on his face.

"What?" I asked, tilting my head.

"You've been working from bed?"

I grinned faintly between sips. "Nolan, I'm better, but I'm still officially sick. I'm not moving away from my bed just yet."

He raised an eyebrow, skepticism etched in his features. "So, you're saying we should discuss the next article like this? From your bed?"

I shrugged, setting the empty bowl down on the nightstand. I knew what it might mean to invite my nemesis-slash-roommate-slash-almost-kisser-slash-freelance employer into my bed, but at this point, we were at least friends, or something close to it. If we'd survived that awkward encounter in the kitchen, surely, we could survive working from one bed.

Besides, guilt nagged at me for not meeting my deadlines. I needed to get things done without letting myself relapse.

"I know you're not telling me how behind we are on your schedule because I was sick," I said softly. "But I also know how much deadlines matter to you. So...it's fine. I get that you don't work anywhere but your desk, but for one day, we can work from bed like most Americans."

He hesitated for a moment, then walked around to the other side of the bed and sat down, stiff and uncomfortable.

"You can put your feet up," I advised. "As tired as I was, I did wash the sheets and pillows today."

Nolan shot me a sharp look, but the slight twitch at the corner of his mouth betrayed his attempt not to smile. He leaned back a little, and after a beat, placed his legs on the bed. A loud, involuntary sigh escaped him as he sank into the mattress.

It was then I noticed how utterly exhausted he looked. His eyes were sunken, his posture weary, and his face bore the telltale signs of overwork. Knowing him, he'd likely been juggling his usual demanding work schedule with running his start-up and taking care of me. Guilt twisted in my chest.

"You look so tired, Nolan," I said softly.

"Thanks for the compliment," he replied, his tone dry, as though I'd offended him.

"No, I mean it's okay to let yourself rest when you're this tired. One can work toward their dreams and still take care of themselves."

"Not when the one is me," he muttered. "Besides, I eat healthy and work out seven days a week. I'm taking better care of myself than most people."

"It's not just physical health that keeps us going," I argued.

"Can we just..." He gestured toward my laptop. "Focus on work? You need to get back to bed soon so you can fully recover by tomorrow."

I nodded, but a heavy worry for him lingered in the back of my mind. It surprised me how much I wanted him to be okay.

I opened my Spotify playlist titled "Palette Cleanser" and hit play.

"I thought we were working," Nolan commented, narrowing his eyes at the screen. "And what kind of name is that for a playlist?"

"We *are* working. It's just background music for brainstorming. And as for the name, I made the playlist for when I need to clear my mind. It refreshes my brain."

Nolan raised his brows but eventually nodded in defeat. "Fine. Let's get started."

As I pulled up the Excel sheet of our ideas, the warmth radiating from his body filled the small space between us. Despite the lingering weakness in me, it felt...nice, and comfortable. Strange, considering everything that had transpired after that dinner.

For an hour, we worked, bouncing ideas back and forth. With each exchange, I could feel my strength returning, one idea at a time.

But as our discussion wore on, Nolan's contributions became fewer and quieter. When I turned to check on him, I found him fast asleep, his head tilted at an awkward angle. He looked so uncomfortable, still in his formal work clothes, belt and shoes included, but I didn't have the heart to wake him.

I knew if I did, he'd dive right back into work. Instead, I decided to finish the topic I was researching, then move to the couch so he could get some proper rest.

But I must have dozed off as well because when I next opened my eyes, it was dark outside, and I had slid down my bed. My laptop rested on its side, its screen black, abandoned. It took me a moment to orient myself, to notice the steady warmth wrapped around my left hand. Strong, steady, possessive.

Nolan's palm.

My pulse quickened as reality came into focus. He was in my bed and we were holding hands.

I turned around cautiously, and my breath caught in my throat.

Nolan was awake. Not just awake. Watching. Waiting. His dark brown, thoughtful eyes were locked on mine. His grip on my hand didn't waver. If anything, his fingers curled slightly tighter around mine, as if daring me to pull away.

There was a faint shade of longing on his face that was impossible to miss. I experienced intense, powerful affection towards him, a feeling I'd probably not forget until my end days. It terrified me how connected I felt to him in that moment.

My chest heated up as I became hyperaware of the warmth of his skin, of the way his thumb moved in slow, absent strokes against the side of my hand.

Memories surfaced unbidden—when I was a child, I used to reach for my sister's hand in my sleep, a subconscious search for comfort. I had forgotten about it, because this had never happened with Trent. But I must have done the same with Nolan. Embarrassment flushed through me. Not wanting him to feel obligated, I gently began to pull my hand away.

Nolan didn't let me.

His hold turned firm. Not harsh. Not desperate. But unyielding.

My gaze darted back to his face. Beneath his longing, there was something else. A quiet kind of dominance. A silent declaration that he wasn't going to let me go.

The intensity of it sent a pulse of heat down my spine.

Nolan shifted closer, his movements slow and deliberate. The moonlight filtered through the window, casting a silvery glow over him. It traced the line of his jaw, his slightly rumpled hair, and a sliver of his shoulder that peeked from his slipped shirt collar. My breath stuttered as he leaned in, closing the distance.

He was too close. He wasn't close enough.

His breath fanned against my lips. My body reacted before my mind could catch up, my fingers twitching against his hold, my chest rising just a little quicker.

He paused for just a beat, as if giving me a chance to surrender.

I didn't pull away.

His hand slid to my jaw, fingers firm but claiming, his thumb pressing lightly beneath my chin as if testing how much I'd let him take.

And then his lips were on mine. Confident. Possessive. A kiss that didn't ask but took.

He tasted like strong, sweet tea, and something richer beneath it, something dark and heady, like temptation itself.

I melted into him, let his rhythm guide mine. He carried me through the kiss, as if he was a choreographer, and I, a mere dancer. But he wasn't just leading. He was consuming.

His chest pressed against mine, solid and reassuring, as his hand tangled in my hair. A low sound rumbled from deep in his throat when I arched into him, the vibration sinking into my bones.

My fingers found the buttons of his shirt, fumbling as I undid the top ones. I wanted more. Needed more.

A sharp inhale. And then his lips left mine.

Not because he was stopping. He had other plans.

His mouth found my neck, his lips tracing a slow, torturous path before his teeth caught the sensitive skin just below my jaw. A sharp nip, followed by the soothing warmth of his tongue.

A shuddering gasp tore from me. "Nolan," I moaned.

It only tightened his arms around me. His restraint, his patience, they were slipping.

I traced the curve of his neck with my lips, brushing against the taut muscle of his shoulder.

His control cracked.

He grabbed me harder. A growl, deep, primal, vibrated against my skin.

Everything about him, his touch, his scent, his presence, felt dangerously intoxicating.

Too much. Too good. Too right.

But then, like a lifeline, a sliver of clarity broke through.

I pulled back, breathless and trembling.

"I can't," I whispered, my voice barely audible over the pounding of my heart.

Nolan's forehead creased, his chest rising and falling as he tried to steady himself.

"Is it because of that Adrian guy?" he said, after a minute. His tone was quiet, but there was an edge of frustration beneath the calm.

"What?" I sat up, adjusting my t-shirt. Leaning against the headboard, I reached for the lamp, casting a warm glow over the room. "No. Adrian is just a friend."

"Then what is it?" he asked, his voice strained. "I thought you liked me too."

"I do," I admitted, my heart aching with the weight of my words. "But..."

"But what?" He sat up as well, running a hand through his hair, the lamp light catching on the tension etched into his features.

"You fix me and break me in the same breath, Nolan," I said, the words tumbling out before I could stop them.

He stared at me, the hurt in his eyes like a physical blow. "What does that even mean?"

I swallowed hard, struggling to find the right words. "It means that you heal the wounds I thought would never heal but then you turn around and look at me like I am a mistake. It's hard to be part of this when it feels like you're fighting yourself just to be here with me."

"That's not true," he said, his voice rising slightly before he caught himself. "Maybe it is. But it hasn't been easy for me." He took a breather, probably to decide his next words. "I planned out my entire life when I was twenty-one. This... you... weren't part of that plan. So yeah, it's throwing me off, Ivy. But isn't it something that I'm still here, wanting to be with you despite my inhibitions?"

"It would be, in a perfect world," I said, my voice laced with a sorrow I couldn't hide. "But I've spent too much of my life being someone's second choice, someone's Plan B. Not just as an adult, but even as a child."

That did it. Admitting that triggered my actual fear, and before I could stop myself, I voiced it.

"I can't do this because you act like being with me will ruin you somehow. As if there are better people you could be pursuing, but you're giving in because of momentary... whatever this is. Lust, infatuation, lapse in judgment." My voice cracked despite my strong rein on it.

That was how he made me feel. Not just a mistake, but like someone lesser, and I refused to feel inferior again.

Nolan looked me in the eye, his voice firm. "I don't see this as momentary anything. While I am having a hard time accepting this, I've *never* been confused in my life about whom and what to pursue. You might be my chaos, but you're also my peace. I really like you."

I shook my head, tears welling in my eyes. "I don't want to be your chaos, Nolan. Sorry," I whispered, slipping out of bed and heading to the bathroom.

Once inside, I locked the door and leaned against it, rubbing my chest. Tears streamed down my face unchecked as I stared at my reflection in the mirror. The girl staring back looked broken in so many more ways than I had thought.

I splashed cold water on my face, trying to steady myself. When I finally emerged, Nolan was gone, his lingering scent on my pillow tormenting me long into the night.

CHAPTER 17

NOLAN

I stood in the hallway, fists clenched, staring at the closed door to Ivy's bathroom. My pulse thundered, frustration building with every second that passed. Rejection stung. A sharp, bitter taste I couldn't shake, and I couldn't decide whether I was more furious at her for pulling away or at myself for caring this much.

I shouldn't.

Because A. No one rejects Nolan Sterling, and B. I've never been the kind of man who looks back. I don't plan for detours, for disruptions. Certainly not for her.

And yet, here I was, losing my footing in ways I never thought possible. Looking back. Wanting someone who had turned their back on me.

This was the result of my mistakes. Three big ones, to be exact.

The first: asking Ivy to work for me.

Hiring her wasn't just logical, it was necessary. Desperation had driven me to it, and desperation wasn't a place I liked to operate from. Elena had talked me into taking the direct approach.

"Stop being childish," she'd said. "Just be honest, Nolan. If you want someone like Ivy to work for you, you'll get further by asking straightforwardly instead of scheming."

In a rare moment of weakness, or idiocy, I'd agreed with her.

So, I'd asked Ivy outright. Like ripping off a Band-Aid. And this little nothing, this woman working for a mediocre company at a barely livable wage, had the audacity to refuse me. My first instinct had been to tell her, Fine. You don't deserve to work for someone like me anyway.

But I didn't.

Instead, I swallowed my pride and laid it all out for her: why I needed her, what I was willing to offer. I even told her I'd waive her rent entirely.

Weak move. It showed her I was capable of bending.

It worked, though. She said yes. And I hated how much it had cost me. Not in money but in ego. Why had I been so willing to let go of my pride for her? I told myself it was strictly for the project. For the sake of the work.

Then I drove her to my office.

Watching her step into my world had been... unsettling. It wasn't just the strangeness of seeing her in a space that felt so distinctly mine. It was how easily she seemed to fit into it.

I sat her at my desk and presented all of it. The mission behind my AI model, and years of work, passion, and sacrifice behind it. I half-expected her to look overwhelmed or indifferent, maybe even a little confused. After all, this wasn't her realm. But then, her first piece of feedback left me stunned.

She didn't just understand it. She challenged it, dissected it, and put it back together in a way that made me rethink my entire approach to presenting my new technology.

As we worked, I couldn't help but notice the way her face lit up when she explained her ideas. It was... magnetic. There was a passion in her that mirrored my own, and by the end of the meeting, I was left wondering why I hadn't asked her to work with me sooner.

But I wasn't a fool. Trust was not something I gave fully. I had her sign a contract before she left. A solid one with ironclad clauses. No loopholes, no room for betrayal. I half-expected her to hesitate, to read the fine print and question my motives, but she didn't. She simply signed it and handed it back.

At least my first mistake had a contingency plan.

My second mistake? Letting her see sides of me no one else gets to see.

After much internal debate, I took her to my favorite restaurant. Not just any place; this was the place. The one that felt like home. The one my mother used to take me to when I was a child.

It was a big deal for me. To put it into perspective, it took me two years to take Elena there. Two and a half for Jay. No one else even knew I went there regularly.

I kept telling myself it wasn't a big deal, that it was just a meal. But the truth was, it felt personal.

I wasn't sure how Ivy would react to the place, let alone to what I was about to share. But she surprised me again. She always did.

She listened, really listened, as I talked about my mother. For the first time, I shared about my part-Indian identity not because I had to, but because I wanted to. In a world where people only needed one reason to make you feel like you didn't belong, she made me feel seen.

And then, his ex showed up.

That guy was a whole other level of jackassery I never saw coming.

He lumbered into the restaurant, with his oversized denim jacket and worn jeans that were too tight around his middle. The whole time, he leaned his elbow on the counter as if he was doing the restaurant a favor and stared down at his phone with a cocky smirk, the kind that made you want to punch him just for having it. The way he spoke to Imtiaz, the busboy, like he was beneath him, only fueled my irritation. I wanted to say something, but I bit my tongue.

Not then. Not when Ivy was trying to stay unnoticed.

But how does an idiot like him come to know my favorite restaurant? And why was Ivy reacting that way?

As soon as she saw him, she turned her face away, as if trying to hide. The entire time he was there, she kept herself shielded behind her palm, her expression shifting between hurt and anxiety. Only after he left did her body finally relax.

Upon asking, she opened up.

She had spent three long years with that loser who had ground her spirit into dust. I wanted to hate him on instinct, but as she talked, I found myself focusing on her face instead.

Until then, I'd only seen anger, confusion, or mockery in her expressions. But sitting across from her in the soft glow of the restaurant, I saw something else entirely. Vulnerability. Depth.

And beauty.

She had this nose, upturned, with the slightest dent in the bridge. It gave her face an almost angelic quality, but it contrasted against the rest of her features, which were sharper, more modern, thoughtful. Intense. She looked...complicated. Beautiful. Like one of those women in museum paintings, but dressed as a nerdy bohemian.

I got so lost staring at her that I forgot what I was going to say. I ended up mumbling something about hermit crabs like an idiot.

What surprised me the most wasn't her story, though, but her self-awareness.

The way she spoke about her past, why she stayed with someone who clearly didn't deserve her—it came from a place of deep clarity. It was the kind of insight I'd spent years chasing but never quite grasping.

For the first time, I was jealous of Ivy. She had something I didn't: the ability to truly understand herself.

It only made me angrier that someone as smart and beautiful as her had wasted three years of her life on an idiot who didn't deserve her.

When we got home, I spent a good hour—time I borrowed from my work schedule, which annoyed me, but felt worth it—digging into everything there was to know about Trent Whitmore. A grown man using bullshit theories to excuse his behavior and spewing tone-deaf videos for clicks. By day, he searched for a new job, having recently left his role as a public relations specialist; by night, he lurked in comment sections, bullying anyone who dared to disagree with him.

Even without hearing Ivy's side of the story in detail, it wasn't hard to conclude that, if there was a jerk in the relationship, it was Trent.

I don't use social media, but his YouTube channel and LinkedIn profile, which read more like an inflated autobiography, were enough to confirm he was a Grade A asshole. He exaggerated, even falsified, claims about campaigns he'd worked on, projecting an image that didn't hold up under scrutiny. No woman, especially not Ivy, should have to hide or live in fear of a guy like him. He needed to be taken down a notch, and by the end of that hour, I had a plan.

Trent was going down.

At first, I thought I was doing it out of ego, a power play to satisfy my pride. But when Ivy called me later that evening from the Gliderport, it hit me like a brick: I was doing it because I had feelings.

Feelings for her.

Yes, I liked her. This "little nothing" who wasn't little in any sense of the word. Except maybe in stature. It was endearing how she always seemed to rise on her toes when she stood next to me, probably without realizing it. I didn't mind. It gave me a chance to see more clearly into her warm brown eyes. Did I mention the tiny freckle in her left eye? Or how her eyes crinkle when she laughs? Or the way she masks her vulnerability with silly humor?

And then there was the Gliderport, her favorite spot in the city, which just so happened to be the only place where I ever felt even remotely human.

Without hesitation, I'd dropped everything when she told me she was stranded, including an important after-work drink with a colleague.

All of this swirled in my head as she sat half a foot away from me on a rock so precarious I wouldn't even trust it to hold my phone. And yet, I obeyed her and sat there anyway, just to be close to her.

By then, I had accepted the truth: I had fallen for her.

And it wasn't just that. I couldn't bear the idea of her being in any kind of trouble or pain. It hurt me. Physically, even. How was that fair?

Watching her shiver on that cliff, I didn't have it in me to pretend. There was no performance, no calculated moves, no weighing the cost of getting myself sick and losing productivity. Just an overwhelming, primal need to keep her warm, to protect her.

The need was paralyzing.

It went against my nature, my code, my carefully laid plans. Yet there I was, sitting like some lovesick teenager on a cold night, unwilling to leave her side.

And then Adrian happened.

Her pathetic little friend who acts like the perfect guy friend but is bound to reveal an ulterior motive sooner or later. I've seen the type. Too insecure to stay in his lane and, when rejected, claims he's been "friend-zoned" to guilt the woman.

Finding him in her room, lying under her blanket, holding her hand. It took every ounce of self-control not to lose it right then and there. Adrian was nowhere near my level. Not with those corduroy pants and half-baked charm. But seeing him there lit a fire in me. A raging inferno.

Ivy wouldn't go for someone like him. But they have history. He was there when she broke up, there when she moved. What if that's what she needs? Someone who's just...there.

No. No one could be there for her like I could. No one had my capacity to be there for her. And I wanted her to choose me.

That realization, that I didn't just like Ivy, I wanted her to be mine, was seismic.

And there it was, my third mistake: deciding to take the plunge and give my all.

After seeing them together, I resolved to stop holding back. I would win her over, no matter what.

One of my strengths? Cooking. So I invited her to dinner, determined to make it perfect. Could I have just asked her on a date? Sure. But my pride wasn't ready for rejection. Or to seem desperate.

Cooking for her turned out to be an act of vulnerability I didn't fully grasp until I was already doing it. As she sat at the kitchen counter, watching my every move, I felt like I was giving my first investor pitch. Scared and exposed.

Why did this tiny woman make me feel the same pressure as a high-stakes presentation?

And the dinner hadn't even started.

Outside, on the balcony, watching her laugh, hearing her make me laugh, I felt...alive. For the first time, I got to look at her face at leisure, without feeling self-conscious about my staring, and she was breathtaking. More beautiful than I'd remembered.

And that nose. That cute-as-a-button nose.

I wanted to grab her, kiss her, and drink her in like the wine that had brought a warm flush to her cheeks.

So I tried.

When she came into the kitchen for water, I made my move. Standing behind her, I nearly caught her in my arms.

The more she surrendered, the more I wanted her. I brushed her hair aside, my fingers grazing her jaw, warm from a rush of blood.

She didn't resist. And for a second, a small, doubting voice in my head wanted her to.

What if she liked me now but later realized I was just like her ex? What if that shook me so much it jeopardized everything. My plans, my company?

But my hands and eyes refused to listen to my brain. My focus was on her lips, soft and peachy, and velvety under the kitchen light.

I leaned in, and then—

She pulled away.

It was like a slap to my face. And if you've known Nolan Sterling long enough, you'd know the slap wouldn't sting me because of the physical pain. It would be the humiliation of it that would destroy me.

Anger surged through my veins like a raging tsunami. I tried my best to maintain my composure, but inside, I was exploding. Why was she leading me on only to pull away? Was it intentional? Was she trying to make me look like a fool? Would she go back to her room, call her best friend, and laugh about how weak and pathetic her roommate was. The one who prides himself on being so focused, so strong?

The rejection clawed at me, tearing apart every shred of control I had.

By the time I finished cleaning the kitchen and starting the dishwasher, it was nearing midnight, but the usual clarity I found in the rhythm of those tasks was absent. So, I changed into gym shorts and a t-shirt, laced up my running shoes, and headed down to the building's first-floor gym.

I set the treadmill to eight miles per hour and ran as if I could leave my frustration behind. My chest burned, my legs ached, and still, I kept going, convincing myself that she wasn't worth the space she was taking in my mind. Ivy Delaney was just a distraction. A terrible one at that, pulling me away from everything important I needed to focus on.

The next day, as I ate my lunch in my office, shuffling meetings on my calendar like a frantic game of Tetris, I got a message from Elena. After some back-and-forth, she asked if Ivy might like to join the barbecue she and Jay were hosting. Distracted, I told her exactly what had happened after she and Ivy had spoken the last time, sparing no detail.

Elena, of course, was livid.

She felt sorry for Ivy and insisted on meeting me at my place to "set me straight." Yet another mess caused by Ivy. Just when I thought I was done with her.

When Elena arrived, she launched into a full lecture on feminism, patriarchy, and the audacity of a man, me, thinking he had the right to interfere in the lives of two adult women. I didn't bother explaining why I didn't want them talking; instead, I nodded, muttered an apology to Ivy, and left them alone to further discuss how I was the epitome of toxic masculinity.

That was it. The final nail in the coffin. I'd resolved to wash my hands of Ivy.

And then she got sick that night.

I'd gone to her room to let her know we needed to start working on the competitive analysis for the company. But when I found her, she was shivering, wrapped in blankets, unable to even sit up. Before I could stop myself, my hand went to her forehead. She was burning up. Her pale, tired face struck a chord so deep it made my chest tighten.

It was like seeing my mother again. Sick, frail, her strength and clarity slipping away day by day. A flood of memories I'd buried came rushing back. My mother leaning on the kitchen counter, elbows sinking into the granite, confused about why she'd gone there in the first place. Me, at seventeen, bluntly asking if she was dying. Her sunken face, struggling to beam for my sake on the rare days she remembered me. She hadn't wanted her son to worry, and I'd wanted to split the world in two to save her.

The weight of that loss crushed me all over again. Seeing Ivy sick awakened the same helpless fear. I knew it was probably just a cold, maybe the flu at worst, but logic had no place in my mind. Every frustration I'd felt toward her dissolved in an instant. It didn't matter if she didn't like me, if she hated me, even. I just wanted her to be okay.

So I did everything I could. Brought her medicine, made sure she stayed hydrated, even cooked for her. The way she looked at me, like she didn't know whether to thank me or question my motives, only made it harder to understand myself. But I knew one thing: it wasn't about me. There was no ulterior motive. It was selfless. I just hoped she could see that.

When she kissed me, it was like the tension between us had finally found its release. Every argument, every misunderstanding, every unspoken feeling had led to that moment. Her lips were soft and warm. She tasted like sweet limes and I wanted more. I wanted to devour her, to pull her closer, to let her know how deeply she'd gotten under my skin. I finally kissed her nose, softly, unable to stop myself from smiling against her skin.

And then she pulled away.

Again.

At least this time, she gave me a reason, as pointless as it was.

"You fix me and break me in the same breath," she'd said.

I'd pretended not to understand, but every fiber of me wanted to respond, "You too, Ivy."

I returned to my room and replayed it all in my head. The way her lips had felt against mine, the way I never wanted to let go, and the way she'd pulled away as if I wasn't enough.

That's what it boiled down to, wasn't it? I wasn't enough. I didn't fit into the neat little box she'd constructed for her perfect partner. Not exciting enough, not funny enough. Wrong in all the ways that mattered to her.

She'd want someone like Adrian. He'd held her hand, carried her moving boxes, been there for her in ways I never had. He was everything I wasn't. She didn't want someone cold, someone distant, someone whose life revolved around his work, someone so broken he couldn't even ask the girl he liked on a date.

This is where my three big mistakes had led me: broken, alone, misunderstood, and more lost than ever.

CHAPTER 18

Nolan's scent on my pillow was more torturous than whatever had happened an hour ago because, unlike him, the scent refused to leave. I tossed and turned on my bed, restless and sleepless, my thoughts spiraling in every direction.

Had I overreacted?

Was I being too demanding?

Were my expectations too high?

Did I ruin what could have been a great night?

I grabbed my phone, seeking distraction, and scrolled through my photo gallery. My fingers hesitated before taking me to a part of my life I wasn't ready to revisit. Photos from the last three years.

I had planned to gather all the pictures of Trent, put them in a single folder, and archive them. A symbolic farewell I had failed to create. So, in all its intrusive glory, my gallery showcased every corner of my past I had left behind.

There was a photo of Trent standing by his car, his hand resting confidently on the hood.

A picture of us at a holiday party, his arm slung over my shoulder as we beamed at the camera.

Another of us hiking, him holding up a water bottle like it was a trophy after reaching the summit.

Us at a friend's wedding, his tie loose around his neck as he leaned in to kiss my cheek.

And another one, his favorite—a selfie at an arcade, our faces squished together under his record breaking score flashing on a screen.

Seeing those pictures, a deep yearning rippled through me. It wasn't love. It wasn't even regret. It was loneliness, raw and unfiltered, clawing at me. I hugged my knees to my chest, trying to fill the hollow ache.

That was one thing Trent was good at: holding me.

He was a big guy, weighing over 200 pounds. His hugs were like those cozy bear hugs that could make anyone feel safe, cocooned, even if the comfort was only physical. Spooning in his bed used to feel like being swaddled in warmth, which, for a long time, I thought was enough.

It was ridiculous that I was missing Trent while I still had the lingering taste of Nolan on my mouth.

As I laid there clutching my pillow, Nolan's scent haunted me again. Frustrated, I flung the pillow away and returned to scrolling.

As I looked through more photos of us, I wondered again why Trent never reached out to me after the breakup. The first time I thought about it was when I saw him at the restaurant with Nolan. A part of me knew why. He was too self-involved to go through the typical post-breakup phase. But even then, our breakup seemed too clean. I had at least assumed he'd be upset, maybe even try to ruin my stay at this apartment.

But he didn't.

I didn't even feel the need to block him, because he never bothered me.

So out of curiosity, I did what you usually and wrongfully do to an ex. Stalk them.

He's a YouTuber, so his Instagram profile was, of course, public, unlike mine.

His latest post was a picture of him posing with a cute German Shepherd in a field, captioned, "Nature therapy." Did he get a dog? The second was a gym mirror selfie, with the kind of motivational quote I used to roll my eyes at when we were together.

Then there was a Reel. A montage of his new life—a mix of scenic travel shots, clips from his vlogs, and moments with his friends. His signature grin was in every frame, exuding confidence, like he had shed every piece of our shared past without a second thought.

The ache in my chest deepened. Seeing his face stirred a pain I hadn't expected. I told myself it was closure, but it felt more like scratching an open wound.

For better or worse, I was glad I stumbled upon his profile. It reminded me that no matter how things ended, I had loved him once. I had so many firsts with him:

The first time I had sex.

The first (and last) time I had smoked.

The first time I drove a car.

The first time I voted.

The first time I left the state I grew up in.

He was a huge part of my life, and I'd been pretending that leaving his apartment meant closing that chapter. But that wasn't how it worked.

With a sigh, I locked my phone and lay back down. My Spotify playlist titled Sedative, played softly in the background, its familiar melodies coaxing me into calm. But as the hours stretched, sleep remained elusive. My body, still recovering from my recent illness, begged for rest, but my mind wouldn't relent.

At 4 a.m., I gave up and got out of bed.

First, I took a long, hot shower. The water cascaded over me, soothing the tension in my shoulders and easing the ache in my joints.

Dressed in soft pajamas and a thick cardigan, I brewed jasmine tea while scrolling through my non-Trent Instagram feed. Cup in hand, I stepped out onto the balcony, a quiet sanctuary suspended more than 300 feet above the sleeping city. It was a routine I had promised myself I'd build but never did.

The night was still, the world quiet. Below, the grid of San Diego's downtown glimmered softly, its lights muted by the faint silver of an approaching dawn. The cool ocean breeze carried a faint saltiness, mingling with the lingering scent of the jasmine from my tea.

I took a sip, savoring its warmth, its gentle floral strength grounding me. For the first time in a while, I felt a small spark of gratitude for this space. The fact that I could walk just a few steps from my bedroom and stand under an open sky was something I hadn't truly appreciated before.

The peace was short-lived. My phone buzzed in my pocket. Adrian.

"Hey," I answered, trying to inject some cheer into my voice.

"You okay? You're never up this early." His voice was warm, laced with concern.

"How do you even know I'm awake?"

"You just liked my Instagram story."

Ugh.

"Right. Yeah. Can't sleep."

A pause. I knew what he was thinking. Adrian had confessed his feelings to me a few days ago, and I'd dodged the conversation ever since. Now, he was probably trying to find a way to bring it up.

"Remember that 24-hour diner in Sprigwing? We used to go there when we couldn't sleep."

The memory made me chuckle. "Oh my god, yes. And their terrible coffee."

"What terrible? I loved that coffee!" he argued, mock offense in his voice.

"Fine. I liked their breakfast potatoes."

"Yeah, potatoes. That's all you ever ate. Weirdo."

"More weird than dunking them in milkshakes?"

"You haven't lived until you've tried it," he countered, laughing.

"Gross."

"I wonder if they're still open," he mused. "Imagine, right now, they'd be serving the next generation of nocturnals."

"Right." I smiled, taking another sip of tea. My gaze stayed fixed on the horizon, the sky now a soft blue.

"So... what's going on?" he asked.

"You know who I started to miss today, out of all the people in the world?" I asked him, clutching my warm mug. The air was crisp and carried a chill that bit at exposed skin, despite the promise of summer lurking just around the horizon.

"Trent?" Adrian responded.

I froze mid-sip. "How did you know?"

"You're not as complicated as you think, Ivy."

"Shut up!"

"I'm kidding," Adrian said with a laugh. "It's natural, isn't it? To miss your ex after a breakup? Though, in your case, it's more like the victim of Stockholm Syndrome missing their captor."

"It wasn't like that, Adrian," I corrected. "Anyway, should I be ashamed that I was missing him?"

"No. You've been thrown into a completely different world. It's normal to miss familiarity. Besides," he added, his voice light, "yours is the cleanest breakup I've ever seen!"

"Right? That's exactly what I was thinking!"

"Yeah. It's bound to bother you for a while."

"Thanks," I said, exhaling deeply. "This night finally feels a little less confusing." But I realized too late that I'd said too much.

"Why? What else happened?"

"Nothing important."

Adrian paused before speaking again. "Is this about your roommate?"

"What?"

"Did something happen with him? You sounded... distracted before."

"Why would you assume it's about him and not about you turning into some Romeo the last time we met?" My words came out sharper than I intended, almost bitter.

"Because if you were upset with me, you wouldn't have answered my call."

I sighed. He wasn't wrong.

"Why are *you* up so early?" I asked.

"Don't change the topic," he said firmly. "Tell me what's going on. I shouldn't have to remind you that I'm still your friend and will always be here when you need me."

His sincerity eased me. He meant it. Adrian had always been good at compartmentalizing.

"Thank you," I murmured.

"Now spill."

I decided to share a little. "We had a big argument, Nolan and I."

"Isn't that normal? You've always fought with him."

"This was different."

"How so?"

I ran a hand through my damp hair, staring out at the faint glow of the streetlights. "He acts like everything is black and white, yet he can't make up his mind on important things."

Adrian chuckled. "You mean like the kind of guy who can arrange his spices better than his emotions?"

I couldn't help but laugh. "Arranges spices better than his emotions. That's creative writing, Adrian."

"Thanks to men like me, the creative humor in the world sustains."

"Yes, thanks to men like you," I mocked.

As we both laughed, the weight of unspoken words pressed on me. I wanted to address the elephant in the room, to tell Adrian how much I valued him as a friend, how I didn't want to lose him to whatever idea he'd gotten in his head about us.

But before I could say anything, a sharp, bitter laugh cut through the air behind me.

I froze, the hairs on my neck standing on end. Slowly, I turned to see Nolan standing near the balcony doors in his gym clothes. His expression was dark.

I'd forgotten he went to the gym at five every morning.

"I arrange spices better than my emotions," Nolan said, his voice low but laced with fury. "Thanks to men like him. Should've guessed."

Adrian was still talking on the phone, oblivious, but I couldn't process his words. Nolan's gaze pinned me in place, sharp and unrelenting.

I fumbled for an excuse, for anything to say, but before I could speak, Nolan strode forward, his jaw tight with suppressed anger.

"You shouldn't have shown interest in me when you were involved with him," he said, his voice unnervingly calm. But as he continued, his teeth ground together. "He's more your type, of course."

"What are you talking about?" I managed to say, my voice small against the storm brewing in his eyes.

Nolan stepped closer, his height and intensity looming over me. I tried to hold my ground, but the sheer weight of his anger made me feel like shrinking.

"I heard, Ivy. How little you think of me. And how much you prefer men like him. Men who say the right things, tell you what you want to hear, and keep you exactly where you are."

I blinked, stunned. "You're crossing a line," I warned, my voice shaking.

"Enough," he snapped. His tone wasn't loud, but it carried a weight that silenced me instantly.

"You're so quick to shut me out," Nolan continued, his voice steady but dripping with resentment. "To assume I'm just some asshole who wants to sleep with you. But what about you, Ivy? You know how to arrange *your* emotions? You can barely arrange your own desires, your own life."

His words hit like a slap, and though I tried to stay calm, my resolve wavered.

"You don't know what you're talking about," I said quietly, but even to my own ears, my voice lacked conviction.

"Oh, I think I do," He growled, his eyes locked on mine. "You want to be accepted as you are but can't see me for who I am. He," Nolan said, pointing at my phone, "is easy. The kind of man you prefer. The one who molds himself according to your needs. A people pleaser. Well, you're right. That's not who I am."

His tone twisted my stomach. I wanted to push back, to defend Adrian, to explain, but I was too flustered, too caught in the intensity of Nolan's anger.

"I don't—" I started, but the words died on my lips as Nolan took another step forward, closing the space between us.

"Don't what?" he asked, his voice a dangerous whisper. "Don't like him? Or don't want to admit you're scared of someone like me and using excuses to keep your distance?"

My breath hitched. His hand flexed at his side as though he was holding himself back, his jealousy crackling like electricity.

The silence between us stretched until Nolan finally stepped back, his gaze still burning into mine.

"I thought so," he muttered, turning abruptly and walking away. The balcony door swung shut behind him with a hollow thud.

CHAPTER 19

The groceries rattled in the backseat as I drove through downtown San Diego, weaving through late afternoon traffic. My thoughts were louder than the hum of the engine, bouncing from one half-formed idea to another. I should've been furious. Nolan's jealousy over Adrian last night had boiled over into a full-blown fight. It was upsetting, the way he talked to me, the way he assumed things about Adrian, how he completely misunderstood me. But instead of frustration or anger, there was a strange, almost pleasant buzz in my chest. I felt like that meme where the girl looks at the camera and grins devilishly as a house burns behind her.

I let out a slow breath as I turned into the lot at my building. This conflict with Nolan had definitely stirred something in me. Even as his words echoed in my mind, there was something undeniable about the way I felt afterward. Alive.

Was this the last stage of my breakup grief. Acceptance? The realization that ending things with Trent was harder than I'd thought? Was it the knowledge that it couldn't get any worse with Nolan? Or maybe it was the eight cups of coffee I'd had since then. Who knows.

One thing was clear: I didn't want to sit in my apartment tonight, stewing in all this restless energy. I needed to do something. To be better at arranging my desires and life.

My thoughts flicked to the artist group I'd met a few weeks ago. They were meeting tonight. I'd seen the post earlier.

Before I could second-guess myself, I made the decision. I hauled the bags of groceries inside, tossed them on the counter, and hurried to put everything away. Then I grabbed my art supplies, including my old sketchbooks, and headed out the door.

This time, the group had decided to meet at a coffee shop in North Park. Tucked between boutique clothing stores and thrift shops, the bohemian charm of the coffee shop appeared like a hidden artist's haven. Murals stretched across the walls outside, vibrant and chaotic, almost alive under the sun's UV light.

Inside, trailing vines softened the edges of the concrete walls, while colorful tiles framed the doorway. The atmosphere was cozy but electric. String lights twinkled overhead, and mismatched furniture filled the space. Some tables were occupied by enthusiastic small groups, chatting, and laughing, while others were occupied by students and writers hunched over laptops, tablets, and notebooks.

The scent of espresso hung in the air, undercut by the beach's aquatic scent wafting through the open patio doors.

I ordered a hazelnut latte for a change and tried not to fidget while I waited for the barista to make it.

"Are you here for the artist group?" the barista asked with a friendly smile as he handed me the drink.

"Yeah," I said, a little surprised. "What gave away?"

"You have that... deep artist persona," he answered without hesitation. It lifted my spirits.

"I'll take that as a compliment."

"It was meant to be," he assured. "The group is usually out on the patio. Enjoy!"

With a quiet nod, I carried my coffee outside, scanning the wooden tables occupied by the meet-up group members, until I found a spot to settle in. I arranged my supplies carefully, like armor against my nerves, and stared out at the potted succulents and palms framing the patio.

I was starting to wonder if I'd made a mistake when Cleo, one of the pirates from my guild, and the girl I chatted with during the last meet-up, arrived. A whirlwind of color and energy, she wore a mustard-yellow dress layered over striped tights, paired with chunky combat boots covered in doodles and patches. Around her neck was a cluster of necklaces, each one more eclectic than the last, and her bangles jingled softly as she waved enthusiastically.

"Ivy!" she called so loudly a few heads turned. I was surprised she remembered my name, because it took me a while to recall hers.

"Hey, Cleo."

She dropped into the chair across from me, looking like an abstract piece of art, as her hair caught the last golden sunlight. Today, they were teal with tiny braids woven in them. A cup of kiwi boba tea sat in her hand, the green liquid almost glowing. I wasn't even sure if this place served Boba.

"You didn't show up at the last few meetups," she stated. "I thought you'd given up on us."

"Got busy," I answered. Before I could expand on that excuse, she spoke again.

"If you don't mind..." She tilted her head, her expression playful yet kind. "What happened last time? You looked really upset."

Heat crept into my cheeks. "I..." What was the worst that could happen if I told the truth? I could always stop coming here if I embarrassed myself too much.

"I was upset because I couldn't draw anything," I admitted, ripping off the Band-Aid. "I couldn't even think of anything to draw."

I took a sip of my latte, hoping to drown the embarrassment.

"Ah, artist's block," Cleo said knowingly, chewing on the boba pearls. "The great nemesis of creativity. Been there, done that, bought the T-shirt. But I have a cure. Wanna try it?"

I raised an eyebrow. "What kind of cure?"

"Action!" Cleo stood suddenly, dragging her chair back with a scrape. "Come on."

Before I could ask where we were going, she was up and bouncing toward the street. I laughed nervously and got out of the patio. My quiet converse followed her solid boots as they clomped against the sidewalk. We must have looked like two schoolgirls walking home at the end of a rainy day.

The mural she led me to was a masterpiece of chaos and creativity. It stretched across the side of a building, a kaleidoscope of abstract shapes, vivid colors, and intricate details. A dragon curled around a tree that sprouted from a clock face, while birds with geometric wings soared overhead. Beneath it all, a small patch of wall was alive with chalk drawings from children and passing artists who had left their marks.

Cleo handed me a thick marker from her belt, her bangles jingling as she moved. "Here's the deal," she said, her expression serious but her winged liner dancing with excitement. "We take turns drawing squiggles, or shapes on the wall, and the other person has to make something out of it. No rules, no pressure, just fun."

I hesitated, glancing between Cleo and the wall.

"Don't overthink it," she urged, nudging my shoulder. "The first step is just... starting."

So I started. I drew a wavy line that reminded me of an ocean current, and Cleo immediately turned it into a pirate ship, complete with a tiny flag.

We went back and forth like that, our wonder and laughter echoing in the evening air. Cleo's art was as expressive as her personality, and the shapes and lines she gave me matched that energy. I turned her concentric circles into a mandala design, an infinity sign into an owl, a sunflower into a swimming pool, a candle into a stack of books, and a pirate hat into a UFO. Meanwhile, she turned my random squiggle into a duck family, a star into a queen with an elaborate robe, a potted plant into a goofy monster, a cuboid into intricate abstract art, and a chair into a fantastical four-legged creature wearing sunglasses.

Even though I was nowhere near Cleo's level of creativity, and I was sure she was holding back to keep me encouraged, it was more art than I had created in the last year. Somewhere along the way, the tight knot in my chest unraveled, and I felt the familiar pull of creativity again.

By the time we returned to the patio, my cheeks ached from smiling.

We slid back into our chairs, and I took a long sip of my latte, which was still warm. Around us, the other artists were immersed in their work. A woman at the next table sketched on a digital tablet, her stylus moving in quick, precise strokes. Behind me, a man with a thick full beard was hunched over his sketchbook, headphones on as he drew manga characters. I recognized him from the last meet-up. His work was bold and dynamic. The kind of art that made me want to peek over his shoulder and ask a million questions.

Another artist sat by the railing, her sketchbook tilted away from view. I could only see her hands, smudged with charcoal, and the occasional glint of her glasses as she leaned forward.

"Fun, wasn't it?" Cleo said, grabbing her tea.

"Super fun! Thank you."

She propped her chin on her hand, the trinkets from her necklace jangling softly. "So... how'd you get into art?"

I hesitated, the question tugging at something tender. "I *used* to do art. Paint. But I stopped for a while."

"That's not an answer to my question. But why did you stop?" she asked, her voice gentle now, her earlier exuberance replaced with quiet curiosity.

I ran my fingers over the edge of my sketchbook. "Life got in the way. Or maybe I just let it."

Cleo nodded, sipping her tea and pulling some boba through her straw. "That happens. I don't know any artist who had not had a dry spell. But you're here now, right? That counts for something."

Her words settled over me like a warm blanket.

"It does."

She grinned, her vibrant energy returning.

We sat there for another two hours, talking about art, our pirate guild, garb ideas for the fall Ren Faire, and her journey—how art helped her embrace her true self. The hum of traffic, the soft scratch of pencils against paper, and occasional laughter from inside the coffee shop provided a pleasant background score for our conversation.

"I grew up in Berkeley," she said, "surrounded by people who knew exactly what they were passionate about. Activists, scientists, writers, you name it. And me? I was this awkward kid who doodled on her math homework and made collages out of cereal boxes."

I couldn't help but smile at the image. "Sounds pretty creative to me."

"Sure, but back then, it felt... small. Like everyone else was doing these big, important things, and I was just cutting up paper." She paused, her eyes drifting to the patio railing, where a few potted begonias swayed in the breeze. "It wasn't until high school that I realized art could be more than just a hobby."

"What changed?"

Cleo's expression softened, her voice quieter now. "My art teacher. She was this fierce, no-nonsense woman who saw right through my insecurities. One day, she handed me this ancient-looking set of oil pastels and said, 'You're good, but you're playing it safe. Stop being afraid to make a mess.'"

I leaned in, intrigued. "What did you do?"

"I made a mess," she said with a grin. "A glorious, chaotic mess. I still remember the piece. It was this giant abstract thing, layers and layers of color and texture. It was like all the noise in my head finally had somewhere to go."

I could picture it: vibrant and unapologetic, just like her. "So, that's your medium? Oil pastels?"

"Yup!" she said, holding up her hands, faintly stained with color. "They're so messy, you know? Like, you can just dig in, smear everything with your fingers, and suddenly—bam!—a whole galaxy on the page. Plus, I kinda like that it's all over me afterward. Like battle scars from the art war." She flipped open her sketchbook and began blending a night sky with her thumb, the hues melting together. "See? Instant magic. I fell in love with it the second I tried it. Total game changer."

I nodded, thinking about my own, far more cautious choice of medium. I picked acrylics because they were forgiving, low-risk. I could make as many mistakes as I wanted and still cover them up without ruining the painting.

"I mean," Cleo went on, her tone shifting to something thoughtful, "eventually, it wasn't an easy choice. My parents wanted me to be a lawyer or a doctor or, you know, a coder genius or something. Something practical."

I wouldn't know. I never had a parent who gave a shit about my studies or career.

"I get it," I muttered. "The assembly line of Bay Area kids."

"Exactly!" she said, pointing at me with the same finger she'd been using to blend. A streak of blue now decorated her cheek where she'd scratched absently. "But I stuck with it. Got myself into the Visual Arts program at SDSU. Because I realized something important: even if my art doesn't bring in big checks, it will bring me happiness. And if I'm happy, I'll find a way to survive."

Her words landed with more weight than I expected, striking a nerve I didn't know was raw.

"Art is how I make sense of the world. If I stopped, I'd probably shrivel up into a boring little raisin-person. I can't imagine doing anything else." She closed her sketchbook with a satisfied snap and leaned back, her grin stretching wide.

"That's brave," I said quietly, her energy making me feel both inspired and exhausted at once.

"Pfft, brave? Nah," she said, waving me off. "I'm just stubborn and a little reckless. Oh! Look at Mateo's Light Yagami's sketch!" She pointed toward the bearded guy behind me. "So cool." Her attention flipped again as she gasped, eyes widening. "Wait, check out her portrait!" She practically bounced in her seat, her enthusiasm contagious. The woman with the charcoal finally turned her sketchbook toward us, revealing a striking portrait of an old woman.

"I wish I was that talented," I mumbled, completely awed.

"Oh, please," Cleo said, rolling her eyes, but her tone was empathetic, like she had been there. "Nothing happens just by wishing. You've got to *do* the thing"

I hesitated. "What if you realize you're not as good as you thought?" The reason I couldn't paint for so long was because I was afraid. Afraid that if I actually tried and failed...then I couldn't blame Trent for my shortcomings. I wouldn't have any excuses left.

Cleo tilted her head, considering my question with surprising seriousness before snapping her fingers. "Then you pivot! Like, if you're not who you thought you were, *you'll discover who you really are*. And maybe that's even better!"

I couldn't help but smile at her relentless optimism. She raised her tea dramatically, as though we were in some grand moment of victory.

"To glorious, chaotic messes!"

I lifted my empty cup and clinked it against hers. "And figuring it out as we go."

"Yes!" she said, tapping the table with both hands. "Okay, now show me what you've got. Sketchbook. Let's see it."

For once, I didn't hesitate. I flipped my old sketchbook open and laid my creative past bare.

CHAPTER 20

Nolan and I hadn't crossed paths since the argument on the balcony four days ago. We'd kept our communication strictly professional, exchanging emails about work without any personal notes. In some ways, I was grateful. I'd needed the space to sort through the mess in my head.

During that time, I'd tackled everything I'd been putting off. Removing Trent's photos from my phone, unpacking my remaining boxes and hanging up my old paintings on my bedroom wall, watering the plants. I RSVP'd to more art meetups and even exchanged fun texts and memes with Cleo.

Adrian had been asking questions as he had heard part of our argument. He was out of the city for an assignment, but I had asked him to meet me as soon as he returned. It's time I clear the air with him.

I stayed up late finishing work deadlines, my body exhausted but my mind full of energy. Clearing every corner of my life felt like an act of rebellion against the chaos Nolan had stirred within me.

But there was one thing I couldn't shake. Him.

When I heard the sound of the front door closing that evening, my stomach tightened. I was waiting for him in the living room, my arms crossed over my chest like a shield. He walked in, looking worn out. Tie loosened, jacket slung over his shoulder, his face drawn with exhaustion. He froze when he saw me.

"Nolan," I said, my voice steady despite the turmoil inside. "We need to talk."

His gaze flickered, weary but guarded. "Can it wait?" he asked.

"No." I held my ground. "I'm done waiting."

He sighed, running a hand through his hair. "Fine. Let me shower first."

While he was gone, I made tea for him. The loose-leaf kind he preferred. I wanted this to be civil. By the time he returned, dressed in fitted joggers and a simple dark green t-shirt, hair still damp, my carefully rehearsed opening felt like it had vanished into thin air.

Nolan sat down across from me at the kitchen island.

"Thanks," he said, grabbing his tea and taking a sip.

"First," I began, "Adrian is only a friend, and I won't explain any further. Second, I don't appreciate how you spoke to me on the balcony. You had no right to belittle him or me."

Nolan didn't flinch. Instead, he nodded, his voice quiet. "You're right. I'm sorry."

The simplicity of his apology caught me off guard, but I didn't let it derail me. "I've been thinking about why I pulled away, why I keep pulling away. And it's not just about you treating me like a mistake. It's about what you represent."

He leaned back slightly, his brow furrowing. "What I represent?"

I nodded, feeling the weight of my own words. "You see the world in black and white, Nolan. Through numbers, logic, efficiency. And that's fine. For you. But I see the world in colors, in textures, in moments that don't have to make sense. You shame me for my choices, my lifestyle, my interests. You make me feel like I'm wrong for being who I am."

He opened his mouth to respond, but I cut him off, my voice rising. "And do you know what that does to me? It brings me back to Trent. To the way he used to look at me, talk to me. Like I was always falling short. Like I wasn't enough."

At the mention of Trent, Nolan's expression darkened, his jaw tightening. "Don't compare me to him."

"Then stop acting like him!" I snapped, my voice trembling now. "Stop making me feel like I'm a failure because I don't live up to your idea of what a person should be."

He stood abruptly, his chair scraping against the floor. "You think I'm the problem? That I'm the one holding you back? Ivy, you've been holding yourself back long before I came into the picture."

"That's not true—"

"Isn't it?" he shot back, his voice rising. "You talk about reaching for the stars, starting a new life here, about wanting to paint, but what have you actually done since you moved here? You've romanticized an idea of yourself instead of facing the reality of who you are."

His words hit me like a slap, but he wasn't finished.

"You know what your real problem is?" he continued, his frustration boiling over. "You're a non-finisher. A quitter. You want to quit on me, on everything, not because I'm the problem, but because you don't have it in you to finish what you start."

"That's not fair," I said, my voice barely above a whisper, my anger giving way to hurt.

"You sit here blaming me, blaming your ex, blaming everyone else for your unhappiness. But you don't take responsibility for yourself. You want to paint? Then paint. You want to reach for the stars? Then jump. Don't point fingers."

I felt my throat tighten, my hands shaking. "Nolan, you have no idea."

"And you," he said, his voice softer now but no less cutting, "you live in a fantasy. The idea of being an artist. The idea of a perfect man. The idea of a relationship that's nothing like the last one. But that's all it is, Ivy. An idea. A fantasy. It's why you can't handle being with someone who's real. When it comes to reality? You run. You try to escape. Every single time."

"Well, maybe I run because I know what happens when I stay," I fired back, looking at him with deep loathing. "When I stay, I see the real picture, and the real picture is always cruel and hurtful. Nolan Sterling, you are cruel and hurtful. You can paraglide all you want, but you'll never be a bird."

The second the words left my mouth, I wanted to take them back. I didn't mean them at all; I just wanted to hurt him.

His face went pale, his shoulders sagging as if the wind had been knocked out of him. For a long moment, he just stood there, staring at me.

"Nolan," I said softly, reaching out, but he stepped back.

"You really think I don't know how broken I am?" he said, his voice quiet. "That I don't know I'll never be able to fly? I know, Ivy. I've always known."

Tears welled in my eyes, but I didn't know how to respond.

He looked at me then, his eyes filled with a vulnerability I'd never seen before. "I'm not the man you want," he said. "And I never will be."

His words broke something inside me. "Nolan," I whispered, stepping toward him. "I never expected perfection from you. I just—"

"But you do," he interrupted. "Deep down, you do."

I shook my head, tears spilling over. "And you make me feel like I'm damaged, like I'm some mistake you regret every time you look at me. You think I don't feel that?"

For a moment, we just stood there, the weight of everything unsaid pressing down on us.

Then, suddenly, he was in front of me, his hands on my arms, his voice low and urgent. "How can I prove it to you? How can I prove how much I like you, want you? Tell me."

I didn't have to answer. With my feet on tiptoes, my hands found their way to his neck, and before I knew it, my lips were on his. All the anger, pain, and longing poured into that one kiss, demanding to be felt, shared, consumed.

He crushed his lips against mine with equal fervor, his hands gripping me like I might vanish if he let go. The kiss was raw, desperate, like he was trying to exorcise all the emotions that had built up between us. His frustration, his desire, they were all there, translating into the way his mouth moved against mine. It was a claim, a demand, and I couldn't stop myself from answering.

I gasped into his mouth, every nerve in my body coming alive. His lips were warm, faintly tasting of Earl Grey, and I found myself savoring it. My hands tangled in his hair, tugging, holding, needing. He growled softly, the sound vibrating through me, as his hands found my hips and pulled me closer.

His fingers slipped under the hem of my tank top, rough against my skin but thrilling in their certainty. I let out a soft groan, and that seemed to break whatever restraint he had left. His tongue slipped into my mouth, first tentative, then deliberate, coaxing a response from me that was almost primal.

He spun me, pinning me against the living room wall with a firm but measured pressure that sent electricity racing through my spine. His body pressed into mine, solid and unyielding, and I was caught between the wall and him. Trapped, but entirely willing.

I clutched at his chest, unsure whether I wanted to push him away or pull him closer. My mind was in chaos, but my body knew exactly what it wanted. His lips left mine, traveling down to my neck, where he kissed and nipped, each sensation sparking through me like a live wire.

"Nolan," I gasped, his name spilling from my lips like a plea, though I wasn't sure what I was begging for.

He didn't answer. Instead, his hands slid higher under my top, his touch firm yet exploratory, as though memorizing every inch of me. He played with the straps of my tank top with deliberate care.

Then, with a sudden, impatient pull, he freed me from them, baring my shoulders and my collarbones. It left me breathless in more ways than one.

As he pressed his hip harder into mine, I felt him. Hard and hungry. The current rushed through me, from his mouth to mine, to my chest, and to between my legs.

Grabbing my jaw, he devoured me again. First my lips, then my shoulder, then down further to my chest. Kissing and tasting. I melted. My head tilted back against the wall, my hands clutching him, desperate for something to anchor me as the world tilted.

In one swift move, he picked me up, like I weighed nothing. I clung to him, my legs wrapping instinctively around his waist as he carried me to the bed. He laid me down gently, his body following mine as though he couldn't bear the distance for even a second. I trembled under him, not from fear, but from the sheer power of his body over mine.

He slipped off my shorts and eased my tank top away, sending my heart racing, partly from shyness, partly from anticipation.

The intensity in his eyes sent a shiver down my body. He wasn't just looking at me. He was seeing me, taking in every detail like I was a painting he couldn't look away from. I'd never felt this wanted before.

When he leaned on me, I instinctively arched into him, my body seeking his warmth, and he responded in kind, his lips finding mine once more, as his hands roamed over me, confident and unapologetic.

Reaching my back, he unhooked my bra with one hand. His lips curled into a faint smirk, the only hint of triumph he allowed himself before his attention returned to me.

"Ivy," he murmured against my skin, "I want you." His voice was rough and low, sending a fresh wave of heat through me.

His mouth descended, trailing kisses down my breasts, his hands cupping and caressing with a reverence that made my heart thump. I felt myself submitting, piece by piece, under his touch. Every kiss, every lick, every movement was deliberate, as though he was claiming me.

I reached for him, pulling him closer with a need that both thrilled and frightened me. My hands tugged at his T-shirt, desperate to feel the heat of his skin against mine. He obliged, tossing it aside before wrapping me in his arms. The press of his bare, muscular chest against mine was dizzying. My lips sought his, then trailed to his neck and shoulder, and chest, kissing and grazing his warm, olive-toned skin.

There was no gentleness in the way our bodies moved. We were raw, exposed, both emotionally and physically, and the intensity of it all was almost too much to bear. But I didn't want it to stop.

Nolan entered with a confidence that made my heart skip a beat, his body guiding mine, and I matched his rhythm, giving in to the fire that burned between us. It was all-consuming. The room seemed to disappear around us. We both were incomplete, but the way our bodies fit together like a complete puzzle was nothing sort of perfection.

When we came together, it was more than physical. It was fire and fury, pain and healing, all tangled into one. He kissed me gently on the eyes, nose, and then on the side of my lips. The walls we'd both built came crashing down, and for those moments, there was nothing else but us.

When it was over, and we lay there tangled together. I looked up at Nolan, my heart still racing, my mind spinning. His eyes met mine, and for a moment, I saw something there, something real. And I knew, even though we had both hurt each other, even though everything was still messy and unresolved, that this, we, weren't a mistake. It couldn't be.

Not tonight.

CHAPTER 21

The city lights painted soft patterns across the walls, casting a faint glow over the rumpled satin sheets that clung to our bodies. We were both still catching our breath, the intensity of the last hour lingering between us like an unspoken truth. Through the cracked window, the cool night breeze slipped in, mingling with the faint hum of downtown San Diego—distant traffic sounds, the soft whoosh of airplanes overhead.

Unlike my room that had a view of the open sky, Nolan's window framed the city skyline, dotted with high-rises that interrupted the view.

A realization hit me: I had never seen Nolan's room before. This was my first time in his bedroom.

I glanced around. It was minimalist, but not cold. Clean lines, dark woods, and neutral tones dominated the space. A sleek standing desk stood beside the window, free of clutter except for a single laptop and a neatly coiled charger. The bed we were lying on had a low, modern frame, with sheets that felt expensive but not ostentatious. On the wall above the bed hung a single piece of abstract art, stark and bold, like it had been chosen with precision rather than sentimentality. Everything had a purpose, a function, and yet it wasn't sterile. There was warmth in the balance, in the subtle details: a beautiful notebook on the nightstand with a faint scent of cedarwood lingering in the air.

It wasn't my kind of space. Too composed, too calculated. But it suited Nolan perfectly. This room was an extension of him: efficient, sharp, in control. The observation sent a jolt through me, a reminder of how different we were. I couldn't imagine having a window and not put my desk facing it!

And yet, it didn't matter. Not now. Not with his arm draped around me and the steady rhythm of his breathing beneath my ear.

My mind drifted to an old memory, unbidden. The first time I'd slept with Trent. The hollowness I'd felt afterward. How he had immediately jumped out of bed to check football scores, leaving me alone in the sheets like discarded trash. The contrast was stark. Here, in Nolan's arms, I felt respected, wanted. Whole.

But I was doing it again, comparing Nolan to Trent.

Nolan had been wrong about Adrian, but he'd been right about one thing: I was seeking perfection, measuring moments and people against impossible standards. I shook my head, pushing the thought away. Not now. Not tonight.

I rested my cheek against Nolan's chest, letting the rise and fall of his breath ground me. His hand moved lazily across my back, tracing gentle patterns on my skin. For a while, we lay there in silence, the world outside fading into background noise.

His voice broke the quiet, low and gravelly. "April 25th. The day we chatted for the first time. I've been falling for you since."

"What?" I lifted my head in surprise, thinking about the heated argument we had when we first met. "At the Ren Faire?"

Nolan shook his head, a faint smile tugging at his lips. "No. Before that. When you first messaged me about the apartment. You said something funny... I don't even remember what, but I thought, 'She's different. I could get used to that.'"

I raised an eyebrow, a smile creeping onto my face. "Really? And when you saw me at the Ren Faire, you knew it was me?"

He chuckled, his thumb brushing against my arm. "Yeah. I knew."

I wanted to be angry, but my laughter betrayed me. "I hate you," I told him, shaking his bicep.

Nolan stilled for a moment, his expression shifting. "That's my biggest fear, you know. That you could hate me."

I pushed myself up slightly, meeting his gaze. "I could never hate you, Nolan."

His brow arched with skepticism.

"Well," I admitted, smiling, "not anymore."

That seemed to console him.

"I think I started having feelings for you during the beach clean-up," I confessed, my voice softer now.

His hand paused on my back. "Why?"

I hesitated, letting the memory wash over me. "It was the way you stood so close to me that day, whispering in my ear. I still remember how you smelled. I got goosebumps."

Nolan's lips curved into a smirk. "That's not called 'having feelings'. That's being horny."

I smacked his arm, laughter bubbling out of me. "You're impossible. It wasn't just that. It was the way you laughed, the way you kept looking at me... it did something."

"You looked beautiful that day," he said, grabbing me. "In that yellow dress. I couldn't take my eyes off you."

My heart thudded in my chest, warmth blooming under my skin.

Nolan let out a tired groan, his head tipping back against the pillow as a grin stretched across his face.

"What?" I asked, amused.

He glanced at me, his brown eyes gleaming. "Just thinking about how this is not what I had imagined when you moved in."

"Oh?" I muttered. "What did you imagine?"

"I figured one of us would end up killing the other."

I laughed again, the sound spilling out of me like marbles. "I thought the same."

Nolan brushed his knuckles against my cheek, his gaze softening. "I love your laugh. And that nose!" He leaned in, playfully capturing the tip of my nose with his mouth, making a soft, exaggerated pop as though he were savoring a cherry. "I've always loved that nose."

The words hit me like a gentle wave.

"I haven't really laughed in years," I admitted, quietly.

"In that case..." He pulled me closer, his arms wrapping around me. "I'll make it my job to make you laugh every day."

His eyes sparkled as he played with a strand of my hair, and I melted into the warmth of his embrace. For a moment, I let myself feel like I was on top of the world, untouchable. But then a pang of guilt nudged at the edge of my mind.

"Nolan..." I started, hesitating. "About what I said earlier, the paragliding thing, I'm so sorry. That was cruel, and I swear I didn't mean it."

A firetruck wailed past on the street below, its siren piercing the momentary quiet.

Nolan's body tensed slightly beneath me, but he exhaled deeply. "It's okay," he said, his voice steady. "We don't have to talk about it right now."

"You fly every day without a paraglider, Nolan Sterling," I said, meaning every word. "You just made *me* fly."

He smiled, his expression softening.

"And you made that condom fly," I said with a chuckle, breaking the tender moment. "I didn't even notice when you put it on. Seems like you've had a lot of practice," I teased, a flash of jealousy rising in my chest. "And having one conveniently in your nightstand? Speaks volumes about its usage frequency."

Nolan laughed, throwing his head back. Oh, that wonderful, musical laugh. It was so rare to see him this carefree.

"Are you jealous?" he asked, biting my cheek playfully.

"No," I said, fighting to keep a straight face.

"Well," he drawled, amusement thick in his voice, "I have a dispenser in the drawer. Just press a button, and voilà, condoms on demand."

My silence only made him laugh harder. "You're so fuckin' cute," he murmured, kissing me deeply.

Once his laughter subsided, he glanced at me, his voice softening. "The reason I was so fast at grabbing and putting on the condom is because..." He lifted the comforter and let his gaze trail over my naked body. "You looked like this."

I squeaked, yanking the blanket over myself, though I couldn't help grinning.

"And as for having them in my bedside drawer, you know I like to be prepared, for anything and everything. It's more about caution than... anticipation. I've always kept them around since I became sexually active."

"Oh yeah?" I said, leaning in slightly. "And when was that?"

He paused, his gaze shifting behind me as if searching his memory. "When I was twenty."

"Twenty?" My eyebrows shot up. "That late?" It was hard to believe that someone as attractive as Nolan hadn't lost his virginity until then.

"I had other priorities," he explained. "And I didn't meet anyone who made me want to change them. Sure, there were girls. Many," he added with a casual shrug, though there was no arrogance in his tone, "who made passes, but I was focused on other things. From the age of fifteen to nineteen, I was also taking care of my mom, almost full-time."

"Why?"

"She suffered from dementia." Nolan's voice was even, but I could hear the undercurrent of loss.

My voice got stuck in my throat, and I failed to say anything meaningful.

"It's why I build that AI model," he explained.

I wrapped my hands tighter around him to comfort him, but also to thank him for sharing that with me.

"That's the best tribute one could give to their loved one," I said. "I am so sorry, Nolan."

He smiled.

"Anyway, a year after she passed away, I went to my first party in ages and ended up going home with someone. That was my first time. Since then, it's mostly been one-night stands."

The information sent a mild warning signal to my brain.

He smiled, reading my expression. "Not as many as whatever number you're imagining right now."

"Why only one-night stands?" I asked.

"You've seen my schedule," he said. "It used to be even worse. A relationship, or even a fling, requires time, energy, and attention. I didn't have any of those to spare. So, instead, I made sleeping with someone more like a self-care ritual...that's the term they keep repeating a lot these days, right? Self-care?"

"Yeah. But self-care, how?" I asked, both amused and intrigued.

"Like a workout. Good for the body, good for the mind. Sex is a basic human need, afterall."

I was surprised by the honesty, and the logic of his reasoning. It was... practical. Very Nolan. It was also the healthiest way to see sex, I had learned.

"Hey," he said softly, his gaze locking with mine. "I never misled or cheated anyone. I was always upfront about what I was looking for. I made sure they were okay, dropped them home, the whole thing."

I smiled, touched by his sincerity. "I wasn't worried about that. You're... wonderful."

He studied me for a long moment, his gaze so intense I almost had to look away.

"But that's not what's going on right now, Ivy," he said, his voice firm. "This time, I am ready to invest my time, energy, and attention. I've never felt like this before. Wanting someone so much that I couldn't help myself. I've always had control over my urges. But you... you broke me."

My heart stopped, and before I could respond, he kissed my nose and added, "In a good way."

We laid there, intertwined in each others arms, talking and sharing and being our most vulnerable and open selves. It was as easy as breathing.

By the time we finally got out of bed, it was eleven at night.

I wrapped my arms around myself, shivering from the cold as I searched for my top and shorts. Nolan, standing by the closet, grabbed one of his button-downs and tossed it to me.

"Thanks," I murmured, slipping on the black shirt, grateful for the warmth and the faint scent of him.

He stood by the door, shirtless, his joggers hanging low on his hips, watching me with an unreadable expression.

"What?" I asked, tilting my head. "Is this some kind of reverse striptease for you?"

He didn't reply, just shook his head.

I walked over to him, barefoot, and wrapped my arms around his waist. Standing on my toes, I kissed him deeply.

"I like you, Nolan Sterling," I whispered close to his ears.

"I like you a lot more, Ivy Delaney," he responded.

As I retracted my arms, my stomach growled. Loud enough to break the moment.

Nolan laughed.

Grabbing my wrist, he took me to the kitchen. "Alright, come on. Let me feed you."

I perched on the kitchen island, feeling the cold granite under my thighs, and watched as Nolan rummaged through the fridge, his bare upper body illuminated by the fridge light. He looked like something out of a Greek painting—broad shoulders, defined muscles, sleek body, and a godlike aura.

"What's on the menu, Chef?" I asked, stopping myself from salivating over my roommate.

He smirked. "Gotta cater to your 'selective' preferences."

"Excuse you!" I shot back, tossing a dish towel at him, which he dodged with ease.

Soon, the aroma of basmati rice filled the kitchen, making my mouth water. I leaned in and kissed his neck.

"Smells amazing," I murmured, my hands slipping around his abs.

"Distracting me won't make it cook faster," he said, though his smile betrayed him.

Once the food was ready, I grabbed two plates, two glasses, and some silverware, setting them on the counter. Nolan picked up the ladle, carefully scooping the chickpea curry and serving it over a bed of fragrant rice on one of the plates. Then, with practiced ease, he poured a generous glass of red wine. Without a word, he carried both the plate and the glass and headed toward the couch.

"I know you've been eyeing this spot ever since I started boiling the rice," he said casually, settling on the floor with his back against the couch and facing the balcony.

I froze, stunned. He had read my mind. I *had* been eyeing the little nook by the balcony doors. A cozy spot to eat where we could stay warm indoors while still looking out at the night sky. But I hadn't mentioned it, knowing how much Nolan preferred eating at the table. I didn't want to push our differing habits tonight.

And yet, here he was, sitting exactly where I had imagined.

Placing the plate and wine on the floor beside him, he patted the space between his legs.

"Come here. Eat from my plate."

My heart flipped, and I couldn't help but grin like an idiot. Of all the incredible things Nolan had done tonight, this simple act might just be the most romantic. I cracked the balcony doors slightly, letting in a cool whisper of night air, then nestled myself between his legs. Moonlight spilled through the glass, bathing us in soft silver. His arm wrapped snugly around me, pulling me closer.

"You're the sweetest," I said, peppering his face with kisses. "This is perfect."

He picked up the plate of rice and curry and held it in front of me, his other hand resting comfortably on my waist. I took a spoonful and tasted it.

"Yummm..." I moaned. Then, scooping another spoonful, I turned to him and lifted it to his lips.

Nolan hesitated, momentarily puzzled, like I'd just done something completely alien. But then his lips parted, and he accepted the bite. A flicker of something unspoken passed through his eyes as he chewed and swallowed.

"Could use more chili," he remarked with his usual pragmatism.

I nudged him playfully with my shoulder. "Not all of us have part-Indian spice tolerance, Nolan. This is perfect for me. Can't believe you whipped this up so quickly."

He chuckled, reaching out to wipe a smudge of sauce from the corner of my mouth with his thumb. Without thinking, he licked it clean, his eyes gleaming with mischief.

We fell into a comfortable silence after that, sipping wine from the same glass, eating from the same plate. The world outside faded away. For the first time in ages, I felt wholly present. No past wounds. No future anxieties. Just the warmth of Nolan, the glow of moonlight, and the rhythm of our shared breaths.

"I have a proposal for you," Nolan said suddenly, breaking the quiet.

I shot my head to look at him.

He smirked at my wide-eyed, nervous expression. "Relax, Ivy Delaney. Not that kind of proposal."

I relaxed, chuckling as he continued. "This Friday, there's an AI and Mental Health Symposium at UCLA. I was planning to go alone, network a bit, meet potential investors for the start-up. But..." He hesitated for just a second, his confidence softening into something more vulnerable. "Would you join me?"

"Me?" I blinked, caught off guard. "Nolan, I don't know anything about this stuff."

"Ivy," he said patiently, leaning forward so his face was closer to mine. "You're the reason I'm going to this symposium in the first place. You're the one who made me look at my work differently. If it weren't for your perspective, I'd probably be at some generic tech expo, pitching to the same boring crowd. Besides, you have also build this company up with your words. Whether you realize it or not, you know enough about this... stuff."

"Oh..." I murmured, still unsure. The idea of walking into a room full of tech moguls and investors was intimidating, to say the least.

"It might be boring," he admitted. "Panels, workshops, endless discussions. But..." He paused, his eyes locking with mine. "It would really mean a lot to me if you were there."

That admission hit me harder than I expected. For Nolan, this wasn't just about work. This was him inviting me into his world, trusting me to share in something deeply important to him.

"I'd love to join you," I answered.

His face lit up with a rare, unguarded smile. "Thank you."

I turned to face him fully, my gaze searching his. "You make everything seem so easy."

His brow furrowed slightly. "What do you mean?"

"You just... do what you want, say what you mean. No second-guessing, no overthinking. It's liberating. It takes so much pressure off me."

He laughed, the sound warm and low, pressing a kiss to my temple. "Trust me, it's not as easy as it looks. But with you... it feels worth the risk."

My heart swelled, leaving me speechless. Instead of responding, I leaned back into his chest, letting his words settle over me. He moved my hair away, whisked his shirt's collar to the side, and kissed me tenderly on the shoulder, his lips refusing to part from my skin.

We stayed like that for a while, cocooned in the night's quiet beauty, gazing up at the stars. The cool breeze from the balcony whispered promises of a thousand possibilities, but for now, I didn't want anything else.

CHAPTER 22

My anxieties had been crushing me ever since Nolan invited me to the symposium three days ago. As if driving up to UCLA with him and meeting a roomful of polished, genius-level people wasn't daunting enough, my mind fixated on a seemingly trivial yet monstrous question:

What am I going to wear?

Nolan had mentioned it was a business-casual event. But knowing him, that probably meant a perfectly tailored suit, a crisp, pressed shirt, and just the right pair of matching shoes and belt that exuded, "I'm the smartest guy in the room, but I'm not trying too hard." If I showed up looking even slightly off-brand, I'd stick out like a sore thumb. And since I'd somehow become his unofficial representative at this event, a role I still couldn't fully wrap my head around, I knew I had to match his energy.

I'd spent hours googling outfit ideas, only to spiral further into self-doubt. Then it hit me.

I now had a friend with impeccable taste in clothes.

Two hours after texting Elena for help, I found myself in the buzzing labyrinth of Fashion Valley Mall, trailing behind her as she scouted racks with the focus of a woman on a mission. The air was infused with the scent of roasted coffee and designer perfume, blending with the distant chatter of shoppers and the faint hum of music from various stores.

"So, when is this event?" Elena asked, flipping through a rack of blazers.

"Tomorrow," I said, bracing myself for her reaction.

"Oh, boy." She shot me a look over the pencil skirt she was examining. "What about shoes? A handbag? Do you have something at home that'll work?"

"No..." I admitted sheepishly.

She shook her head, chuckling. "Okay, let's get you the clothes first. We'll figure out the rest later."

We'd done one loop through the stores, and I'd tried on four outfits, none of which made the cut. Now, we sat at a small table in the courtyard for a much-needed break, sipping our drinks. The coolness from a splashing fountain near us dampened the afternoon heat.

"So," Elena began, leaning back and taking a sip of her caramel frappuccino, "when were you going to tell me about you and Nolan?"

I nearly choked on my cold brew. "Nolan told you?"

"And then some!"

My face flushed as my mind raced, wondering just how much Nolan had shared.

She laughed, leaning forward conspiratorially. "I'm kidding! He only told me you two were together. I had to drag it out of him, though. He got all coy when I mentioned your name this morning. But seriously, I am so happy for you two." She reached over and pulled me into a half-hug.

Relief washed over me. I'd felt bad keeping Elena in the dark, but I wanted to leave it up to Nolan to decide when and how to share the news.

"Thank you," I said, smiling.

"I knew something would happen between you two," she teased, taking her seat again.

"What are you talking about? We bickered all the time."

Elena rolled her eyes. "Oh, please. You know what Nolan never does after meeting a girl? Talk about her. Yet he couldn't stop talking about you. Granted, they were rants, but you were definitely in his head. Right from the start. Why do you think I tried so hard to get to know you?"

"Clever." I blushed. "But that's Nolan's reaction. Why were you so sure I'd go for him?"

"The way you tried to understand him, even after clashing so hard at the Faire. The way you both steal glances at each other like a couple of awkward teenagers."

I groaned, holding my temple.

"You think no one notices the tension? You two have the whole 'enemies-to-lovers' trope written all over you."

I couldn't help but laugh, feeling both embarrassed and oddly touched.

"I like you for him," Elena said, her tone softening. "You've had such a positive influence on him. I can already see it."

Her words left a warm glow in my chest.

"I'll be less worried about him now, knowing he has you," she added, her voice quieter. "It'll make it easier for me when I'm not here."

My brows furrowed. "What do you mean? Where are you going?"

Elena's smile faltered as she stared into her drink. "I've been thinking about taking a break. Visiting my dad in Idyllview."

"That sounds nice," I said, watching her carefully. "For how long?"

"I've been...thinking about moving back. For good."

Her words hit me like a small punch to the gut. "Wait, what? Leaving San Diego? Permanently?"

"I haven't told anyone yet," Elena admitted quietly. "Not even Nolan."

"And Jay?"

Her expression darkened. "Not him either."

A heavy silence fell between us, broken only by the distant chatter of shoppers and the occasional squeak of a passing trolley.

"Why do you want to leave?" I asked.

"I just can't with this city anymore," she spat. It was the strongest tone of voice she had ever used in front of me.

"Are you sure it's the city?" I asked gently.

She hesitated, looking at me like I'd caught her in a lie. "Of course. I mean, San Diego's amazing, but it doesn't feel like home. Never has. The problem is, I feel selfish to even think about moving because I know Jay hates Idyllview. He'd never move back."

"Elena," I said, placing a hand on her arm, "there's nothing selfish about wanting to be in a place that makes you happy. Trust me, I stayed in a place I hated for someone else, and I still regret not listening to my gut." I paused, choosing my words carefully. "But... I do think you should talk to Jay about this."

"I want to," she said weakly. "But I already know how it's going to end." She blinked rapidly, pressing a finger to the corner of her eye.

"Elena, is it the city you've grown out of, or the person?"

Her eyes glistened as she shook her head. "I don't know. I just know I'm not happy. I haven't been for a long time."

Then she broke into tears. "Oh God, I'm crying at the mall."

"Hey!" I scooted my chair closer, wrapping an arm around her. "It's okay. That's why they build fountains. To mask the sobbing."

She gave a watery laugh.

"Listen," I said, my voice soft. "Take it one step at a time. Talk to Jay. Be honest about how you're feeling. You deserve to be happy, wherever and with whoever that may be."

Elena sniffled and gave me a small smile. "Thanks. Now, let's go get you a nice dress." She stood from her chair, wiping her cheeks.

I hesitated, pulling out my phone and glancing at the time. An idea struck me.

"You said you're free until dinner, right?" I asked, slipping my phone back into my pocket.

"Yeah."

"Perfect. Let's go." I grabbed her arm.

She blinked. "Go where?"

"To the movies," I said, already steering us toward the AMC. "My treat. As a thank you for today. Inside Out 2 starts in ten minutes, and I know you've been dying to see it."

Her steps faltered slightly. "Movies? Now? But what about shopping?"

I glanced over my shoulder at her, jogging, and beamed. "Shopping can wait. Now, run fast. We don't want to miss the trailers."

Elena let out a laugh, her earlier tears drying as she matched my pace. "And popcorn!"

"That's why I like you!" I shouted through the chaos of the outdoor mall, as we weaved through the crowd, and reached AMC right on time.

AT FIRST, WHEN THE movie started, I thought bringing an emotionally overwhelmed Elena to something so heavy might've been a bad idea. But when we walked out of the theater, all cried out, we both felt lighter. Almost happy. The movie had been a catharsis, not just for Elena but for me too.

"I'm going to recommend this movie to all my patients," Elena said, pulling out her phone and typing a quick note.

"I'm going to watch it again with Nolan," I added, smiling at the thought.

The sun had dipped below the horizon, mall had transformed into a glittering wonderland. String lights wrapped around palm trees glowed warmly, and the reflection of shopfronts shimmered on the polished cobblestones. The air carried a faint chill, mixed with the comforting aroma of freshly baked pretzels.

We grabbed another round of coffees before hitting the stores again, this time with renewed energy. After some back and forth, Elena found the perfect dress for me: a sleek navy number that hugged in all the right places and was elegant and formal enough to speak for itself. Paired with understated nude heels, the outfit practically screamed confidence.

As we walked toward the parking lot, our shopping bags swinging lightly by our sides, Elena turned to me. "Thank you for today."

"Thank *you*," I countered. "I won't look like a lost kid at UCLA, all thanks to you."

She laughed.

"Can you keep the whole moving and Jay thing between us... just until you're back from L.A.?" she asked hesitantly. "I don't want to burden Nolan with it right now, especially with the symposium and everything else he's dealing with. I'm sure he'll have strong opinions about me moving away from here."

"I bet he will," I said, nodding. "But yes, I'll keep it between us. Just remember, I'm here if you need to talk more about it, okay?"

Elena pulled me into another hug, a full one this time, and an unexpected wave of melancholy swept through me. For a moment, she reminded me of my sister, Amber, and the ache of missing her burned my chest.

"Good luck in LA," Elena said, giving me a final smile before heading to her car.

As I drove home, my emotions churned in a bittersweet mix. I was glad I could be there for Elena, yet the thought of her leaving San

Diego left an ache I couldn't shake. Still, deep down, I knew she had to follow her heart, just like I was learning to follow mine.

NOLAN CAME HOME LATE that night, juggling his dry cleaning and keys, his tie slightly loosened and his sleeves rolled up in a way that made him look effortlessly dashing even after a long day. Welcoming him with a kiss every evening had been weird. Good weird. Except, like every night, it didn't stop there.

The kiss turned into us tangled together, breathless and desperate, this time in my room. His hands were on me the second the door shut, and we didn't even make it to the bed at first. "I've been waiting all day for this," he murmured against my lips, his voice low and rough. The way he said it made my entire body melt. It was impossible to keep our hands off each other, the pull magnetic, as if we'd both been holding our breath for this moment.

Afterward, as we lay catching our breath and putting our clothes back on, I told him about my day with Elena, carefully skirting around the parts she had confided about Jay. Guilt nudged at me, but I knew Elena was right to want to wait.

"I wish you'd warned me that she knew about us," I said, pulling my hair into a quick bun. "She caught me off guard."

Nolan chuckled as he unbunned my hair, keeping the hair tie to himself. "Sorry, I forgot."

I escaped his grip and ran to get another tie, a teasing smile on my face.

"It was a busy day," he added, buttoning his shirt. "She got it out of me just before you two met. And honestly, I didn't mind sharing. It felt... good."

His words were a relief.

"So... you're *really* okay with Elena and me hanging out?" I asked tentatively.

"Of course. I don't have to worry about my friends liking you. She already does."

"I like her too," I replied.

"Maybe next time, we should all hang out. Jay included," he suggested, surprising me. "You'll like him."

The way Nolan was pulling me into his world so quickly was both thrilling and terrifying. He was a man with a clear vision of his future, moving toward it with unstoppable precision. I couldn't help but feel the pressure to match his energy, to show him I was just as serious, even though I didn't have a polished plan for my own life.

Not that I had anyone close to introduce him to in return. No friends, no family. Except one person. Adrian. But even his name was a sore subject in this house.

I made a decision. That weekend, when I met Adrian, I would tell him about Nolan. I would ask him to be happy for me, to accept him. He had always had my back, and I needed him to have it now too.

Later, since Nolan and I had already had dinner, we shared tea and pears in the kitchen for dessert while prepping for the symposium. Watching Nolan work was like witnessing a conductor directing an orchestra. He had this innate ability to tie every detail together into a flawless plan. His confidence and clarity were almost contagious, and as the evening went on, my anxieties about tomorrow began to melt away.

When we wrapped up, we headed to his room, where I introduced him to the wonderful world of Stars Hollow and the whimsical chaos of Gilmore Girls. Nolan had a TV mounted on the wall, and as he worked on his laptop in bed, I lay beside him watching Lorelei and Rory talk like their life was on line.

"You sure you don't mind?" I asked, pausing the episode. "I can do something else."

"No, leave it on," he said without looking up. "I'm already working from bed. Might as well increase the difficulty level."

"You're so weird," I commented, unpausing the show.

Throughout the episode, Nolan kept glancing at the screen, making comments and asking questions, his expression a mix of disbelief and amusement.

"This town is a circus," he muttered. "How are they all so free all the time? Just... chatting, eating, and gossiping? Do they even have jobs?"

I laughed. "Oh, you haven't seen Lorelei at the inn. You *have* to see the Inn!" I got out of the current episode and scrolled to a further season. "Besides," I added, "that's the charm of small-town life, you know. Being completely unrealistic."

"Unrealistic is right," he said, shaking his head.

The quaintness of Stars Hollow reminded me of Elena's hometown. "Have you ever been to Idyllview? Elena's town?" I asked.

"Yeah," he said, typing something on his laptop. "After my mom passed, I spent most Thanksgivings there with Elena's family. Jeremy, her dad, is a solid guy."

"Do you like it there?"

"It's okay for a day or two. After that, the slowness suffocates me. I like the city."

"Me too," I said, pleased to find we were on the same page about at least one thing.

"If you're curious, we could go there someday. Elena would love to show you around."

"That sounds lovely."

"Okay, enough chit-chat," Nolan said, "You need to sleep. We leave at six tomorrow morning. Sharp."

"Yes, sir," I said, mock saluting as I turned off the TV and slid under the comforter. "But the rules should apply to you too. You need to rest. You can't look tired tomorrow."

"I look tired?" he asked, sounding genuinely surprised.

"All the time. I mean, you still look like a million bucks, but it shows. And I don't care if it's on your face, but I don't want it to affect your health."

"Why didn't you tell me sooner?" He set his laptop aside, turned off the lights, and got into the comforter. Then he pulled me into him by the waist, his body warm and solid against mine.

"You know what else is great for health besides sleep?" he whispered.

"Sex?" I guessed from the look in his eyes.

"Sex."

And just like that, we found ourselves wrapped up in each other again, losing track of time. Later, as I drifted off to sleep in his arms, his steady breathing against my forehead, I thought, it couldn't get any better than this.

CHAPTER 23

I stood proud by the kitchen counter at 5:50 a.m., waiting for Nolan to get ready. Determined not to make us late, I woke up earlier than I needed to, took a quiet shower in my room so I wouldn't disturb him, and got ready with time to spare. Usually, I'm scrambling at the last minute whenever I have somewhere to be, so it felt like a small luxury to take my time for once.

When Nolan finally stepped out of his room, his mouth parted slightly as his eyes scanned me.

"You look... stunning," he said, his voice sincere, before leaning in to plant a kiss on my lips.

I smiled, feeling my cheeks warm under his gaze. I was wearing the cinched navy blazer dress and nude heels we'd shopped from the mall yesterday. A dainty pair of gold earrings and soft waves in the hair added a touch of femininity to the otherwise polished outfit. I also used some of the make-up I had and wore a perfume I'd owned but never opened.

We continued kissing, his hand sliding to my waist as he pulled me closer. Nolan looked as delicious as ever in a slim-fitted charcoal gray suit and a white shirt underneath perfectly tailored to his frame. It was hard to stop when he looked at me like that.

"Okay," I said, catching my breath between kisses, "we're going to be late."

He smirked, his hand still lingering on my face. "We need to leave," I repeated, firmer this time.

He nodded but didn't let go, stealing kisses as we walked to the elevator and all the way to the car in the underground parking. By the time we got in the car, I was laughing, half-annoyed, half-amused. "Now I have to redo my makeup and hair," I said..

Nolan grinned, unapologetic. "Worth it."

Once on the road, we made a quick stop at a local café. Nolan brought me a tall black coffee and a warm, flaky croissant. For himself, he grabbed an Earl Grey tea and an avocado bagel sandwich.

As we got back on the freeway, San Diego stretched out behind us in soft, muted hues. The early morning light bathed the city in a warm glow, the kind that feels full of quiet promise. A faint chill still hung in the air, just enough to make the warmth of the coffee in my hands feel comforting.

We drove north on I-5, the highway hugging the coastline. To our left, the Pacific Ocean sparkled like liquid gold under the rising sun, waves crashing gently against the shore. On our right, the mountains rose in lush, green folds, their usual dryness replaced by a vibrant carpet of wildflowers and foliage. Thanks to the generous winter rains, spring this year had transformed Southern California into a lively landscape.

Nolan let me take over the music since he usually preferred audiobooks. I flipped through my playlists, picking a mix of upbeat and calming tunes to match the mood of the drive. He was distracted, of course. I could see it in his furrowed brow and the way he drummed his fingers lightly against the steering wheel, rehearsing his presentation in his head, running through every possible detail.

The drive felt peaceful despite his quiet intensity. I couldn't stop staring out the window, captivated by the world floated alongside me.

As we passed the Irwindeal highway sign, a pang of memory hit me. The years I'd spent there felt like a distant life, one I was finally leaving behind for good. I thought about all the pain I'd endured in that chapter, but it didn't bother me as much as it used to.

I glanced over at Nolan, his sharp jawline catching the light as he concentrated on the road. This wasn't just a new chapter; it was a whole new book. I felt like I wasn't just running away from something. I was running toward a future that was mine to create.

Not just with Nolan, but with my own life.

THREE HOURS LATER, we arrived at UCLA, beating the morning traffic. The campus stretched out before us like something out of a postcard, its iconic red-brick buildings glowing under the morning sunlight. Towering palm trees swayed gently against the clear blue sky, and students hurried past on bikes or clustered in groups, chatting animatedly. There was an energy to the place, one that felt both vibrant and intimidating.

I couldn't help but slow down to take it all in as we walked across the sprawling grounds. The landscaped gardens, the neatly trimmed hedges, the sound of fountains bubbling faintly in the distance; it was all so beautiful, so alive with possibility. I had never been on a campus this grand before. It felt like the kind of place where brilliant ideas were born, and brilliant people walked the halls. I glanced at Nolan, who seemed completely at ease, like he belonged here.

When we reached the conference hall, my confidence faltered. The tall glass doors reflected a sea of polished professionals, all dressed sharply and moving with purpose. The hum of conversation spilled into the air as people checked in, collected badges, and mingled in small, energetic groups.

"Ready?" Nolan asked, his voice cutting through my hesitation.

I nodded, clutching the strap of my bag tightly.

Inside, the space was sleek and modern, with high ceilings and large windows that let in plenty of natural light. A digital banner near the entrance read, AI & Mental Health Symposium: Innovating for a Better Future. Tables lined the walls, each showcasing different companies, research groups, or projects. Screens displayed colorful graphics and charts, while sleek pamphlets offered details about cutting-edge advancements.

Before heading to the main conference room, we stopped at a breakfast station. There was an impressive spread—pastries, fruit platters, yogurt parfaits, freshly brewed coffee, and teas. Nolan grabbed a cup of breakfast tea and a plate of fruit, while I opted for coffee and a small Danish.

We found a table to sit at, sharing it with a couple of other attendees. One was a woman in her late thirties with short-cropped hair and glasses perched on her nose. She introduced herself as Dr. Park, a cognitive neuroscientist studying the impact of creative activities like painting and writing on mental resilience. It instantly piqued my interest. The other was a middle-aged man with salt-and-pepper hair named Siddharth Nair, a health tech entrepreneur who ran a startup focused on teletherapy solutions for under-served communities.

Nolan immediately launched into a conversation with them, asking pointed, intelligent questions about their work.

"I'm fascinated by your approach, Dr. Park," Nolan said, leaning forward slightly. "Are you finding it difficult to gather enough diverse data points for your models?"

"It's definitely a challenge," Dr. Park admitted, adjusting her glasses. "But we're partnering with hospitals across different regions to address that. The real hurdle is convincing people to trust AI when it comes to mental health diagnoses."

"Exactly," Siddharth chimed in. "That's why education and transparency are critical. If people don't understand how the AI works, they're not going to trust it."

I sat quietly, sipping my coffee, feeling out of place. Their conversation flowed effortlessly, filled with technical terms and concepts that were far above my head. Every now and then, Nolan glanced at me, his eyes soft with reassurance, but it didn't help much.

My mind drifted to Trent, to the times he'd mocked my intelligence in front of his friends. "You're a creative, Ivy," he'd said once with a condescending smirk. "Leave the smart stuff to brainy people." The memory made my chest tighten.

Excusing myself, I rushed to the restroom, my footsteps echoing down the marble hallway. Inside, I locked myself in a stall and leaned against the cool metal door, taking deep breaths. You're not stupid, I told myself. You don't have to be like them to be worth something.

My phone buzzed.

"Everything okay?" It was Nolan.

I smiled faintly, his concern pulling me back to the present.

"Yeah, just needed a moment. Be right out," I replied.

After a few more deep breaths, I fixed my hair in the mirror and headed back. When I returned, Nolan was standing with a group of new people.

"There you are," he said, smiling warmly. He placed a hand on my back, guiding me closer. "Everyone, this is Ivy, an incredibly talented writer who's been helping me with the content for our project."

I swallowed a knot in my throat, surprised by the pride in his voice.

"Her ideas have been brilliant," Nolan continued, "especially her approach to structuring our presentation today. Honestly, it's what's going to make it stand out."

The group nodded politely, offering a few kind words about the work they had read on our website. Some shared their frustrations about the lack of good copywriters for their projects, while others handed me their business cards, encouraging me to reach out if I was open to more freelance opportunities. My cheeks warmed. Not from embarrassment this time, but from a deep sense of pride.

The rest of the day unfolded in a blur of panels, networking, and conversations. Nolan introduced me to more people than I could count, each one as passionate and knowledgeable as the last. Despite my initial nervousness, I found myself soaking up the energy of the event, asking questions here and there, and even sharing a few of my thoughts.

When it was finally time for Nolan's presentation, I took a seat near the front, my heart pounding as I watched him take the stage. He began with his usual calm confidence, explaining the vision for his startup and how predictive analytics could revolutionize mental health care.

As he wrapped up the technical portion, he turned to me, nodding slightly. I stood, walking to the podium. My palms were sweaty, but I pushed through.

"In closing," I said, concluding my speech, my voice steady despite my nerves, "I'd like to share some quick but powerful data. Studies show that the average person remembers the last thing they hear the most. And the last thing I want you to remember is this: one in four people will struggle with mental health at some point in their lives. That's 25% of the world's population. I believe the actual number is even higher. If we can leverage technology to identify the signs early, imagine the lives we can save."

The applause that followed will ring in my ears for days.

By the end of the day, a potential investor approached us, a tall man with a warm smile named Henry Clarke.

"I'd love to discuss this further over dinner," he said, looking at both of us. Then he turned to me specifically. "And Ivy, your perspective was refreshing. You don't often hear that kind of authenticity and emotional appealing in presentations like these. You should be proud."

I did feel proud, and more than anything, I truly felt belonged.

CHAPTER 24

Instead of asking Adrian to come over, I decided to visit him. His studio apartment in Pacific Beach was small but inviting, with a charm that was unmistakably his. It sat on the second floor of a weathered beachfront complex, the kind of place that had seen its fair share of sunsets and salty sea air. Through the large windows facing the ocean, the Pacific stretched out endlessly, its waves entertaining the surfers and tourists. Adrian had always said that having the ocean as his front yard was all that mattered, and honestly, I could see why.

His studio interior was a perfect blend of Scandinavian simplicity and minimalist modern warmth, according to him. A low-profile dark teal sofa sat against the wall, paired with a simple oak coffee table that held a stack of architecture magazines and a single potted plant. Beneath the large window overlooking the ocean was a white desk with slim, tapered legs, set up with his laptop and an assortment of sketchpads. In the corner, his well-worn surfboard leaned casually, while the faint scent of sandalwood lingered in the air.

I perched on his sofa, gazing out at the view as my eyes fell on his bookshelf. I snorted a laugh as I noticed a stack of romance and self-help titles he never admitted to buying.

Adrian was pacing back and forth near his desk, finishing a phone call. His voice was calm yet commanding, probably wrapping up another deal or handling a client who wanted a mansion in La Jolla with an infinity pool and a wine cellar. It was ironic, really.

Adrian spent his days immersed in talks about lavish houses and sprawling estates, yet he came home to this cozy, unassuming studio. But then again, Adrian had always been about quality over quantity.

As I waited, my thoughts drifted to yesterday, to the incredible day I had at UCLA. The symposium had been far better than I'd imagined. After the conference, Nolan and I were invited to dinner by some of the attendees, and for once, I didn't feel out of place. I'd held my own in conversations, especially with Dr. Park, whose brilliance I had come to admire throughout the day. We connected over shared interests, especially art, and for the first time, I felt truly fulfilled in my work. Not just for what I'd accomplished, but for the way others saw and respected me.

Nolan and I got home late, exhausted but happy. We barely managed to change before collapsing into bed, wrapped in each other's arms. As tired as I was, a quiet kind of joy hummed within me. This was the life I wanted. Not just the work, but the feeling of being seen and valued.

"Sorry about that," Adrian's voice pulled me out of my thoughts. He hung up and turned toward me with an apologetic smile, running a hand through his slightly messy hair. "Real estate waits for no one."

"You are lucky you have this view, or I'd have left," I joked. "Seriously, Adrian, I keep forgetting how perfect your place is."

He grinned, grabbing two bottles of beer from his fridge. Sierra Nevada Pale Ale for him, ginger for me.

"Let's sit on the beach," he said.

We walked barefoot through the cool sand, the grains sticking to the damp soles of our feet. The ocean rested before us, preparing to swallow the sun.

Adrian waited until we sat down before speaking. "You got laid," he announced casually, taking a sip of his beer.

I froze mid-sip. "What?"

"Or you won the lottery," he said, tilting his head. "You look obnoxiously nonchalant."

"What does that even mean?"

"You're never this relaxed," he replied, pressing his fingers between my neck and shoulder. "Yup, no knots!"

I batted his hand away, laughing. "Stop it."

He leaned back on his elbows, looking at me expectantly. "So? What's going on?"

I took a deep breath, unsure of how to start. "Adrian, you do know I love you, right? As a—"

"Ivy, no beating around the bush. Just tell me."

I exhaled sharply. "Nolan and I are seeing each other."

His grin disappeared as he turned to stare at the water. The sudden quiet felt like a weight pressing down on my chest. Somewhere nearby, a frisbee landed awkwardly in the sand, and a golden retriever dashed past us to retrieve it, its tail wagging furiously.

Adrian broke the silence. "You hated him."

"What?"

"Your roommate. You hated him."

"I did, but..."

"But what? He's different now? This is just Trent all over again, Ivy."

"It's not!" I snapped, the sting of his words cutting deep. "Nolan is nothing like Trent. He's... thoughtful. He's kind—"

"Kind?" Adrian interrupted. "The guy who tricked you into staying with him and then made you work for him? For rent? That's not kindness, Ivy. That's manipulation. That's power play."

I clenched my beer. "He didn't trick me into anything. I stayed because I wanted to. I worked for him because I wanted to."

"Did you, though?" Adrian's voice softened but held its edge

"Yes. They were my choices."

"Ivy, when the other option disrupts your status quo, it's not a choice."

His words felt like needles, pricking at the doubts I'd buried. "I know Nolan has rough edges, Adrian, but since we've been together, he has treated me with nothing but respect.

He scoffed. "Respect? The guy who insults your way of life every chance he gets? What's next, Ivy? Are you going to let him chip away at you until there's nothing left? Because that's what Trent did. That's the pattern you keep falling into."

"That's not fair," I whispered, my voice trembling.

"It's not fair to you," he shot back, his tone rising. "To keep chasing men who don't see your worth. It's like... like some cry for help."

Tears burned at the corners of my eyes, but I refused to let them fall. "You don't know him like I do."

"And you don't know him at all," Adrian said, his voice intense. "He's shown you who he is. Time and time again. Just like Trent did at the beginning of your relationship. Are you so blind or you're ignoring it because you're afraid of being alone?"

For a moment, I wavered. Adrian's words echoed in my mind, dredging up old fears. But then, anger replaced my hesitation.

"Afraid of being alone? Look who is talking." I didn't have to say more on that subject, for we both knew how afraid Adrian was of staying alone. "And are you saying all this because I didn't reciprocate your feelings?" I asked, my voice cutting through the air like glass.

Adrian flinched. "You know it's not about that."

"No, it is," I pushed. "You think Nolan and I are transactional? That he has an ulterior motive? What about you? Aren't you trying to cash in on all the years of friendship we've had?"

His face twisted with hurt. "That's absurd, Ivy. I've always been there for you, no matter what. I would have been there even if you'd rejected me. My love, my friendship, for you has never been conditional."

His words melted my anger because I knew they were true.

"I know," I said, my voice softening. "Adrian, you deserve the kind of love you've been waiting for your whole life. The kind where there's no math in your brain, no compromises. And you won't find that by forcing yourself to love me."

He looked away, pulling his knees up and resting his arms on them. His jaw was tight, and I reached out to touch his arm gently. "Look, I am not the poster girl for love. I have no clue what I'm doing myself, but I do know that you can't make these kinds of relationships happen. They need to fall into place on their own. You deserve that. I deserve that."

When he didn't reply, I scooted closer to him and laid my head on his shoulder.

"I'll always be here for you," I said, my voice barely above a whisper. "Just not in the way you were hoping."

Adrian's shoulders slumped, and he nodded, his eyes glistening against the setting sun.

"And I'm okay, I promise," I said, more to convince myself than him. "You will be too. You just have to be patient. The right person will come along when it's time."

My phone buzzed in my pocket, breaking the quiet between us. Nolan's name lit up the screen.

"I have to go," I said, standing. "But think about what I said, okay?"

Adrian nodded again, his expression unreadable. As I walked away, I glanced back once. He was sitting in the sand, staring at the ocean, the neck of his beer bottle dangling loosely from his fingers.

CHAPTER 25

The evening was lazy yet warm as Nolan and I pulled into Elena's townhouse community. The faint scent of grilling meat hung in the air, mingling with the tang of freshly cut grass. Even before stepping out of the car, I could hear the hum of cheerful conversation, underscored by the occasional splash from the pool.

Elena's community sat in the heart of a bustling San Diego neighborhood. The tightly packed townhouses, with their pale stucco facades and terracotta roofs, looked almost cramped at first glance. But the spacious communal area in the center, alive with energy and laughter, brought a sense of balance. A large barbecue grill stood as the centerpiece, surrounded by Jay and Elena's group of friends. Music blared from a portable speaker, while kids squealed and cannonballed into the pool.

I adjusted the strap of my sundress, suddenly feeling self-conscious about meeting Nolan's circle for the first time. Following him closely, I watched as he carried a six-pack of craft beer with that unhurried, effortless grace I had come to associate with him, nodding politely to familiar faces.

"Nolan!" A booming voice called out, cutting through the buzz of conversation.

I turned to see Jay approaching—a ball of unrestrained energy in neon sneakers and a bright muscle tank that screamed "weekend bro." He tossed a football mid-stride to someone behind him before closing the distance between us.

"Hey, dude," Nolan greeted him as he neared.

Jay slapped Nolan's shoulder in an exaggerated manner that would have knocked over anyone less steady. But Nolan didn't so much as sway.

"And this must be the elusive Ivy!" Jay exclaimed, grinning at me before turning to Nolan and punching him lightly in the arm. "You actually brought her out in public? Miracles do happen!"

I flushed at the comment, momentarily thrown by his larger-than-life energy.

"Jay." He extended a hand toward me with an exaggerated bow. "Nolan's better-looking, funnier, all-around cooler friend."

I couldn't help but laugh, shaking his hand. "Ivy. Nolan's slightly confused, moderately amused girlfriend."

Jay raised an eyebrow. "Ah, so she's witty too."

"Nice to see you. Again," I teased, reminding him that we had briefly met before.

It took him a second to remember, but when he did, he let out a loud laugh and clapped Nolan on the back again. "Oh yeah! The day Nolan got his ass handed to him. Good times."

Nolan rolled his eyes, his expression hovering between exasperation and amusement.

"Welcome to the madhouse," Jay said as he ushered us toward the grill. "We've got burgers, grilled veggies, beers, iced tea, and just the right amount of awkward work vibes. Help yourself."

Jay's personality was a sharp contrast to Nolan's quiet intensity, but somehow, they worked. I had imagined Jay as someone entirely different based on Elena's comments about their relationship. Instead, I found myself liking him almost immediately.

As we made our way through the crowd, Nolan leaned toward me and murmured, "Don't mention my start-up. Some of these people are colleagues, and I'd rather keep it under wraps for now."

I nodded, silently brainstorming a few neutral conversation topics to bring up if needed.

We mingled with different groups, Nolan introducing me here and there. I couldn't help but notice something. Nolan had that same small, distant smile for everyone—a polite façade, respectful but detached. But every time he faced me, his smile reached up to his eyes. It wasn't just that. It was the way his entire expression warmed, as if the barriers he kept up for everyone else dissolved just for me. It did something to my chest, seeing that shift.

Before I knew it, I was standing on my toes, cupping his cheek, and pressing a light kiss to his lips.

Jay immediately let out a joyous whoop. "Well, that was cute."

Nolan looked startled, the tips of his ears turning faintly red, but there was no missing the shy, almost proud smile that crept onto his face.

Elena's voice cut through the moment. "Ivy, you're making Nolan look like a softie."

I turned to see her approaching with open arms. She hugged me warmly, her energy as welcoming as ever.

We caught up briefly before she floated away, the consummate host, greeting guests, chatting effortlessly, and ferrying plates of food and drinks.

I stayed close to Nolan, navigating the sea of new faces with him. Most conversations revolved around light, work-related banter or the latest gossip in their circles. Occasionally, someone would offer Nolan a half-joking remark about finally bringing a girl along, to which he responded with his usual dry wit.

At one point, my attention drifted to Elena, who was standing by the grill with a spatula in hand. She wasn't cooking, though. Just staring across the patio with a faraway expression. Her gaze lingered on Nolan and me for a beat too long before she caught my eye and offered a faint, fleeting smile.

Leaning closer to Nolan, I whispered, "Elena seems... distracted."

"She always gets like that when she's hosting," he said dismissively, though his eyes followed her for a moment longer.

Later, Elena circled back to me, holding out a perfectly grilled corn cob.

"Your favorite," she said with a knowing smile.

"Yummm," I replied, eagerly taking it.

"Eat. You haven't had anything all evening."

"Thanks. I just feel... awkward with so many new people around."

She glanced between Nolan and me, her eyes thoughtful.

"What's going on?" I finally asked, half-laughing. "You've been creeping me out with all the staring."

She hesitated before replying, her voice low enough for only me to hear. "Nolan looks so happy, Ivy."

I blinked. "Does he?"

"Of course. He looks... grounded. Content. I haven't seen him like this. Ever."

She reached out and grabbed my arm, her tone dropping into something both playful and earnest. "Please don't ever leave him."

I laughed it off, but her words stuck with me as we joined Jay and a few others in the middle of a game of beanbag toss. Nolan and I exchanged reluctant glances before agreeing to join.

Jay tossed a beanbag first. It hit the edge of the board, wobbling precariously before falling off. He threw his hands up in dismay. "This game is rigged!"

"Or maybe you're just bad at it." Elena crossed her arms, a faint smirk tugging at her lips. There was an edge to her tone, almost challenging.

Jay puffed out his chest, grinning. "Babe, you know I'm a pro at this."

Nolan chuckled beside me, his focus unbroken as he took his turn. The beanbag soared through the air and landed squarely on the board, sliding effortlessly into the hole. Jay groaned, tossing his head back in mock defeat. "Show-off."

The group laughed, but I noticed the subtle flicker of tension in Elena's expression as her gaze lingered on Jay. Her smile didn't quite reach her eyes.

When it was Elena's turn, Jay leaned against the table, his tone light but carrying an undertone of condescension. "No pressure, babe. Not everyone's got my skills."

Elena straightened, her movements slow and deliberate as she picked up a beanbag. "Maybe if you spent less time talking, you'd actually score." Her aim was sharp, her throw precise. The beanbag landed neatly on the board, teetering for a moment before settling. She turned to Jay with a tight, forced smile.

Jay's laugh was a little too loud. Then his posture stiffened. "Oh, come on. I'm just trying to keep things fun. No need to get all serious."

Elena's expression hardened, though her voice remained calm. "I wasn't being serious, Jay. But maybe you should stop assuming how I feel."

A noticeable crackle of tension filled the air. Nolan and I exchanged a glance, uncertain if we should intervene. Jay shrugged, his tone more defensive now. "You're always in your head about something. Maybe just relax a little?"

Elena froze, her knuckles gripping the edge of the table. Her voice, though quiet, cut like glass. "And maybe you should stop dismissing everything I say like it doesn't matter."

The playful atmosphere evaporated. Jay's smile dropped, replaced with a defensive frown. "Elena, I'm not—"

She cut him off, her words sharper now. "You are. You always do."

The group that had gathered to watch the game fell silent. The weight of their words hung in the air. Jay's jaw worked as though he wanted to retort, but his eyes darted to the onlookers. With a frustrated sigh, he muttered, "Can we not do this here?"

Elena stared at him for a long moment, her face unreadable. Finally, she nodded curtly. "Fine. Let's go."

Without another word, they walked away toward their condo, leaving Nolan and me standing there in awkward silence. Nolan's shoulders were tense as he watched them retreat.

"I hate to say this, but I saw this coming," I murmured, mostly to myself.

Nolan's head snapped toward me, his brow furrowing. "Did you know about this?"

I hesitated, unsure of how much to reveal. "Elena mentioned... things weren't great. She's been unhappy here in San Diego and wanted to move back to her hometown."

His frown deepened. "What? When did she say that?"

"When we went to the mall," I admitted reluctantly. "I'm sorry I didn't tell you. She asked me not to. She wanted to tell you herself, after the L.A. conference."

Disappointment flickered across his face. "You should have told me, Ivy. I could've helped her. Made her understand."

"Nolan, she doesn't need us to make her understand her own relationship," I said gently but firmly. "She's been clear about how unhappy she is."

Nolan crossed his arms, his tone defensive. "She's just overthinking, like always. You don't know her like I do. She's always been like that. Jay loves her. And she loves him, just as much."

"Maybe things changed," I argued softly.

"That's not possible," he snapped, his voice rising slightly. His jaw clenched. "She's devoted herself to him. Too much, in fact. I even told her to find balance. She's always been all-in with Jay."

I sighed. "Sometimes love isn't enough, Nolan. From what Elena told me, their priorities don't align. They're too different."

"So are we," he countered, his gaze locking on mine with such intensity it churned my stomach. "That doesn't mean it doesn't work."

I opened my mouth, searching for the right words, but nothing came. Instead, I nodded, uncertain.

Nolan sighed and rubbed the back of his neck. "I'll talk to her when they come back. Maybe it's just stress from work."

"Nolan," I said gently. "Maybe you should let Elena decide how she feels about her own relationship."

His gaze darkened. "And maybe you shouldn't have interfered."

The sharpness of his words stung, but I forced myself to stay calm. I walked to a nearby bench and sat down, letting the tension dissipate. Nolan followed silently, sitting next to me, his focus on his phone. He was likely texting Jay, while I stared at the crowd milling around, blissfully unaware of the turmoil their hosts were going through.

Almost an hour later, Elena returned, looking drained. Her eyes were red-rimmed, her face blotchy.

"Sorry, guys," she said, fidgeting with her phone. Her voice wavered.

I stood and pulled her into a hug. "It's okay. How are you holding up?"

Nolan remained seated, his expression unreadable. He watched Elena carefully. She met his gaze and, without hesitation, said, "We're over."

Her voice cracked on the last word as she burst into tears. Nolan stood quickly, wrapping her in a tight hug. He rubbed her arms soothingly, his voice soft but steady. "Hey, it's okay. You'll get through this."

Elena sobbed into his chest, her tears soaking his shirt.

"Don't give up yet," Nolan murmured. "You two will figure it out. I know it."

Elena shook her head and pulled back slightly. "I've been watching you all day, Nolan," she said, her voice trembling.

Nolan and I exchanged a confused look.

"You seemed so... relieved," she continued, her tone steadier now. "Like something heavy had been lifted off your shoulders. And I know how hard it was for you to take this plunge," she glanced at me with a faint smile, "to be with Ivy. That was really brave of you. It made me realize that if someone like you, who's always so cautious and calculated, can take a leap of faith and follow their gut, then I need to do that too. I need to listen to my heart and be brave."

Nolan frowned. "What exactly happened, Elena? Did Jay do something?"

Her lips quivered, but she held her ground. "This has been happening for a while. I can't be with someone who loves a version of me that does not exists. It's unfair. To both of us."

Nolan looked like he wanted to argue but stopped himself. Elena's conviction left no room for doubt.

"I feel... relieved," she said quietly, wiping her face. "I wish it didn't have to end this way, but it's for the best."

Nolan nodded, pulling her into another hug. I walked off to get her some water, giving them space. By the time I returned, Elena looked calmer, though her shoulders still sagged with the weight of her decision. Jay, she informed us, had left to be alone, but he and Nolan planned to meet the next day.

For now, though, the evening was over.

NOLAN HAD BEEN ON EDGE since Elena's and Jay's argument. He barely spoke a word the entire way back to the car. When we reached the car, I grabbed the passenger door, but before I could open it, Nolan walked up and caught my hand.

His face was tight with worry, but there was a calmness in his eyes that felt deliberate, like he was trying to steady himself. "I'm sorry for the way I talked back there," he said quietly.

I nodded.

Leaning against the car, Nolan pulled me closer, his hands wrapping firmly around my waist. His touch was grounding, yet there was an ache in the way he held me.

"I've watched their relationship from the very beginning," he started, his voice heavy. "I dropped Elena on her first date with Jay. I was there when Jay told he loved her for the first time. Elena asked me to accompany them when she introduced Jay to her dad. Through all the chaos in my life, their relationship was like this... anchor. It wasn't perfect, I knew even though I didn't admit it, but it gave me hope. They're so different. Jay's all about barbecue nights, and Elena hates even the smell of grilling meat. But they made it work, year after year. It made me believe that differences don't have to break people. That maybe... if they could do it, so could we. But if they can break..."

I felt the unspoken words hanging in the air between us. His voice faltered as his fears surfaced. He wasn't just grieving Elena and Jay's breakup. He was afraid for us, too.

I reached up, brushing my fingers against his cheek, the roughness of his stubble tickling me as always. I leaned in and pressed a soft kiss to his jaw, inhaling the faint scent of smoke. "I know," I murmured.

His grip on my waist tightened as he spoke again, his voice breaking slightly. "They're the closest thing to family I've ever had. Watching them fall apart... it feels like I'm losing something too."

"Hey," I said, wrapping my arms around his neck and pulling him closer. I wanted him to feel it, to know he wasn't alone. "No matter what happens between them, they'll still be a part of your life. Elena loves you, and that's not going to change."

He nodded, but the tension in his shoulders didn't ease.

"And as far as family goes," I continued, cupping his face and tilting it until his eyes locked onto mine, "I'm your family too. You're not alone, Nolan. Not anymore."

His eyes searched mine, raw and vulnerable. For a moment, it felt like time stretched. His lips parted as if to speak, but instead, his gaze deepened, and I knew he was waiting. Hoping.

"I love you, Nolan." The words spilled out of me effortlessly, as natural as blinking my eyes.

His reaction was instant. His hands rose to frame my face, his thumbs brushing against my cheeks. Then he kissed me, the intensity of it stealing my breath.

When he pulled back, his voice was hoarse and thick with emotion. "I love you, Ivy."

There was something in the way he said it. It broke something in me, and I felt tears sting my eyes. We clung to each other, standing in the quiet of the parking lot. And yet, beneath the overwhelming joy of our confessions, there was a shared awareness that love alone wouldn't shield us from what lay ahead.

On the ride home, the weight of the night pressed down on me. My mind raced, a chaotic loop of voices and memories crashing into each other. Nolan telling me he loved me. Elena crying, saying it was over. Adrian's words, warning me about Nolan's character and my relationship patterns. And my own thoughts, dark and unspoken, surfacing like unwelcome guests.

I glanced at Nolan, his profile lit by the glow of the dashboard. His grip on the steering wheel was tight, his jaw clenched in concentration, but I could see the cracks in his composure.

We didn't speak, but the silence between us wasn't empty; it was filled with the weight of everything we'd said, and everything we hadn't.

By the time we reached home, I wasn't sure if I wanted to cry or collapse into his arms.

CHAPTER 26

We entered the apartment in silence, the echoes of our friends' breakup still lingering in the air between us. Nolan looked exhausted, his shoulders slumped under the weight of whatever he wasn't saying. The lines of tension on his face made my chest ache.

"You should sit down," I said softly, not wanting to break whatever fragile peace we had managed to maintain. "I'll cut some fruit and make you tea."

He didn't argue, just nodded and slid onto one of the stools at the kitchen island, resting his elbows on the counter. I turned to the fridge, grabbing some mangoes and berries, and tried to focus on the simple task in front of me.

"Any updates from Mr. Clarke?" I asked, steering the conversation into safer waters.

He exhaled deeply, running a hand through his hair. "He said he needs time and could use a follow-up pitch. We have to polish our call to action. I think that's where he started having questions. It's ridiculous how people mindlessly throw money at something as silly as a luxury dog collar but take forever to invest in a technology that could change lives."

The frustration in his voice tugged at me. I peeled the mango carefully, thinking about something that had been nagging me ever since Nolan told me about his start-up.

"Nolan," I said cautiously, looking up from my cutting board. "Have you ever thought about sharing your technology with a nonprofit instead? I mean, if your goal is to help people, wouldn't that make more sense than… selling it to a corporate machine?"

The shift in his demeanor was immediate. His body went rigid, and his eyes snapped to mine, sharp and unyielding. "Ivy," he said, his tone suddenly cold, "that's not how the world works."

I blinked, taken aback by the edge in his voice. "But you can change that, can't you? Teach the world something new?"

"And what?" he shot back. "Live off nothing? Sacrifice everything I've worked for?"

"I'm not saying it's easy," I said carefully, "but if this is about changing lives, about making sure no one goes through what you and your mom went through, then shouldn't this tech's access be your priority and not—"

"Not what? Surviving? Paying the rent? Making a good living?" he interrupted, his voice rising slightly. "Do you know why my mother wasn't diagnosed early? Because we couldn't afford it. We didn't have the money for yearly mental checkups or fancy treatments. I don't ever want to be in that place again where I have to worry about money."

"So you'll make others pay the same price?" I shot back, frustration bubbling to the surface.

His arms flexed, and he stood abruptly, pacing the kitchen like a caged animal. "You don't get it," he muttered. "You don't know what it's like to fight for something, to work for it. You live in a bubble. In the real world—"

"Enough," I interrupted, my voice rising with a mix of anger and hurt. "Don't ever lecture me about the real world again."

Nolan stopped pacing, turning to face me, his eyes dark and surprised at my tone.

"You keep acting like you're the only one who's ever faced reality," I continued. "You want to know what my reality looked like? While your mom was teaching you how to cook and feeding you homemade food, you know what *my* mom was doing? Starving me. While you got sisterly love and support from a woman who wasn't even your sister, my own sister abandoned me. While you were paying for paragliding lessons to manage your grief, I was giving up therapy because I couldn't afford it. You were deciding how to fly again and I was planning to jump off that same cliff."

My chest heaved, the words tumbling out before I could stop them. "You don't get to stand there and judge me, Nolan. You've had your struggles, but don't you dare act like mine don't matter."

For a second, he just stared at me, his expression unreadable. I thought he might say something, something that would cut me even deeper, but instead, he turned away, grabbing his laptop and shutting it with a decisive click.

"Goodnight, Ivy," he said, his voice cold and final.

Without thinking, I grabbed the knife again and went to slice the mango, my mind far from the cutting board. The blade slipped, and a sharp pain shot through my hand.

I yelped.

Nolan spun around, his eyes narrowing as he rushed to me. "What happened?"

"I—" I rushed to the sink, blood already pooling and trailing down my finger. "I cut myself."

His brows furrowed with worry before his expression shifted into something calm and controlled. Without a word, he darted out of the kitchen.

I stood there, rinsing my bloody finger under the running tap, the sting of the cut making my eyes water. By the time he returned with a first-aid kit, I already felt foolish for crying over something so small.

He turned off the tap and tried to reach for my hand.

"Let me see," he said softly.

I hesitated but extended my hand after patting it dry on my pants. His touch was warm and steady, a contrast to my shivering arm. His fingers brushed mine as he held my hand firmly, tilting it under the kitchen light to examine the cut.

"It's deep," he muttered, his voice tight. "But not bad enough for stitches."

I bit my lip as he cleaned the wound with a damp cloth, the antiseptic sting sharper than the initial cut. My instinct was to pull away, but his grip on my wrist was firm. Not forceful, just anchoring, like he wouldn't let me escape even if I tried.

"Hold still," he murmured, his tone softer now, almost soothing.

I watched his face as he worked. The way his brows drew together in concentration, the way his lips pressed into a line. There was no mistaking the concern etched into his features.

Once the wound was clean, he carefully wrapped a bandage around it. When he finished, he placed his thumb over the edge of the bandage to secure it, his touch lingering just a second too long.

"It's going to hurt for a while," he said quietly, finally looking up at me. His voice caught, as though he realized the depth of his words at the same time I did. "But you'll be okay."

I froze, my chest tightening as his words hung between us. The way he said them. It was like he wasn't just talking about my finger, like he was saying something neither of us wanted to admit yet.

Tears pricked my eyes. "Nolan..." I whispered, my voice breaking.

He looked at me then. Really looked at me, and I saw it in his eyes: love and devastation, all at once. I knew what I had to say, and I hated myself for it.

"I have to move out," I said.

His face darkened as if I'd just struck him. The pain in his eyes was so vivid it almost made me take the words back.

"You can't," he said, his tone low and clipped.

I breathed in, steadying myself. For a second, I thought he was going to say it. Say that he loved me, that he couldn't bear for me to leave. But his expression hardened, transforming from the face of my Nolan to the Nolan that appeared at meetings and conferences.

"Why?" I asked, my stomach twisting.

His eyes met mine, cold now, calculated. "It's in your contract," he said, his voice sharp and businesslike. "You can't quit until you finish the job you were hired to do. And since your salary is the rent payment for this apartment, you have to stay until the sublet is paid off."

I stared at him, stunned. "What?"

"It was in your contract, Ivy."

His words hit me like a punch to the gut. I took a step back, my hand curling into a fist. "You never mentioned anything like that," I said, my voice rising.

"It's there," he said coolly. "You should have read the contract before signing."

The weight of his betrayal settled over me, heavier than anything I'd ever felt before. A new kind of hatred surged in my chest, so intense it left me trembling.

"You tricked me. Again," I said, my voice shaking with anger. "Adrian was right. You're just a man who uses people for his own gain, who profits off someone else's pain. You—you're worse than I thought."

His jaw tightened, but he didn't respond, his silence only fueling the fire inside me.

I stepped closer, the tears burning in my eyes now from pure rage. "You can do whatever you want, Nolan. Sue me, withhold my pay. I don't care. But I refuse to share a roof with you for another second."

I turned and stormed out of the kitchen, my heart pounding so hard I felt the floor shake. In my room, I grabbed my luggage and began packing, my hands shaking too much to fold anything properly.

I didn't let myself cry. I didn't let myself think about what had just happened or the way he cheated me.

Instead, a cruel taunt rang in my ears.

It's your fault. You should've known.

CHAPTER 27

NOLAN

The apartment was silent, but my head was loud.

I paced from the living room to the kitchen, then back again, every creak of the hardwood under my feet grating on my nerves.

I stopped at Ivy's bedroom door. My hand hovered over the handle, my chest tight with the weight of what I was about to do. It had been over three weeks. I had to confront the nothingness she'd left behind.

When I pushed the door open, the emptiness hit me like a punch to the chest.

The walls that had once been covered with her chaos. Paintings, sketches, photos, even those needless Post-it notes, they were stripped down to their cold, impersonal plaster. The air smelled faintly of lavender, a scent that clung stubbornly to her absence. Everything of her was gone. She'd even taken that stupid ceramic mug with the chipped edge, the one she drank from every morning.

She hadn't just left. She'd erased herself.

My throat ached as I breathed in.

"What the hell were you thinking, Ivy?" I muttered under my breath, pacing the room now like I'd been pacing the rest of the apartment. Anger bubbled up, sharp and biting.

She'd walked out like none of it mattered. Like I didn't matter. Like the nights we stayed up talking, the work we'd done together, the goddamn contract didn't matter.

I clenched my fists, my breathing hard and uneven.

I'd gone out of my way to make space for her in my life. I'd taken her to meet my friends, shared parts of my world I'd never shared with anyone else. Hell, I'd even shared my mother's favorite dishes with her.

But she couldn't even stay long enough to talk things through. She ran.

I glared at the bed where I first kissed her. It was easier to hate her for leaving. Easier to resent her for not giving me a chance. For throwing it all away.

Except I couldn't.

Because no matter how much I wanted to stay angry, it didn't last.

I sank onto the sheet-less mattress, my arms on my knees.

The memories bled through, softening the sharp edges of my fury. She couldn't take away that night. No matter what she did, no matter how far she ran. I'll always have the night we finally came together.

It wasn't just the way her body had felt against mine, though that alone was enough to undo me. It was the way she'd laughed in my arms, her head thrown back like she didn't have a single care in the world. The softness in her eyes when she looked at me, like I was more than my work, my successes and my failures. The way her angelic nose scrunched up when she teased me, and how easy she made it for me to bare myself.

Hell, we'd shared a plate of food that night, and she had fed me with her own hands like it was the most natural thing in the world. If only I could have explained to her what that had meant to me.

That's why I had to ask her to be a bigger part of my life. Inviting her to join me at UCLA wasn't just a business decision; it was so much more. It was personal. I wanted her beside me, to stand with me, to prove, to the world, to myself, that I wasn't as broken as I had feared.

But then Elena and Jay broke up.

If they couldn't make it work, what chance did Ivy and I have? That thought had followed me home, urging me to dissect it. I'd replayed Ivy's every glance, every word, wondering if she was having doubts. Wondering if I was already losing her.

But then she had said the three words I never thought I'd hear. She said she loved me.

And I believed her. The way she looked at me, the way she said I was her family, it was the only time in my life I hadn't felt the need for anything else. Not even success.

I had to tell her I loved her too. Of course I loved her. How couldn't I?

But it hadn't been enough. Not for her.

I'd thought those three words would save us. But they didn't.

Her careful voice replayed in my mind. "Have you ever thought about sharing your technology with a nonprofit instead?"

At the time, I'd been so stunned that she could even suggest something like that. Her words hadn't just questioned my strategy; they'd questioned my entire purpose, everything I'd built, everything I'd sacrificed.

I hadn't been able to stop myself from snapping.

It wasn't just her words. It was the crushing weight of everything she didn't understand.

She didn't know what it was like to grow up watching my mother fall apart, piece by piece. She didn't know what it was like to sit in those waiting rooms, month after month, praying that some low-cost clinic would have an opening, only to walk away empty-handed.

Ivy meant well, I knew that. She wasn't trying to tear me down. But those words ruffled me.

Because I'd spent my entire life fighting to make sure I'd never end up in the position my mom was in. To make sure I'd never have to worry about scraping together pennies for something as essential as healthcare.

What Ivy didn't see, what she couldn't see, was that by building a profitable business, I could scale this technology far beyond what a nonprofit could ever dream of. By selling it to a "corporate machine", I wasn't selling out. I was ensuring its survival. And my survival.

But I hadn't been able to make her understand that. I hadn't been able to make her see that my ambition wasn't selfish. It was the only way I knew how to live.

I wasn't a revolutionary, and I wished I had the courage to be an idealistic dreamer like her.

Ivy didn't live in a bubble. I knew that too. I knew she had her own struggles, her own pain, and yet, I hadn't even known about her mother and sister. All she'd ever told me was that they weren't in the picture.

Why didn't she share those parts with me? Not even after I'd told her about my mother, my struggles, my fears. Did she think I wasn't strong enough for her truth? Did she not trust me yet?

I rubbed a hand over my face and dropped on the bed, my feet still grounded to the floor.

Why couldn't she see how much I'd been trying to change, to be worthy of her? Why couldn't she see that my priorities had shifted, that she was no longer just a part of my life? She was my life.

And instead, she blamed me for everything, and she left.

I wanted to ask her not to go, to tell her how I couldn't bear her absence. But I didn't. I used the excuse of a contract I could barely remember.

Because, in that moment, while her finger was split open and we were both more hurt than ever, her first instinct was to abandon me. And I didn't know how to fight that.

Of course, I wasn't going to sue her or plot some scheme to make her stay again.

I held my head in my hands, and my eyes landed on something small, tucked beside the leg of the bed.

It was Ivy's hair tie, the one I kept unfurling from her bun because of how much I loved her hair cascading over her shoulders.

I picked it up, and my heart fluttered. It was unbearable, and shocking, how much her absence affected me.

The last twenty-five days had been hell. Work felt hollow, even when I threw myself into it with everything I had. Even when I was the closest I had ever been to achieving my dream.

Coming home was worse. The silence of the apartment was suffocating.

I missed her.

I missed her laughter, her fire, even her goddamn clutter and those annoying conversations from her TV shows. Most of all, I missed the way she made me feel. Like I wasn't broken.

The anger that had burned so brightly when I first saw her empty room had dimmed into something fragile.

I sat there alone, my chest hollow and aching.

I had to fix this.

Because life without Ivy wasn't life at all.

CHAPTER 28

The hum of the ceiling fan filled the quiet apartment as I sipped my guava boba tea, the pearls dancing up the straw, sweet and chewy—a small indulgence while I waited. The coffee table was set with fruit platters, cheese, crackers, chips, guac, salsa, and flavored sparkling water chilling in the fridge. Everything was ready.

I glanced around my one-bedroom apartment. Beige popcorn walls, thrifted, mismatched furniture, and a soft, well-worn rug that Cleo had helped me pick out. The kitchenette was barely big enough for a toaster and my new French press and the couch creaked when I sat on it, but I didn't mind. I had lived in larger spaces, spaces that weren't truly mine. This one, though, this was snug, imperfect, and a work in progress, just like me.

My favorite spot was the tiny dining nook where sunlight pooled in the afternoons. I had turned it into a creative space. A secondhand desk sat against the wall, stacked high with notebooks, sketchbooks, brushes, tubes of paint. I had started painting again. The bristles had felt foreign at first, my strokes hesitant, but the colors had come back to me—bright, bold, unapologetic. Besides pursuing my passion, I was also taking an online SDSU class on the craft of writing which was surprisingly enjoyable.

Through the single window of my living room, I could see a sliver of the San Diego skyline in the distance, the golden hour light spilling across the streets below. Not the ocean view I had once had, but something. And on days when the old doubts crept in, whispers of maybe I should have stayed, I walked to Balboa Park, which was right next to my neighborhood. I would lose myself in the winding gardens, sit in the museum courtyards, and remind myself that I had built this new life, brick by brick.

I took another sip of my drink, sinking into the couch. A month ago, I had been in a completely different place. Physically, mentally. When I had walked out of Nolan's apartment, I hadn't been sure if I was running toward something or just away from him. I only knew I couldn't stay.

I hadn't wanted to call Elena. She had enough going on. And Adrian... after our last conversation, I wasn't sure if we were even friends anymore. So, I had called Cleo.

"Stay as long as you need," she had said without hesitation.

But by the second day, I had started looking for my own place. No matter how much Cleo insisted, I didn't want to overstay my welcome.

After a week of searching, I had found this apartment. It wasn't perfect, but it was a great start.

My days had settled into a rhythm. Same old copywriting work during the week, regular meetups with the artist group on weekends, hanging out with friends every now and then, and spontaneous late-night painting sessions, sometimes with Cleo, sometimes alone.

Cleo had become a constant in my life, always pushing me out of my comfort zone and filling my days with laughter and bold ideas.

She was also the one who had gotten me addicted to boba.

It wasn't the healthiest habit, but I had cut sugar and junk food from my diet, started taking better care of myself, and made small changes to feel better. This was my one guilty pleasure.

Speaking of taking better care of myself, I had even started cooking every now and then, when I wasn't too exhausted. Just last night, I made Pad Thai for dinner.

I set my cup down, my gaze drifting to the light spilling through the window. The heat pressed against the glass, and my midi dress clung lightly to my skin.

My thumb traced the faint scar on my finger, a souvenir from that night, when I had cut myself mid-argument. A tiny mark, but it held the weight of something heavier.

Nolan.

I hadn't spoken to him in a month.

I had thought about emailing him once, asking him if he'd want me to finish writing the content for his start-up. Not because I needed the money anymore, but because it was a job I had agreed to do. I wanted to be professional.

But I couldn't bring myself to message him.

He had betrayed me. Tricked me into signing a contract he knew I wouldn't read. He was the one who had been unprofessional.

And yet, there was still a part of me that missed him.

Not in the way I had missed people before. This was different. His absence felt like a gnawing wound.

The main door thudded with a knock, snapping me back to the present.

My heart leapt due to nervous excitement. For three weeks, Cleo and I had been working on making this apartment guest-ready, and the time had arrived.

I exhaled slowly, smoothing down my dress.

This was my home. My life. And tonight, I was stepping into it.

THE DOOR SWUNG OPEN, and before I could even say hello, Elena pulled me into a tight hug. She smelled like ginger and gardenias, a familiar scent that had always felt like sisterly comfort.

"I missed you," she murmured.

I hugged her back, squeezing just a little tighter. "I missed you too."

When she pulled away, her face broke into a grin as she held up a neatly wrapped package. "Happy Housewarming!"

I took it, the paper soft under my fingers. "You didn't have to—"

"Of course, I did. Open it."

I peeled back the wrapping, revealing a beautifully woven blanket in deep blues and earthy browns, the kind that looked like it belonged in a cozy cabin in the woods. Running my fingers over the fabric, I marveled at its softness.

"You always get cold easily," Elena said with a knowing smile. "And I figured you'd need something comfy for the incoming cold fall nights."

Warmth bloomed in my chest, thick and bittersweet. "This is perfect. Thank you."

Elena flopped onto the couch, stretching her legs out. "You have no idea how much I needed to get out of Idyllview for a bit."

"How's the move been?" I sat beside her, draping the blanket over the armrest.

She let out a breath, placing her hands on her thighs. "Good. Not as exciting as I had hoped, but Jay and I... we're on amicable terms now, so that makes things easier."

"That's great. I'm glad."

"He wasn't a bad guy, you know?" Her smile was small, a little sad. "It wasn't completely his fault that I changed myself instead of actually talking or setting boundaries."

I nodded, understanding more than I wanted to admit.

Elena's expression softened, but then her brows knit together slightly. "But I gotta say, I'm really upset with you."

"What? Why?" I asked.

"You didn't reach out. Not once. I had to hear from... Nolan that you moved out. You know I would've been there for you."

Guilt settled heavy in my chest. "I know. And I'm sorry. I just... I needed to figure things out on my own. I didn't want to burden you."

Elena scoffed. "Ivy, that's what friends are for." Then, after a beat, she added, "But I'm here now. So tell me everything."

I exhaled, rubbing my temple before giving her a rundown of what had happened since the barbecue at her place.

"To be honest," I added, "I'd thought about moving out of his place long before that. The day we went to the mall, when you told me about Jay, I realized I was doing the same thing. Building my life around a guy. Again. But I didn't know how to leave without ruining things with Nolan. In the end, that fight gave me the push I needed."

Elena frowned. "But you guys were doing so well. How did it get this ugly?"

I let out a slow breath. "I don't know. I don't know how much of it is my fault, how much stems from my own issues. But I do know what he did with the contract, that was unacceptable."

She pursed her lips. "Yeah... I get that. I wish he had told me about the contract. I would have stopped him."

"I think he and I, we're just too different to coexist, let alone be in a relationship."

Elena studied me for a long moment, then said carefully, "I don't doubt your judgment, Ivy, but I do want to say this... from a completely objective perspective, of course. The fact that your differences are becoming an issue isn't necessarily a bad thing. It means you're both living authentically. As yourselves.

"Jay and I never fought for the first couple of years because I molded myself into the person that worked best with him. But you and Nolan? You two chose closeness despite knowing your differences. That's something worth thinking about."

Her words lodged in my chest, stealing the warmth from my skin.

I hesitated before asking, "How is he doing?"

Elena exhaled, glanced toward the window. Then, shaking her head, she said, "You know what? Let's not talk about men. Or relationships. Or sad adult things. This is your day, Pirate Girl! Your first place of your own. We have to celebrate that."

As if on cue, another knock sounded at the door. Louder this time, followed by Cleo's voice calling out, "Put on your pants, Ivy, because we have arrived!"

Before I could ask Elena to stop giggling at the announcement, the door swung open and Cleo burst in like a one-woman parade, arms full of gift and balloons, her violet hair flying wildly.

"Welcome to Ivy's casa, everyone!" she declared, stretching her arms wide.

Behind her, the rest of the group piled in—Mateo, the bearded manga artist, carrying a leafy pothos; Mira, the quiet but observant portrait painter, holding a tiny succulent in a dinosaur-shaped pot; and two more unexpected guests.

One was Liam, a bartender Cleo and I had met a few months back, a sharp-witted guy with an easygoing grin and a knack for making every situation feel like an inside joke. The other was a lanky, tattooed guy with a septum piercing and a slightly lost expression.

"Uh, so... I brought a plus-one," Cleo whispered to me and gestured toward the tattooed guy. "Evan. He's my friend, and he kinda just tagged along. That okay?"

I grinned and said the four words I'd never imagined myself saying. "The more, the merrier."

Evan gave a lazy salute. "Sweet. I brought beer. Happy Housewarming."

"Thank you," I said, stepping aside to let everyone in. "And beer? You're already forgiven."

Mateo set the pothos on my windowsill with a flourish. "For oxygen and vibes," he said, smirking.

Mira handed me the little succulent. "This one doesn't need much care," she said softly. "Thought it'd be a good fit."

I smiled at the thoughtfulness and placed the little dino dude by my art nook. "You guys are the best."

"And this," Cleo thrust her gift into my hands, eyes sparkling, "is from me."

I ripped off the wrapping and burst out laughing. A disco ball. With a note attached: For emergency dance breaks and spontaneous joy.

Elena, still lounging on the couch, chuckled. "I love that!"

I hung the ball from the ceiling fan's chain as Mateo turned on my Goodwill portable speaker. The light from the sunset streamed through the window, catching the disco ball and scattering tiny rainbow flecks across the walls. In an instant, my once-muted apartment burst to life, a kaleidoscope of color, music, and pattern.

Once everyone settled in, the apartment pulsed with chatter and movement. Mateo took over as DJ for the night, flipping through my playlists until he landed on something upbeat. Mira, true to form, meticulously rearranged the snack table into an Instagram-worthy spread. Evan, despite his initial lost-puppy energy, quickly proved himself useful, cracking open beers, tightening the screws on my wobbly coffee table with a pocket screwdriver, and tossing out quiet but unexpectedly funny observations. And then there was Elena, effortlessly slipping into the role of co-host, making sure everyone was comfortable, fed, and hydrated. That, more than anything, made my heart swell.

Meanwhile, Cleo took it upon herself to conduct a house tour. Never mind that the apartment was barely 450 sq ft.

"Here we have the artist's sanctuary!" she announced, sweeping her arm toward my tiny nook. "Where masterpieces shall be born!"

"Or where unfinished projects go to die," I muttered.

"Not on my watch," Cleo shot back.

"She's right, though," Liam added. "This setup is dope. I mean, look at that light." He gestured toward the large window beside my easel. "If I were an artist, I'd be jealous."

"Are you not?" Mira murmured, genuinely curious.

"Nah, I just mix drinks and pretend it's an art form," Liam said with an easy grin.

"Mixing drinks is definitely an art form," Cleo said. "Speaking of, please tell me someone brought something stronger than sparkling water?" She rolled her eyes at me.

Evan stuck up his head like a meerkat. "Umm... I got tequila in my backpack?"

Cleo gasped, placing a dramatic hand over her heart. "Evan, you beautiful menace."

That was all it took. Within minutes, shots were being poured, music was turned up, and someone (probably Mateo) started passing out makeshift party hats made from paper towels and rubber bands.

Liam leaned over to me, watching Cleo put a funny hat on Elena, who had given up on resisting. "So, is this how all your housewarmings go?"

I smiled, taking a sip of my drink. "This is my first one. But if they all turn out like this, I won't complain."

As the night went on, the apartment buzzed with more energy. Cleo started an impromptu dance party under the disco ball, its light spinning across the ceiling. Elena, even with her usual composed demeanor, got dragged into it, laughing despite herself.

Mira and Mateo ended up in a fierce, silent competition over who could build the most structurally sound cracker tower from the snack tray. Evan, who had initially seemed quiet, turned out to be a low-key party instigator, challenging Liam to a one-minute cocktail-making contest using only what was in my fridge. The results were questionable, but the effort was appreciated.

And in the middle of it all, I sank into my couch, watching these people fill my tiny space with warmth and laughter.

For the first time, I had a group of friends, my own people. People who stayed. Growing up, I never thought someone like me could make friends, let alone keep them. But here I was, wrapped in their glorious presence. It had taken effort, stepping outside my comfort zone, sacrificing solitude, trusting, but it was worth it.

I raised my glass. "To new beginnings."

The others lifted their drinks, voices overlapping in agreement.

Tonight, I was happy. And for now, that was enough.

CHAPTER 29

As I loaded the dishwasher, another knock echoed through the quiet apartment. My heart jumped. It was 11:30 at night, and in a new place, the unfamiliar creaks and shifting shadows still unsettled me.

"Not a serial killer," a familiar voice called out.

A grin spread across my face as I practically ran to the door.

"How did you find me?"

"Through the asshole I still hate," Adrian said, leaning casually against the doorframe.

My smile faltered. "You talked to Nolan?"

Adrian scrunched his brows. "Aren't you supposed to invite me in first? Where are your manners, Ivy?"

"Sorry. Come in."

He stepped inside, his sharp, observant architect's eye scanning the space. His gaze flicked to the empty glasses and bottles scattered around. I wished I had let Elena help me clean.

"New apartment. New life." Adrian nodded toward the mess. "New friends."

Then, settling onto my couch, he gave me a look. Serious, tinged with sadness. "You swore I'd always be your friend, but you replaced me in record time."

He said it like old Adrian. My Adrian. My best friend. I rolled my eyes and sat beside him.

"You're irreplaceable," I said, nudging his shoulder. "I just... didn't know if you wanted to talk to me."

That was a lie. I knew he would have. I was the one who hesitated. I had vouched for Nolan while Adrian had warned me. And in the end, everything he said had been right. I was embarrassed.

Adrian shook his head, disappointment flickering across his face. "Talk to you? When your life was turned upside down? When you were basically homeless? Ivy, why wouldn't I talk to you in that situation?"

"I wasn't homeless," I muttered.

He arched a brow. "Semantics." Then, his expression softened. "Are you okay?"

"More than okay," I assured him. "But tell me, how did you end up talking to Nolan?"

Adrian leaned back, resting an arm on the couch. "He came to see me. At work. The man had the audacity to order me to check on you. To make sure you were okay."

A lump formed in my throat, but confusion distracted me. "He could have asked Elena to do that," I said, thinking out loud. "Why did he come to you?"

Adrian shrugged. "Maybe he knew, there is no one as close to you as I am."

A smile spread across my face, my lips still tight.

"And... the sociopath apologized to me," he added.

"For what?"

"For never treating me well."

The words hung between us. My fingers tightened around the fabric of my sleeve. It wasn't easy for Nolan to apologize, even when he knew he was in the wrong.

"And what did you say?" I asked.

Adrian shrugged again. "I was in a hurry, so I..." He paused, watching my expectant expression.

I braced myself for some testosterone-fueled response.

"...told him it was okay. That I had no hard feelings."

I snorted. "Lies."

Adrian grinned. "No, really. He didn't bother me that much. In fact, for the first time, I actually didn't hate seeing his face."

I narrowed my eyes. "That's sus."

He exhaled, his gaze turning distant. "Listen, you were right. About everything." His voice dropped slightly. "That day outside my house... when you left so abruptly, I came after you. I don't know why. Maybe I wanted to change your mind. But I was in your building's lobby when you and Nolan came down in the elevator."

I froze. Elena's barbecue. Nolan and I had been running late, so he'd called for the valet.

"You were adjusting his collar or something," Adrian continued, "and he was messing up your hair. You looked happy, Ivy. Really happy. Like yourself." He let out a small chuckle. "And you know what's weird? I didn't feel jealous. Or sad. I felt proud. Like... when your best friend finally gets it right."

I pressed my lips together, another lump knotted in my throat.

Adrian shook his head. "I was a fool. I was so afraid of being alone that I clung to the one constant relationship I had and tried to force it into something it wasn't."

I threw my arm around him, hugging him tightly. "It's okay. I'm just happy you're back in my life. I missed you so much."

He didn't say anything right away, but when I pulled back, there was something in his eyes. A shadow, an exhaustion I couldn't fix.

"I'm sorry," he said quietly. "I wasn't there when you needed me."

I suddenly got up and rummaged through my bookshelf, pulling out a small model house. The one Adrian had given me. I placed it in his hands.

"Remember this?"

Adrian turned it over, his thumb tracing the roof. "My maquette. Yeah. I gave it to you."

I nodded. "When I was at my lowest, you told me that one day, I'd have a home of my own. A place where I could do what I love and feel safe. A place where I could paint and live freely, with no one to stop, judge, or hurt me." I glanced around the apartment. "I finally made it, Adrian. I'm in a place that I'd dreamed of my whole life."

I met his gaze. "You never really left me. I looked at this little house every day, and I'm here because your faith in me kept me going."

His grip on the model tightened slightly, but he didn't speak. He just nodded.

And then we sat there, catching up on the month we had lost. I told him about my art, my classes at SDSU, my new friends, and my work. He told me about his parents, finally, completely out of each other's lives, making his own life easier. He already knew Nolan and I were broken up, so I told him I didn't want to talk about him anymore. He didn't push.

An hour later, I handed him a beer and curled up beside him as we queued up our favorite episodes of Gilmore Girls.

"Don't you dare leave me again," I muttered, playfully smacking him in the face with my Stars Hollow throw pillow. The same one he once helped me pack.

Adrian turned to me, his gaze suddenly serious and intense. My heart dropped. I wanted to beg him not to go there again, but before I could, he spoke.

"So..." He placed a hand on my leg. "That Cleo girl. Is she single?"

I stared at him for a beat before bursting into laughter, nearly falling off the couch.

I DRAPED ELENA'S NEW throw blanket over Adrian, propping his head on a pillow as he softly snored into the night. The TV hummed with the low static of a paused screen, casting flickering light across the room. With a sigh, I turned it off and made my way to my bedroom.

The day had been long, physically exhausting, yes, but it wasn't just that. As I settled into bed, the ache returned. That dull, persistent void in my chest.

I knew this feeling. Had carried it for years.

It wasn't about Nolan, or even about Adrian, despite the emotional whiplash of getting my best friend back. It was something older. Deeper. Despite the warmth of the housewarming party, the laughter, the people who had shown up for me today, I still felt hollow. Like I was standing in the middle of a crowded room and yet completely alone.

It hit me, then.

Having people around me, letting them in, it only reminded me why I had never tried to hold on too tightly.

Because, eventually, they leave.

Just like she did.

The thought had lingered all day, surfacing when Elena arrived. Her presence, as always, stirring something in me. A memory. A resemblance. I pushed it down, burying it beneath the chaos of the party. But when I spoke to Adrian about wanting a safe house, the thought pressed harder, refusing to be ignored.

Now, in the silence, there was nowhere left to hide from it.

A cold wave of fear settled in my bones. What if these friends left, too? What if I was just a stop on their journey, something temporary?

I shook my head, forcing the thought away.

But my fingers moved on their own, reaching for my phone.

I opened Facebook. My breath caught as I typed in the name.

Amber Branco.

Her married name. She had stopped using our last name long before she got married.

Dozens of profiles appeared. I scrolled, scanning each face. My heart pounded. The sixth one stopped me cold.

A wide smile, dimples still as deep as I remembered. But her cheeks were fuller now, softer. A child, maybe three, sat beside her, giggling at a dog.

I stared, my vision blurring.

She looked happy.

She looked like someone who had built a beautiful life out of the ashes of our childhood.

Like she barely even remembered that she had a sister.

Like I had never mattered.

My fingers clenched around my phone as I scrolled through every picture she had made public. Each one sent another surge of anger through me. A perfect family. A beautiful home. A life untouched by the wreckage she left me in.

I had loved her more than life itself. And she had walked away without ever looking back.

My chest ached. My hands trembled. Before I could stop myself, I clicked Message and started typing.

"Hey, sis. Guess what? Your little burden of a sister actually made it. Got my own place, my own life, my own people who didn't up and disappear on me. Crazy, right? Bet you thought I'd never make it without you."

I hovered over the Send button, my thumb hesitating. Then, before I could change my mind, I pressed it.

Less than a minute after it went through, my phone vibrated in my palm.

Incoming call. Facebook Messenger. Amber.

The air rushed from my lungs. I stared at the screen, my stomach twisting.

She actually called.

Before I freaked out, I swiped to answer.

"Hello?" My voice was tight and cautious.

"Ivy!" Her voice was bright, warm, like nothing had ever happened. Like she hadn't abandoned me. "It's been so long! Congrats on the new place! That's amazing."

A lump formed in my throat.

"Yeah. It is." My voice came out clipped.

Amber laughed softly. "I'm so proud of you. I miss you, you know?"

I inhaled sharply.

"You miss me?"

"Of course I do!" she said, like it was obvious. "I think about you all the time."

A beat of silence stretched between us. My fingers curled into a fist, more by the way she talked, like we chatted every week.

"You do?" My voice trembled, low and unsteady.

"Of course," she repeated, softer this time. "Ivy—"

"Then where the hell have you been?"

Amber faltered. "I—"

My breath shook. My pulse pounded.

"You left." The words came out raw, shaking. "You just... left. And you never looked back. You were the only person I had, and you walked away like I was nothing. You said nothing. You didn't check in. Not once."

"I know, and I—"

"You knew!" My voice cracked. "Do you have any idea what that did to me? I was thirteen!"

Silence.

A slow, painful breath. My vision blurred with unshed tears.

"A child with no father. A mother who came home drunk every night. But you, you were mine. You were my person. My best friend."

I swallowed back the sob threatening to break free. "And you left me in that house. Alone. You knew how bad it was. And you still left."

"Ivy," she whispered, her voice heavy with regret. "I had to go," she admitted, voice shaking. "I... I couldn't stay in that house."

A hollow, bitter laugh escaped me.

"And I could?"

"I thought—"

"You thought what?" I snapped. "That I'd be fine?"

The dam broke. The years of silence, the weight of every unspoken word, every unanswered question, I couldn't hold it back anymore.

"I spent years wondering what I did wrong. Why my own sister didn't want me anymore. Why I wasn't worth staying for. You punished me for everything Mom did. I was just another burden you had to escape from."

Amber let out a broken sound. "No, I—"

"You were my whole world!" My voice shattered on the words. "And you left me to rot with that woman! You don't even know..." I took quick short breaths. "You don't know what it was like after you left."

A pause.

"When you were there, at least she had someone to keep her in check. After you were gone..." My voice wavered. "She started hitting me, Amber. If I didn't clean fast enough. If I spent too much on groceries. If I went out of the house for something. If I spoke back."

A choked sob filled the line.

"Oh, god," she whispered, her voice wet. "Ivy... I don't know what to say."

"Yeah," I whispered. "Neither did I. For a long time."

She started crying.

"If I could do it over, I wouldn't have left," she choked out. "But you have to understand, VeeVee."

The last word caught my breath. It's what she had always called me. My heart burst from pain and nostalgia.

"I was a kid, too," she added. "I was also thirteen, a child, when I started taking care of you. I loved you to death, but I... I couldn't do it anymore. I wanted to have a life of my own. So I left. At first, I didn't call because I had nothing. No money, no job, no home. I had nothing to offer you. And by the time I could, it had been so long... I was scared. But I never stopped missing you."

I let out a shuddering breath. "I get why you left. But you had years to contact me. To come back. And you didn't."

Her breath caught.

"If you had, my life would have been different." My voice was hoarse. "I wouldn't have clung to love in the wrong places. I wouldn't have pushed and distrusted people who actually cared. I wouldn't have been this big bundle of insecurities, constantly worrying if I did something wrong. You hurt me more than anyone, Amber."

Silence.

Tears streamed down my face as I whispered, "More than Mom."

A sharp inhale on the other end.

I wiped my face, swallowing hard. "I have to go." My voice was barely there. "Have a good life."

And I hung up.

The room was unbearably quiet. My chest ached, but I was glad I wasn't carrying all of it alone anymore.

Curling into myself, I stared at my phone, wondering if she would ever call again.

CHAPTER 30

Instead of going to the artist meet-up, I decided to spend the day with myself and drove out to Coronado Island for a change. I wore my favorite summer dress, the one I bought a couple of weeks ago. It was white, backless, reached just above my knees, and had a deep V-neck with spaghetti straps. Not overly revealing, but it still exposed more of my skin than I was used to. The first time I tried it, I felt a little self-conscious, but I felt so pretty in it that I ended up buying it in two colors. Now, I couldn't stop wearing them.

Coronado Beach was quieter, more peaceful than the downtown beaches. I perched in a quiet corner, the iconic red-roofed Hotel del Coronado proudly standing behind me. The ocean stretched before me, its horizon on the left touching the Mexico border.

Slipping off my sandals, I sank my feet into the warm, cream-colored sand and let the grains slip between my toe. Free spa treatment. The breeze tugged at my hair, brushing cool against my skin.

I put on my sunglasses and gazed out at the waves rolling in, their rhythmic crash against the nearby rocks blending with the distant cries of seagulls. Then I spread out my beach blanket, pulled a book from my tote bag, and lay down, the sun draping over me like a gentle, golden embrace. For almost an hour, I read, enjoying the salty scent of the ocean, mingled with the faint, sun-soaked fragrance of my sunscreen. The warmth seeped into my skin with each passing minute, as a pleasant sense of peace washed over me. It was wonderful. Solitude had never felt so blissful. I savored every second of it.

At some point, I picked up my phone and opened my messages. Amber had been calling and texting me for the past two days, trying everything—emotional pleas, entitled demands (I'm your big sis, and you *have* to talk to me!), even a cute video of her son saying, "Aunty VeeVee, you won't talk to me etheer?" That one nearly broke me. But what finally did was the picture she sent. A box filled with what looked like fragments of our childhood. Random stones, sticks, and feathers I had collected near the river, our spot, and gifted to her. She had kept them all. Along with those little trinkets, there were old photographs of us, little scraps of memories I hadn't thought about in years. The sight of it had finally thawed me.

I took a deep breath and typed out a message.

"I'd like to be a part of your life if you'll have me."

On my drive home, I put her on speaker, and we talked the entire way back. She caught me up on her life—a good-paying job, now divorced, a single mom. I shared pieces of my world in return.

We weren't quite our old selves yet, but we were miles ahead of where we had been the night I first messaged her.

Feeling a rush of happiness I couldn't contain, I texted Adrian.

"My sister is back in my life!"

"That's awesome!" he responded. "I'm so happy for you. Where are you, btw?"

"About to reach home. Why?"

"Just asking."

I PARKED AT THE CURBSIDE and stepped out of the car. The evening air was humid, pressing against my skin as I walked up the familiar path to my apartment.

Then I saw him.

My heart leapt, then plummeted to my feet, a free-fall that left me breathless. Nolan stood by my door.

He wasn't supposed to be here. Not after a month. Not after everything.

"Nolan?" My voice barely made a sound.

He looked up at me, his mouth parting slightly as if he had words ready, but they never came. Instead, his gaze swept over me, slow and deliberate, taking in every inch of me.

"Hey," he finally said, voice rough, unsteady.

He looked...different. Not in the subtle ways I'd noticed before—his stubble growing a little too thick, or his hair messier than usual. This was something else. He wore gym shorts and an activewear t-shirt, a look I'd never seen on him outside a workout. Nolan never wore gym clothes in public. It was a thing for him, a matter of pride. And yet here he was, his hair disheveled, his eyes darker, shadowed with something deeper than exhaustion.

I inhaled sharply. "What are you doing here?"

"Can we?" He nodded toward the door.

I hesitated, my fingers gripping the strap of my tote bag a little too tightly. The moment felt fragile, like if I moved too quickly, it would shatter, and I wasn't sure I was ready for it.

I reached for my keys, but my hands were shaking. My fingers fumbled through the bag, and every movement felt clumsy, my anxiety growing under the weight of his restrained gaze. His hand twitched at his side, as if he wanted to reach for me, but stopped himself.

Where the hell are they? I checked my dress pocket, and, oh. There they were.

I pulled the key out with an awkward tug, unlocking the door and pushing it open. I stepped inside without looking back, hoping my racing heart wasn't as obvious as it felt.

I heard him follow.

The apartment felt smaller with him in it. His presence filled the space, stirring up the air, memories, emotions I had worked too damn hard to push away.

I placed my bag near my reading nook, next to the painting I'd been working on. A quiet scene of two little girls by a river, one sitting on the edge, watching the younger girl pick up sticks.

Nolan's voice pulled me back. "You've been painting again."

I didn't answer. Instead, I opened the fridge. "Water?"

"Yeah." His voice was low.

I poured a glass, my hands steady despite the storm in my chest. When I turned back, he was still standing by the door, like he wasn't sure if he was allowed to step further in.

I handed him the water, which he drained in a single go. His Adam's apple bobbed with each gulp, sweat glistening along his throat. I noticed how his shirt clung to his damp chest and how his hair was more tousled than disheveled.

I crossed my arms. "Why are you here, Nolan?"

His lips parted slightly, and then, unexpectedly, his face lit up.

"I ran on the beach today," he said, as if he had just uncovered the answer to the universe.

My forehead creased, involuntarily. "What?"

His expression shifted, and suddenly he was in front of me, closing the space between us, close enough that I could feel the heat radiating off his skin. His chest still rose and fell with the remnants of his run.

Then he gently took my wrist and placed my palm against his heart.

It pounded beneath my fingers, strong, steady. Alive.

"Ivy," he said. "I am not heartless, like you once said, but this..." He pressed his hand over mine, holding it there. "It had been lying cold, dark, and dead for almost three decades."

I stopped breathing.

"I never learned how to handle emotions the right way," he continued, his voice quieter now. "I've spent years being afraid. Afraid that if I let my guards down, I'll lose. I had been afraid of slowing down, of wasting time. I sacrificed everything, relationships, happiness, even myself, just to keep running. Until I met you.

"You taught me something." He held me. "You taught me that life isn't just about the big, monumental moments and victories. There's beauty in small things, like running on the beach, something I never allowed myself to do because it didn't serve my purpose. But today... I ran for no reason at all. I let the ocean air fill my lungs, and I felt..." He exhaled shakily. "I felt free, Ivy."

My throat tightened.

He looked at me then, something wild and unguarded in his eyes. "And it scared the hell out of me, because I had only felt that kind of freedom with you."

I shook my head, fighting against the swell of emotions. "Nolan..."

"I was angry," he cut in, his grip tightening slightly. "I was unfair to you. You challenge me in ways no one else ever has, and it made me lash out. I did ridiculous things, like drawing up that damn contract. I convinced myself you were the one being unrealistic, but the truth was, I wasn't ready to let go of my own ways."

I stared at him, feeling my chest tighten. "The contract..." Anger rose in me for a moment, and I almost wanted to pull away from him. How could he do that to me?

He saw the shift in my expression and rushed to continue. "There is no justification for that. I am really very ashamed of it, I swear. But if it helps, I did that to protect myself, not to hurt you. I am so sorry for all the pain I've caused you, Ivy." His voice was calm and sincere.

My shoulders relaxed a bit, but my gaze stayed fixed to the ground.

"I don't want to talk about my start-up," Nolan said. "There are some things I can't change, and that's one of them. But I can't..." He exhaled sharply, like the words pressured him down. "I can't live without you."

Tears burned the back of my eyes, but I fought them back.

"I love you, Ivy. So much it hurts."

His words hit me like a collision against my ribs. Nolan didn't throw those words around lightly. I'd thought he was incapable of admitting his own vulnerability.

I took a shaky breath, trying to steady myself. "I was wrong too," I admitted quietly, my heart still conflicted. "I had no right to judge you for how you choose to build your life. You have every right to chase your dreams. That doesn't make you selfish. It was my own insecurities, my own shortcomings, that made me disagree with your lifestyle and ambitions."

A silence hung between us, heavy with understanding, but also with the lingering tension of everything unspoken. I gathered my courage, letting my voice break through the quiet.

"I love you too, Nolan."

He stepped forward, and I thought for a moment he was coming in for a kiss, but instead, he hugged me. His arms wrapped around me, pressing me tight to his chest. I closed my eyes, inhaling the familiar scent of him, and wrapped my arms around him in return.

He held my face. "Come back with me," he pleaded. "Come home."

I pulled away slightly. Not in rejection, but in hesitation. "I can't."

His face faltered. "What?"

"I want to be with you," I said, voice thick. "But now it's your turn. I needed to see if I loved you even after stepping away from your world, and now I know I do. But I need to know if you love *this* Ivy. The one who doesn't live in your oceanfront condo. The one who doesn't only socialize with people with six-figure salaries. The one who doesn't just eat at your favorite restaurants. The one who orders takeouts but is also learning to cook. The one who tries, but still ends up surrounded by organized clutter." I glanced around. "An Ivy you've yet to fully know."

Silence.

Then, Nolan sighed, looking around as if seeing my space. Really seeing it, for the first time.

"So show me," he finally said. "Show me your life. I know I will love you either way."

Then, before I could process it, he leaned in, his lips brushing mine, soft, tentative. It wasn't like the fire we'd shared before, but something gentler.

I melted into him.

His hand slid into my hair, fingers threading through the strands, his other arm circling my waist. I kissed him back. Just as tenderly.

When we finally pulled apart, his forehead rested against mine, breath heavy.

"I don't ever want to lose this," he whispered, his eyes closed. "You are my peace, Ivy. The peace that keeps me away from chaos, and I'm ready to do whatever it takes to never let you go."

I didn't respond with words but my hands, clutching the back of his t-shirt and pulling him closer, as if afraid this fragile moment might slip away.

The next kiss was more urgent, tenderness still there, but wrapped in the intensity that was so uniquely Nolan. His hands slid down to my hips, and then, in one sweeping motion, he lifted me into his arms. As he carried me toward the bedroom, his gaze never left me, drinking me in.

"I can't take my eyes off you," he murmured, pressing a kiss to my neck. "I wanted to grab and kiss you the moment I saw you at the door. You are looking so fucking sexy, I can't bear it."

Blood rushed to my cheeks.

He lowered me onto my bed, carefully, never breaking the connection between us. All I could focus on was the heat of his body pressing into mine, the way his lips moved over my skin with a mix of reverence and hunger.

We fumbled with the last barriers of clothing, our breaths quickening, every touch, every kiss growing more urgent. The streetlight from my window cast a soft halo around us as we tangled together, wrapped in emotions and apologies.

This time, when Nolan looked at me in between, I felt more seen than ever.

The distant hum of traffic faded into the background, as we moved together, lost in each other. There was something about making love to him in this house. It made everything more real, like this wasn't just a fleeting summer fling.

And when it was over, as we lay there, bodies still entwined, Nolan pulled me close, his breath warm against my neck. He pressed a soft kiss to my nose, and I smiled, resting my head against his chest, listening to the steady rhythm of his heart.

YOUR HAIR'S LONGER," Nolan murmured, his fingers threading through the strands as we lay tangled together in my bed, skin against skin.

"It's only been a month."

"I know, but still..." His voice was muffled, his lips buried in my hair. "This whole month. It was the worst. I missed you so much."

I smiled, but my heart clenched at the rawness in his tone.

"So much that you had to visit Adrian?" I teased.

Nolan lifted his head from my neck, a ghost of a grin playing on his lips.

It clicked.

"Did Adrian tell you I was getting home right now?" I asked, recalling my chat with Adrian just before Nolan had dropped in, unannounced yet perfectly timed.

Nolan nodded, looking almost guilty, like I'd just caught him mid-theft.

"I had asked him to inform me when you were home next. He messaged when I was running at the beach."

I didn't know whether to laugh or be mad at my boyfriend and best friend conspiring behind my back.

"You do look happier," he said, studying my face.

"I am. Happiest, in fact, now that you're with me too."

Then I remembered. I hadn't told him about Amber.

"Come, I wanna show you something." I wrapped the sheet around myself and grabbed Nolan's wrist.

"Where are we going?" he asked, pulling on his boxer briefs.

"Just the living room. You don't have to put on your clothes." I arched a brow, eying him up.

He shook his head, smiling.

I led him to my nook and made him sit in my chair before climbing onto his lap. He didn't protest, just rested his hands on my waist, watching me with that sharp, assessing gaze that always made me feel like he could see straight through me.

I reached for the painting I'd been working on and placed it in front of us.

"I finally found Amber, my sister," I said, my voice quieter now. "She's back in my life."

I told him everything; how I'd finally tracked down my childhood best friend, how it had felt like piecing together a missing part of myself, how her leaving me had wounded me for life.

Nolan was silent for a long moment, his thumb tracing absent circles on my hip. "I hated not knowing," he finally said. "Finding out about your childhood during a fight, it hurt."

Guilt tightened my chest. "I'm sorry," I whispered. "I didn't know it impacted me so much until I said it out loud that day."

He exhaled, shaking his head slightly before turning his attention to the painting. His gaze softened as he took in the details.

"This is incredible."

His genuine appreciation, the way he studied my work like it mattered. It helped me make the decision I'd been hesitating over for days.

"I've made up my mind," I said. "I don't want to pursue art as a career."

Nolan's brow furrowed, his grip on my waist tightening. "What?"

"The past two days, working on this painting, I realized, I used to paint because it made me happy. But the moment I started thinking about monetizing it, the joy was gone. I don't want that."

He studied me for a long beat, searching my face. "Are you sure?"

"More than anything." I kissed his cheek. "But I do want to write. I want to use my words to help people like you. The ones making a real difference in the world. That's where I'll thrive. I know it."

Saying it out loud felt like setting myself free. A weight I hadn't even realized I was carrying lifted.

"I've been taking an online writing program at SDSU," I added.

Nolan's brows lifted in surprise. "What? That's amazing!"

I smiled. "Two days after I left your apartment, I got an email from Dr. Park."

His expression was blank. "Who?"

I let out an exasperated laugh. "Nolan. Dr. Park. The neuroscientist we met at the symposium? The one researching how creative activities impact mental resilience?"

"Oh. Right." He nodded, but his expression told me he still had no idea who she was.

I rolled my eyes. "She wants me to work with her, writing grants and content for her research and helping with her studies on artists and mental health. Two things I'm familiar with. Being an artist myself and having my own struggles with mental health."

His posture shifted slightly. "Ivy, I don't know her. She was just an acquaintance. I don't know how far along her research is. You should wait until I—"

I pressed my fingers against his lips. "Even better that you don't know her. I only hesitated because I met her through you, and I wasn't sure how you'd feel about it."

Nolan's jaw tensed. He was wired to assess risk, to analyze every variable before diving in.

"Of course, I wouldn't mind," he said, but I could see the gears still turning in his head. "But we should inves—"

"It's set then." I cut him off with a smile. "I'll email her."

His lips parted, but then he exhaled, shaking his head. "You really won't let me win, will you?"

I grinned. "Not when I'm right."

Nolan sighed, then pressed a kiss to my shoulder. "You do that. You're really good at writing. I know you'll make a difference."

A shaky breath left me, relief washing over me like a tide.

"Now, I'll do what I'm good at," he said, grabbing the bedsheet covering my naked body with his teeth and pulling it away from my chest.

CHAPTER 31

At midnight, we lay tangled in the sheets, the warmth of his body pressed against mine. We were in Nolan's bedroom. My second night sleeping there after he'd spent an entire week at my place. We had been switching apartments for night stays. I knew it frustrated Nolan. He thrived on routine and order, but he never complained. He was willing to adjust, as long as it meant keeping me close.

Our days were consumed by work. Nolan immersed in his day job, while I dedicated myself to my new role with Dr. Park. Evenings, however, were ours. We'd first tackle any lingering tasks for his start-up, then slowly ease into quieter moments together. The month apart had pushed Nolan into a kind of unhealthy, robotic mode, working around the clock without pause. But there was a silver lining: his efforts had paid off. Henry Clark was officially on board as an investor, buyers were lining up, and Nolan had refined his pitch decks to perfection. He wanted me to rework them, though. "You're better at making things sound like they need to be heard," he had said, pressing his laptop into my hands.

It was strange at first, working together again after breaking up because of this very project. But thirty minutes in, we had slipped back into our seamless co-worker mode.

I had also introduced Nolan to Cleo and the gang over dinner at a Mexican restaurant in Ocean Beach. Nolan had stood out like a sore thumb. Polished, precise, and annoyingly put-together, while the rest of us reveled in our chaotic artist energy. But he didn't let it phase him. Instead, he charmed everyone, especially Mateo, whose approval he won almost instantly. It was during their conversation that I learned Nolan had been an avid Manga reader as a kid. He could name almost all the characters from Mateo's sketchbook, which warmed my heart incredibly.

Sometimes, I forgot just how magnetic Nolan could be when he set his mind to it.

Cleo had texted me afterward: "He's woven too tightly, Ivy. Feels like a man who'd alphabetize his bookshelf. But damn, the way he looks at you? You're doomed."

On weekends, I took Nolan to new places I had discovered in the city. Last weekend, we had a video call with Elena, promising we'd visit her soon. She was thrilled we were back together.

Now, Nolan's breath was steady beside me as he stared at the television. Something had been stirring behind his eyes for minutes. He finally turned to me, exasperation clear on his face, and let it out.

"So this grumpy diner guy who pined after her for God knows how many years just lets her go because he couldn't handle two things at once?"

I laughed, pausing the TV. He had been watching Gilmore Girls with me every night. "You need to know the characters well, Nolan," I responded. "It's not that simple."

"To me, it is." His hand slid around my waist, pulling me flush against him. His voice was low, edged with certainty. "If I want you, nothing will stop me from being with you. I'd split the world in two before losing you to something as simple as miscommunication."

His words hit me like a slow, lingering touch, sinking deep into my bones. I cupped his face in my hands.

"I love you."

He exhaled, a rare softness flickering in his eyes. "I love you too." Then he glanced at his watch, beaming. "And, happy birthday, Ivy."

I chuckled, butterflies unfurling in my stomach. "It's barely midnight, Nolan."

"Doesn't matter." His fingers ghosted over my cheek, tucking a stray lock of hair behind my ear. "I've planned the whole day tomorrow."

The way he said it, like a promise, like a certainty, sent warmth curling through me.

"You're going to love it." His lips brushed against my forehead, lingering there for just a second too long.

THE NEXT MORNING, I woke earlier than usual, my heart racing with anticipation. I showered, washing my hair, and pulled out the emerald green dress that had been tucked away in my closet for far too long. It fit me perfectly, flowing with a quiet elegance that felt just right for the day ahead. A swipe of eyeliner, mascara, and a peach blush that I also dabbed onto my lips. The waves in my hair cascaded softly over my shoulders. I wanted to feel like myself. Only better.

When I stepped out of the room, Nolan was waiting, standing at the kitchen island with his laptop open. His crisp white button-down was undone at the collar, sleeves rolled up just enough to reveal his forearms. Dark chocolate trousers, perfectly tailored, framed his lean, powerful build.

His gaze locked onto me, intense, unyielding.

"You look..." He trailed off, his jaw tightening slightly, as if restraining himself. But this was Nolan. He never faltered. "...like a precious emerald."

Heat bloomed in my cheeks. I glanced down, smiling. "Thank you. You're looking very—"

Before I could finish my sentence, he reached for me, his fingers curling around my wrist, tugging me effortlessly into his arms. He held me there, firm and unwavering, as if reluctant to share me with the rest of the world just yet. His scent, like the dewy air of a rain forest.

His thumb traced slow circles over my back. "Ten minutes," he murmured against my hair. "Then we leave."

We stayed like that, swaying, breathing each other in, his hold on me possessive yet reverent.

"Thank you for being born," he whispered.

And then, reluctantly, he pulled back, took my hand, and led me out the door to celebrate my birthday.

OUR FIRST STOP WAS a beautiful oceanfront brunch spot. The view stole my breath away—the endless stretch of blue meeting the sky, from hundreds of feet above. We sat outside, the wind licking at my skin. I felt free, weightless.

I ordered French toast with fresh berries and a glass of mimosa, while Nolan, true to form, had a veggie tofu scramble with potatoes, orange juice, and tea.

As we clinked our glasses together, Nolan's gaze lingered on me.

"I can't get over how beautiful you look today," he said. "You make my cold heart beat twice as fast."

That hurt, hearing him speak of himself that way. Nolan wasn't cold. Not really. He just guarded his warmth fiercely.

"Your heart is warmer than the sun, Nolan," I stated, my words final, unwavering.

As we stood together, his hand brushed lightly against my back, his fingers grazing the fabric of my dress. The touch was almost too subtle to catch at first, but then he smoothed my dress down, ensuring it was in place. It wasn't a grand gesture, but the tenderness of it, the way he made me feel cared for, fluttered my heart.

After brunch, Nolan drove us through Chicano Park and City Heights. It surprised me at first. This wasn't his usual scene. But I was delighted nonetheless.

The murals of Chicano Park stood tall, bold colors breathing life into stories of heritage, struggle, and triumph. City Heights revealed art in its rawest form. Vibrant, unapologetic. I rolled down the window, letting the wind tickle my face as I drank it all in. Each mural whispered to me, urging me forward, telling me that art, real, soul-deep art, was always worth the pain and disappointment.

Nolan didn't speak much as we drove through the streets, but his silence wasn't indifferent. He was giving me this moment, letting me take it all in without distraction. That alone touched me more than words ever could. He might not connect with art the way I did, but he knew what it meant to me. That's why it mattered so much that he brought me here. The same man who claimed to have a cold, dead heart was warming mine in ways I never expected.

Our next stop was the Spanish Village Art Center in Balboa Park. Walking through its cobblestone paths felt like stepping into a painter's dream. Brightly colored tiles, small studios with artists lost in their own worlds of creation. I had lived in Irwindeal for two years, less than two hours away from all these wonders, yet I had never ventured out to see them.

Now that Nolan had brought me here, regret settled in my chest. How much had I missed out on because I had been too afraid to step outside my comfort zone?

As we wandered through the village, something shifted inside me. The energy, the creativity in the air, it was infectious. It felt like every artist was daring me to share my art with the world.

Nolan, always composed, always structured, was quiet beside me, absorbing it all in his own way.

"If you're bored, we can go somewhere else," I said, suddenly self-conscious.

His response was immediate. "I'm good." Then, in a rare, unguarded moment, he pulled me into a side hug—bone-crushing, warm, real. "Never in a million years, I'd be bored beside you."

We shared a coffee and split a churro at a small café in the village. I watched him sip his drink, his sharp gaze occasionally drifting toward the artists at work. It was as if he was trying to understand, trying to see the world the way I did.

The effort he was putting in was proof enough. He wasn't Trent. He wasn't any other guy I had known before.

He was Nolan. My Nolan.

As the day wore on, a small knot of anticipation formed in my stomach. Every place we had visited today had been carefully chosen, places that spoke to my soul. The murals, the art center. Nolan had mapped out a day that reflected me, not him.

But now, as we drove deeper into the city, I couldn't help but wonder where he had chosen for dinner. Knowing Nolan, I expected something grand, upscale, and polished.

But when we parked, and I stepped out, I almost gasped.

Mothership.

An interplanetary, space-themed restaurant.

The décor was wild and eclectic, like stepping into a sci-fi dreamscape. Each table was a spaceship cabin with glowing neon lights around them. Strange alien artifacts adorned every surface, and the ceiling was covered in stars, some falling like shooting stars every now and then. It was a bit upscale, sure, but in the quirkiest, most imaginative and creative way possible.

I looked at Nolan for a moment and then laughed out loud.

"This... is the most adorable thing you've ever done for me," I said, still grinning.

Nolan's lips curved into a rare, soft smile, the kind that reached his eyes. "I figured you'd like it. Happy birthday, Ivy." He kissed me on the head, then, without hesitation, on my lips.

And in that moment, surrounded by the whimsical, surreal atmosphere, I realized just how deeply he understood me, even though he didn't express it in words every day. He got me more than anyone in the world.

The hostess led us through the dimly lit interior, past tables that seemed to hover under strange, ethereal lights. We reached our table, tucked into a cozy corner beneath a mural of a distant planet. As we sat down, Nolan's hand found mine across the table. His grip was firm, but his touch was warm, sending little shivers through me.

Once we placed our order—something experimental and exotic for me, and something filling and healthy for Nolan—he turned to me.

"Did you have a good day?" he asked.

I smiled, squeezing his hand. "Nolan, it's the best birthday I've ever had. Honestly."

A flicker of something passed over his face. Relief? Pride? "I'm glad. I wanted it to be perfect for you."

"It was more than perfect. I know how much work you must've put into researching these places."

He opened his mouth to speak, but I shook my head, cutting him off gently. Reaching into my bag, I pulled out a carefully wrapped package and placed it on the table between us. His eyes widened, confusion flashing across his face.

"What's this?" he asked, still holding my hand. "Why are you giving me a gift on your birthday?"

"I have to," I said softly, my heart racing. "You've given me so much, Nolan. Not just today. I wanted to give you something, too. Open it."

Nolan looked at the package, stunned, his brow furrowing slightly. "You didn't have—"

"I know why you took me to all those artistic places today," I said, interrupting him.

His expression shifted, something guarded slipping into his gaze. "Ivy," he said, "I understand why you decided not to pursue art as a career. But it feels like such a Nolan-decision. Calculative. Something I would do. I don't want you to do something because of my influence. Please don't let the dreamer in you die because of me. Don't give up on your art. You are amazing at what you do. Don't stop."

His words were like a balm to an ache I hadn't realized I was still carrying. I swallowed, my throat suddenly tight and said it again. "Nolan, open the gift."

He held my gaze for a long moment before finally reaching for the package. He untied the ribbon with deliberate slowness, as if bracing himself. His large, strong hands carefully peeled away the wrapping, revealing a framed canvas.

He stared at it, his breath catching for a moment.

It was a Van Gogh-inspired portrait of him, bare from head to waist. I had painted everything in swirling blue and yellow shades except for a single, vibrant, throbbing heart in dark red on his chest. The contrast was striking, capturing the intensity, the quiet storm, that Nolan always seemed to carry within him.

I didn't argue much today when he said again that he had a cold, dead heart, because I had the perfect gift to remind him just how much of a giver he was.

He looked at the portrait for a long moment, completely still.

"Ivy..." His voice was low, almost a whisper.

I leaned in, my eyes searching his face. "Do you like it? I had never done this kind of portrait before. I had to watch a tutorial, I'm not going to lie," I chuckled. "But this is what I wanted to do for you."

He cleared his throat, his gaze still locked on the painting. "I—" He trailed off, shaking his head, as if words weren't enough. "It's... it's incredible. But why paint me?"

I smiled, tracing the edge of the frame with my finger. "Because this is how I see you. Not heartless. Not with a cold, dead heart. But as someone strong, steady, always holding so much inside. People, even you, may see yourself in one shade, but I see all colors of you, Nolan."

His Adam's apple bobbed as his gaze lifted from the painting to me. He squeezed my hand tighter.

"Promise you won't give up on art," he said again, his voice rough with emotion.

I nodded. "I won't."

And in that moment, I knew we weren't just talking about art. He was asking me not to give up on myself. And on us.

NOLAN CLICKED THE SEATBELT and turned to me.

"One last stop," he said, his voice smooth and happy.

I groaned, leaning my head back. "I'm so full, Nolan. I don't think I can handle another bite."

He laughed, shaking his head as he started the car. "We're not going to a restaurant. Don't worry."

Relief washed over me, and I smiled, settling back into the seat as we pulled away from the restaurant. The soft hum of Ed Sheeran's Thinking Out Loud filled the car as we left San Diego behind. The conversation between us flowed easily, like a gentle current, with laughter and stolen glances, the world outside slipping away. It felt like we were leaving everything behind. Just the two of us, lost in our little universe.

After over an hour of driving, the city lights were long gone, and all I could see were faint outlines of distant mountains and wide-open desert. The car finally slowed, and Nolan pulled into a small clearing, parking under the most breathtaking sky I'd ever seen.

"We're here," Nolan announced, turning the engine off.

I looked up and gasped. The sky above was an endless sea of stars. So dark and full, it was like the entire universe had spilled out before us. The Milky Way stretched like a hazy ribbon across the night, and shooting stars already streaked the vast expanse. It was beyond perfect.

"Nolan..." I breathed, stunned. "I've never seen anything like this."

"Epsilon Perseids meteor shower today."

"I've never seen a meteor shower before!" I exclaimed, then chuckled at a thought. "Stars, Mothership... are you planning to send me to my home planet?"

Nolan smirked, that signature, arrogant tilt of his lips appearing before he stepped out of the car. He rounded the vehicle, and opened my door.

Without a word, he lifted me by the waist and placed me gently on the trunk of the car.

"Never." He answered. His hands lingered just a second too long on my hips before he sat beside me. "I am your home planet."

A deep warmth spread through me at his words. I reached out, grazing my fingers through his hair before pressing a soft kiss to the side of his neck.

We were completely alone, no one else for miles. Just the dark desert, the endless sky, and us.

Nolan turned toward me, his eyes drunk with want, and before I could even speak, his lips were on mine, hungry, as if he needed me more than air itself. His fingers slid up to my neck, tracing the sensitive skin there before trailing down my shoulders, sending shivers through me.

"Ivy," he murmured, his breath hot against my skin, "I want to rip this dress off you right now."

My heart raced.

But then, in a surprising shift, he paused, his hand still resting lightly on my thigh.

"But..." He exhaled, as if forcing himself to regain control. "I have something for you."

Curiosity flickered through me as he reached into his pocket and pulled out a small gift-wrapped box.

He smiled smugly at my expression. "Relax, Ivy Delaney. I'm not proposing." Then, after a pause, he added with a teasing glint in his eyes, "Yet."

I laughed, nervousness evident on my face.

Then his snigger turned into something serious as he placed the box in my lap.

"Open it."

I carefully unwrapped the gift, my fingers trembling with anticipation. Inside, a small wooden box awaited, intricately carved with swirling patterns that mirrored the night sky. I lifted the lid, revealing a delicate water-drop glass vial nestled in soft velvet. Inside the vial, layers of sand and earth rested in quiet harmony. A piece of weathered string looped through its top, holding a real silver seashell, its sheen catching the light.

I looked at Nolan, confused but intrigued.

"It's from our beach cleanup," he explained, touching the seashell. "Found it over your footprint after you left. I didn't think much of it at the time, but I kept it."

I ran my fingers over the shell, feeling its cool surface. "Nolan... that's so sweet."

He took the vial pendant from my hands, holding it up to the starlight. "The dirt and sand in here is from all the places we've been together. A little from the beach, some from your apartment, some from mine. From the restaurants we've been to. Gliderport. The Spanish Village. And now," he scooped up a handful of the soft desert sand from the ground and let it slip between his fingers, "I'll take some from here, too."

I stared at him, my heart swelling. It wasn't just a gift. It was us, our good moments and our hardships, all woven into something tangible.

Then, he reached into his pocket and pulled out another vial, this one not in pendant form.

"This one's mine," he said, holding it up. Inside, the same blend of sand and earth rested.

Nolan leaned in, pressing his forehead gently against mine. "You mean a lot to me, Ivy. More than I've been able to show." He lifted his vial between us. "This is my way of telling you that no matter where life takes us, I'll always carry a piece of us with me. And I hope you'll do the same."

I couldn't hold back the tears that welled up. I kissed him. Slowly, deeply, pouring everything I felt into that moment.

When I pulled back, my voice was barely a whisper. "I love it, Nolan. This is the most meaningful gift I've ever received. I'll always carry you with me."

Nolan's gaze softened, but the fire in his eyes never dimmed. His hand came up, brushing my hair back, and then his lips captured mine again, slower this time, as if he wanted to make sure I felt everything. His kisses trailed down my neck, lingering, leaving warmth in their wake.

Under that glimmering sky, surrounded by nothing but the vast universe, I knew, this night, this moment, this man, would stay with me forever.

NOLAN CARRIED ME BACK to the car and gave another birthday gift on his lap. Twice!

It couldn't be said for most of my life, but I was supremely, unabashedly happy.

It made me even happier to see how happy Nolan was. His laugh was unrestrained, reaching his eyes, his chest vibrating beneath my cheek as he guffawed at his own joke. My head bobbed with the motion, and I sighed contentedly, inhaling the scent of him that was now layered with the crisp desert air.

I knew it was a cliché, but as I lay in his arms, the driver's seat reclined all the way back, I felt like I could have stayed there forever, just listening to the steady rhythm of his heartbeat.

Nolan's fingers traced lazy circles on my back. Then he said, "You know what's the most efficient thing I've ever achieved?"

I tilted my head up to look at him.

"Finding perfection through you." His voice was confident, utterly sure. "I was right to be relentless about getting the best. How else would I had remained single until I found you. You are my ultimate perfect find, Ivy."

The openness in his voice was beautiful, disarming. But as his words settled, so did something uneasy inside me.

Perfect.

That word. I had once made the mistake of expecting perfectness from Nolan and had regretted it, but now he was making the same mistake.

It shouldn't have bothered me, but it did. Especially coming from him, a man who demanded perfection in everything he touched.

Nolan didn't tolerate flaws. He optimized. Improved. And I was far from flawless.

I was doing much better than before. I am currently being the best version of Ivy, but there were still wounds that needed time and healing. Even after that, I'd never be "perfect". What happens when he realizes that?

I forced a smile, pushing the thought away. Nolan was still beaming, looking up at the sky through the back window, pointing out shooting stars as they streaked across the darkness.

Then, after a long stretch of silence, he spoke again.

"Ivy."

There was a shift in his tone, the kind that made my chest tighten. I moved from his lap to the passenger side, as he straightened his own seat.

"I know this is a sore topic between us, but I need to tell you something." A pause. "Ask, actually."

I nodded, though my mind was still tangled in my own thoughts.

He turned slightly toward me, his expression more serious now. "Next Saturday is my final meeting with Henry Clarke and the group. My one chance at a better life. A life I now dream of for us."

His hand found mine, his thumb brushing over my knuckles.

"You've been more than a copywriter on this project," he continued. "You've helped me shape it. Hell, you helped *me*. So when this deal goes through..." He exhaled, as if steadying himself before saying, "I want you to be a 25% shareholder in my start-up."

My face scrunched up. "Wait. What?"

"That's my final birthday gift to you," he said, his voice firm, decisive. "Twenty-five percent equity. You belong in this. It's why I was urging you to not give up on your art. With this, you can sustain yourself and continue pursuing your passion."

His expression was expectant, hopeful. He was waiting for me to react, to light up with excitement.

But I just stared at him, my stomach twisting.

Twenty-five percent.

Of a company I had nothing to do with, aside from writing content and giving my opinion in the last stretch of its creation?

Was this his way of making sure I never ended up a starving artist? Of putting me on his level so I wouldn't feel like I was living on scraps while he built an empire?

Was this why he'd invited me to UCLA in the first place?

"Ivy?" He leaned in slightly, searching my face.

I inhaled. I wanted to say something, anything, but the words caught in my throat.

"It's on Saturday, the meeting?" I finally asked, my voice quieter than I meant it to be.

"Yes." His shoulders relaxed, as if he'd taken my question as a good sign. "I know it's short notice, but Clarke's schedule is impossible. I was lucky to get a Saturday slot. So..." He gave me a crooked, expectant smile. "You in?"

I hesitated. "I have the Ren Faire that Saturday."

The second it was out of my mouth, I regretted it.

Because the truth was, of course I would have skipped the Faire for Nolan. It wasn't even a question. The Faire was a piece of my world, yes, but this? This was his whole life.

Nolan stared at me, his expression unreadable at first. Then, slowly, his jaw tightened.

"What?" He said it carefully, controlled, but the shock beneath his voice was unmistakable.

I cleared my throat, shifting under his gaze. "I—I promised my guild I'd be there. I've been part of it for years. They need me... I can't just stand them up."

He let out a slow breath, rubbing his temple.

"Let me get this straight. You're telling me you'd rather skip the biggest moment of my career, possibly yours, for a..." His jaw clenched, and I could see him reining himself in. "A fair?"

I bristled at the way he said it. Like it was insignificant.

"I'm sorry, Nolan, but this is important to me, just like your meeting is to you."

Even as I said it, I knew it wasn't true.

The Faire was important to me. But not like this. Nolan's entire life, everything he had worked for, everything he had faced, it depended on that one meeting.

I could see the storm in him, the way his hands gripped the steering wheel, the way the muscles in his forearm flexed, the slight grind of his teeth.

He wanted to fight this. I could feel it. If he did, if he so much as hinted that he was trying to buy me, to mold me into a woman who fit neatly into his world, I was ready to tell him exactly where he could shove his 25% stake.

But instead, Nolan inhaled sharply, then exhaled just as slow.

And when he finally spoke, his voice was low.

"...Okay."

It wasn't an okay. Not really.

"I'm sorry, Nolan," I whispered.

"It's fine," he said, but the way his fingers gripped the steering wheel told me otherwise.

We got dressed in silence. I put my earrings back on, the same ones he'd taken off with his teeth, and he started the car.

The engine rumbled to life.

"It's late," he said, his tone clipped. "We should go."

I turned to him, my stomach sinking. "Are we... okay?"

His hand found my thigh, his grip firm, reassuring. Too reassuring.

"Of course."

But I knew.

We weren't okay. Not at all.

CHAPTER 32

We were standing at the reception of Nolan's building. He was asking the receptionist if there were any packages for him while I stood beside him, silent, still reeling from the words we had exchanged in the car. The silence back home had been worse—heavy, damaging, filled with all the things we didn't say.

Just as we turned toward the elevator, someone big rushed past me, a blur of denim and fury. Before I could react, Nolan was yanked back by his collar.

"You bougie psychopath!"

The voice curdled my blood.

It took me a moment to register the familiar face.

Trent.

His square jaw was clenched, veins bulging at his temple. His blond hair, which he always styled with hairspray, was disheveled, and his blue eyes were wild with rage. He was breathing hard, chest rising and falling like he'd sprinted through hell to get here.

Did he... stalk me? Follow me here? Was he jealous of Nolan?

"Trent?" I breathed, my heart hammering.

At the sound of his name, his grip loosened, his aggression momentarily faltering. His shoulders relaxed slightly as he turned toward me, eyes scanning my face with something that almost looked like disbelief.

"Ivy?"

Nolan barely flinched. With effortless strength, he grabbed Trent's wrists and yanked them away from his collar like he was dusting off lint. Then, without a word, he flicked his gaze toward the receptionist, a silent command. The receptionist immediately picked up the phone to call security. Trent, being Trent, was too caught up in himself to notice.

His gaze snapped back to me, then to Nolan, then back to me.

"You?" He jabbed a finger at me, accusatory and seething. "You're behind this. I didn't know you could be this petty."

I frowned, my confusion mounting. "What the hell are you talking about?"

"Ivy." Nolan's voice was low but firm as he grabbed my hand, gently but insistently pulling me toward the elevator. "Let's go."

Before we could step away, Trent jumped in front of us, blocking our path.

"Like hell I'm letting you leave after what you did to me!" His voice cracked with rage. "You ruined my career, my life!"

I stopped short, my pulse thrumming in my ears. I turned to Nolan, but his face was unreadable. Calm, composed... too composed.

Something was off.

"What is he talking about?" I demanded.

"I'll tell you," Trent sneered, crossing his arms over his chest like he was about to drop the winning hand in a poker game. "Your boyfriend here? He sent an army of bots and trolls to flood all my platforms with hate and threats. Then, oh, this is the best part. He hacked my YouTube account and posted personal videos of me talking shit. Thousands of followers, gone. And not just that." He took a step closer, eyes blazing. "He emailed my new employer. Fed them a bunch of bullshit about me. Now I'm out of a job."

My stomach twisted.

"Nolan?" I turned to him, searching for an explanation.

He finally spoke, peering at Trent, his voice even, almost bored.

"You falsified your employment records. I merely notified that. And if you didn't want to lose followers, you shouldn't have recorded yourself being the misogynistic, sexist, borderline racist that you are. I just showed your fanboys your true face."

Nolan's admission sucked the air out of my lungs.

"You did what?" I mumbled.

Trent let out a sharp, mocking laugh, stepping in my direction. "Typical, naive Ivy. Always out of the loop. Always a joke."

Nolan moved, placing himself between Trent and me.

It wasn't dramatic, it was deliberate, measured. He closed the space between them in a single step, towering over Trent, his shoulders squared, his presence almost threatening.

Trent, always the cocky, loudmouthed showman, stepped back.

Nolan didn't lay a hand on him, didn't need to. His expression alone, cold, merciless, spoke volumes.

"Say that again," Nolan said quietly, daring Trent, his voice like steel wrapped in velvet.

Trent hesitated. His bravado cracked, just for a second.

Before anything else could happen, the security guards arrived, moving swiftly to restrain him.

Trent thrashed as they grabbed his arms, his voice rising as they dragged him toward the exit.

"Ivy, your boyfriend isn't who he says he is! Ask him what he did!" His voice echoed in the lobby as they shoved him out the door. "Ask him!"

Silence.

I turned to Nolan, my pulse still racing.

"What did you do?"

His jaw clenched. "Let's talk at home."

Then, without waiting for my answer, he reached for my hand again and led me toward the elevator.

I followed.

But I wasn't sure if I wanted to.

WE STOOD IN THE COLD on the rooftop terrace of Nolan's building instead of his apartment. I needed neutral ground. Not his space, where he had the upper hand.

The city stretched beneath us, glittering with headlights and neon, the ocean a dark void beyond. Wind lashed against the glass railing of the forty-story-high-rise, tangling my hair, stealing my breath. It was past eleven, and the night was heavy with the scent of incoming rain.

Nolan stood with his hands in his pockets, jaw tight, his usual self-assured presence unreadable in the dim lighting.

"I'm going to tell you this straight," he said, voice sharp as the wind. "After we saw that douche at the restaurant, after you told me everything, I looked him up. And the more I read, the more he pissed me off. Someone that empty, that fraudulent, had the audacity to put you through all that? So I gave him a taste of reality."

His lip curled in disgust.

"I did what he said. I let some bot accounts loose on his platforms, exposed his lies. Hacking his YouTube was a joke. He had videos sitting in drafts, full of disgusting comments about women and black and brown people. I didn't add anything. Just hit publish. His LinkedIn was a mess of fake credentials, so I alerted his employer." Nolan exhaled sharply, shaking his head. "Honestly, it was done in a week after I saw him and then I forgot about it. And I don't regret it. He deserved it, for what he did to you. For what he is." He turned to me, voice a blade. "A waste of space."

I took it all in, wrapping my arms around myself, not just from the cold, but from the weight of what Nolan had done.

"I can grab a jacket from the apartment," he offered, watching me.

"Nolan." My voice was quiet but firm. "I don't doubt that Trent is a terrible person. I was with him for three years. But you can't do this. You can't destroy someone's life just because you think they deserve it."

Nolan's expression darkened. "I didn't destroy his life; he did that all on his own. He had already lost his original job in L.A. before he ever set foot in San Diego. That new employer he said I contacted? He was nothing more than a cheap temp there. You know why he was at that restaurant? Picking up an order. He's a part-time delivery driver now." Nolan let out a sharp scoff. "Pathetic."

Something inside me erupted like a volcano.

"Why is delivering food pathetic? Why is temp work cheap? Because those jobs doesn't come with a six-figure salary? Because they don't put you in two-thousand-dollar suits? Not everyone wants to, or can, do your kind of work. And that doesn't make them any less."

Nolan's hands shot up to my arms, gripping them like he could keep me from slipping away.

"You know that's not what I meant."

"But that's how you see the world, isn't it? Efficiency. Success. Worth measured in numbers and status. Trent can be the absolute worst, but you had no right to do that to him or call his work pathetic."

His eyes flashed. "So now you care about him?"

I clenched my fists. "I'd say the same thing if it were anyone else. What you did was petty, Nolan."

Something in his face shifted. Like my words had pressed on an old wound.

"You don't think I know that, Ivy?" His voice was quieter now, but still razor-sharp. "Every move I make in life is calculated. Thought out. And yet, I did this reckless, destructive thing. Why do you think that is?"

I didn't answer. But I knew.

"It's because of you," he said, softer this time. "I was angry. Protective. I couldn't stand the thought of someone like him putting you through hell." His thumb brushed over my wrist. "You deserve the world, Ivy."

I swallowed hard, the lump in my throat making it hard to breathe. But instead of letting his words settle, I blurted out what had been gnawing at me since he made his offer.

"All of your moves are calculated. Right. Is that why you offered me twenty-five percent of your company?"

His brows knit together. "What?"

"Because you see my work as pathetic as delivering food?"

His hands dropped from my arms, like I had slapped him.

"What the hell are you talking about?"

"You don't see it as a partnership, do you? It's charity. You're handing me something I didn't earn. Is that because you, someone who's rich, super ambitious, and successful, is ashamed that I'm just a struggling copywriter? A *temp worker* at your company? A broke artist with nothing to show for herself?"

Nolan took a step back, his breath coming heavier now, anger flickering beneath the hurt in his eyes. "This is why I did, what I did, to that asshole ex of yours. This is what he had done. Shattered all your self-esteem." Then his tone softened. "You are so much more than that. You know I don't see you that way."

"Then why?" I pressed. "Why do you feel the need to update me?"

"You want to know what's really offensive, Ivy?" He said, quietly. "That you think I'm nothing more than a type. Yeah, I like structure. I like order. I arrange my spices and go to the gym seven days a week, and, yes, I'm ambitious. But I'm so much more than that. And you—" He pointed at me. "You've type-casted yourself, too. You've decided who you are, locked yourself in that box, and you're too damn scared to be anything more."

A sharp gust of wind rushed past, stealing the breath from my lungs. But I held my ground, refusing to meet Nolan's gaze.

Between us, the air howled, the city humming forty floors below.

Nolan exhaled. "I'm tired, Ivy. Of having the same conversation. Of running in circles about how different we are." His voice softened, breaking at the edges. "We have always find our way back. We love each other. So tell me, what are you really afraid of?"

Tears blurred my vision.

"I fear that..." My voice cracked.

"Say it, Ivy."

"I fear that I will never be enough for you." The words fell out of me like stones. "You are perfect. And you expect me to be perfect, too. But I'm not. I'm flawed. I'm chaotic. And one day, you'll wake up and realize you deserve better."

His expression shattered.

"Are you breaking up with me?"

"No," I whispered.

But his face said he didn't believe me. The fear in his eyes, it was heartbreaking.

I threw myself at him, arms around his neck, pressing desperate kisses to the side of his face. "I love you," I choked out. "I'm not breaking up with you."

His breath was ragged. "Then why does it feel like you are?"

I sobbed.

He cupped my face, brushing his thumb over my cheek. "I've never wanted perfect, Ivy. I've only ever wanted you."

But I shook my head. "You don't help get rid of that fear when you do things like this. Offering me a part of your company, fixing my problems, it makes me feel like you're not happy with who I am. That you're trying to shape me into someone else."

I stepped back before he could say something that would pull me back in. "I'll spend the night at my apartment."

His face twisted like I'd stabbed him.

"You just said you are not breaking up with me." His voice was hoarse. "Are you?"

I shook my head violently. "I don't know."

Nolan stood there, his entire body tensed. His face clouded with a shadow. When he finally spoke, his voice was barely above a whisper.

"You fix me and break me in the same breath, Ivy," he repeated my words to me. "I'll never bother you again."

And then he walked away, leaving me alone on the rooftop, the wind stealing the rest of my breath.

CHAPTER 33

NOLAN

It wasn't easy, being rejected again and again by that infuriating, impossible little-nothing woman.

Ivy had turned me inside out, exposing my pain for the world to see, and dragged my pride through the mud.

That night on the terrace, when she broke up with me, I walked away, not giving her another chance to walk away from me. It had been for the best. It had compelled me to fall back on my original plan—dominate the world, one technological revolution at a time. I had everything lined up: success, expansion, power. There was no shortage of distractions.

And yet, the next morning, I woke up to a void so profound it stunned me. None of it, wealth, recognition, the company I was building, meant anything if she wasn't beside me.

How dare she do this to me? Make me this incapable?

After everything, after every battle we had fought together, she still left.

I slammed my laptop shut, shoving back my chair hard enough to scrape against the floor. The office was quiet now. Too quiet. The celebration earlier with Jay and the others felt like it had happened in another lifetime. My company was days away from its inauguration, but none of it meant a damn thing.

I had plans. Big ones. Once the deal was signed and Ivy had accepted her place in the company, I was going to put her name on the apartment's deed and ask her to move in permanently. I was going to tell her I wanted forever. I had imagined the moment so clearly, the life we would build shimmering ahead of me. Marriage, someday. A life filled with her laughter, her fire, her chaos.

And now?

Now, all of it was gone. And my world felt empty.

My jaw clenched as I paced the room, fists tight at my sides. She had no right to throw everything away like it was nothing.

First, she asked me to turn my company into a non-profit. I should have laughed in her face. Should have cut her out of my life entirely for even suggesting it. But instead, I swallowed my pride and went back to her. Because she meant more to me than her silly suggestions.

Next, I offered her a 25% stake in my company. It was proof that she was a part of me. That I wasn't just building a company; I was building something that included her, revolved around her.

And what did she do? She threw it back in my face and called my love "charity." It was as if she had always had a problem with my start-up. If she had known me half as well as I knew her, she would have known Nolan Sterling didn't just give part of his life's work to anyone.

Instead of understanding that, she accused me of wanting to mold her into some perfect version of herself, one she thought she could never live up to. As if she hadn't already been perfect in the only way that mattered. To me.

She mattered so much that I decided to apologize to Trent, a man who deserved a solid punch to the face on his best day, and sacrifice my self-image. But I did. For her.

Adrian had been worse, because that idiot actually loved Ivy. There was a conflict of interest. But I apologized to him too.

Surprisingly, Adrian hadn't gloated. He had just given me a look. The kind that saw straight through me.

"If you love her, stop trying to trick her."

I argued with him, told him I wasn't into tricking people.

But deep down, I knew.

I was tricking her.

I had been updating her, molding her into something I thought would fit into my world. Ivy was right. And in doing so, I had made her feel like she wasn't enough just as she was.

But she was.

I was the one who wasn't. I was the failure, and she proved that when she left me the first time.

I had watched her move out, start over, build a life without me, with her own house, her own friends, her own routines. And I let her. Even though her absence wrecked me. So much that I slipped from my own healthy habits and routines.

I maintained my distance, let her make her own world, let her prove she could stand on her own.

And she did.

She thrived without me. And I crashed without her.

Yup.

The truth was, I needed her more than she needed me. I was the one who was lacking. Not her. It's why I tried to trick her, mold her, update her.

My throat tightened as I dropped into my chair, running a rough hand over my face.

I saw her in my mind, standing on that terrace, looking at me not with anger, not even with sadness, but with exhaustion. Like she had already lost before she even said the words. Like she had given up on me.

Why was I so afraid to just tell her that I was afraid to lose her? Why did I have to be so Nolan and choose the complicated way?

My eyes fell on the photo on my desk. My mother, beaming at me from inside the frame.

I inhaled a lungful of air.

At a very tender age, I had to be the man of the house, taking care of my mom, the bills, the meals. Any sign of weakness could have derailed Mom's health or our future. Everything depended on my calculations and lack of emotional breakdown. So I became that. Wore that armor permanently. First for my mother and then to protect myself.

But that wasn't Ivy's fault.

She deserved unfiltered emotions. Actual, real love, without caution or manipulation.

If I had a chance to win her back, I couldn't do it with business deals or calculated moves. I couldn't pull her back into my world by being the Nolan I had to be.

The only two things that could bring her back were something I had never given to anyone before.

Complete honesty.

Total vulnerability.

And if she let me, if she gave me just one more chance, I would show her exactly what she meant to me.

Starting now.

I pulled out my phone and made two calls. First to Henry Clarke.

Then to Elena.

Because it was time to do this right.

CHAPTER 34

I hadn't spoken to Nolan since that night on the terrace, and now, Saturday loomed over me like a storm cloud.

He'd be walking into his final investors meeting in a sharp suit, armed with the brilliance of his AI project. One designed to detect early signs of mental disorders, inspired by his mother, whom he had lost to dementia. And me? I'd be striding into a Renaissance Faire dressed as a pirate, spinning make-believe tales and clashing tankards with my guild.

I caught the thought before it turned self-deprecating. My life wasn't lesser. Just... different.

Pulling the string on my corset, I tightened the knot until the familiar pressure settled around my torso, gently hugging the curves I had come to love. The deep crimson fabric clung to me like a second skin, its black lace trim brushing against the soft linen of my white blouse. My long, layered skirt billowed as I shifted, burgundy and black cascading around my boots, the same ones I wore to every Ren Faire, scuffed and worn like old friends.

The mirror reflected a woman who looked bold. Untamed. A far cry from the one who had stood in front of Nolan the other night, unraveling, throwing words like daggers.

Yet, I couldn't ignore the memory of how fragile I'd felt dressing up for the Faire in spring, right before I met Nolan. That Ivy would have never accomplished what I had, despite everything.

Today, I felt strong. Unshaken. Like I could brave any storm.

Then I caught a thought again and stopped myself from falling into an old habit, one Nolan had called me out on. Typecasting myself. Old Ivy, new Ivy... That was nonsense. Every version of myself was me and I accepted and respected them all. I had done my best, and I wouldn't gaslight myself anymore.

Smiling at my reflection, I adjusted the belt at my hips, its pouches and potion bottles clinking softly. My tricorn hat lay on the bed. I ran my fingers along its worn brim before settling it on my head.

It was Nolan's most important day. And no matter where we stood, I cared about him.

I grabbed my phone and typed out a message.

"All the best, Nolan. I am very proud of you. Go break a leg. You deserve the world too."

I didn't expect a response. Nolan wasn't one to linger in uncertainty. He either took it or left it. And the fact that he hadn't spoken to me since our fight made it clear. He had made his choice.

I couldn't blame him.

All I wanted was for him to be happy. To succeed. To find someone better than me.

No.

To find someone who *suited him* better than me.

I shoved my phone into my bag and left.

THE DRIVE TO IRWINDEAL stretched through winding roads lined with the burnt orange and deep gold of fall. The air carried the crisp scent of the season, and the coastal fog had long burned away, leaving behind a sky so blue it almost felt unreal.

But my mind kept circling back.

To everything that had happened since the last Faire.

Moving out of Trent's. Moving in with a stranger, who became my nemesis, then something else.

Working with him. Fighting with him. Loving him. Breaking up with him.

Why did I keep doing that?

A biker roared past my car, the sudden rush of sound jolting me. I steadied my grip on the wheel and pressed the gas.

I did what I had to do to protect myself.

Everyone who was supposed to love me, to stay, had left.

Dad. Mom. Amber.

Trent, too, in his own way. He had emotionally abandoned me long before I walked out of that apartment.

And now it was Nolan's turn.

Of course he didn't accept me the way I was. And when he realized I couldn't be molded into something more up to his standards, he would have left too.

So I did his job for him.

My fingers tightened on the wheel.

But this time, life didn't feel as bleak as it had the last time I wore these clothes.

I had a life now. An apartment of my own, friends I could count on, and work I was proud of. Colors had returned to my world, and so had my sister. Even better, I had an incredibly cute niece I'd be meeting next month.

Nolan would leave a void. But I would keep moving forward.

The rolling hills of Irwindeal came into view, and I forced the thoughts away.

Today, I had a role to play. My guild counted on me to be present, to transport patrons into another world, a world where none of this mess mattered.

That's why I loved the Ren Faire. It was an escape. A place where I could be someone else.

I pulled into the dirt parking lot, inhaled deeply, and smiled.

For today, I was a pirate.

THE FAIRE'S GATES SWUNG open, and just like that, I was in another life.

The scent of woodsmoke and roasting meat wrapped around me. Laughter echoed through the air and the sound of a lute wove through the chaos of knights, fair maidens, and thieves.

"Ahoy, Ivy!"

Cleo's voice rang out as she waved a cutlass my way, grinning like a pirate ready for trouble. She was clad in a patchwork coat, a ridiculous feather sticking out of her wide-brimmed hat.

I grinned, tipping my hat. "Ahoy, me hearty."

The crew was already in full swing, draping tattered banners, setting up props, and arranging our little corner of controlled chaos. Tankards of coffee were passed around like trade secrets, the warmth seeping into my throat as I took a sip.

I let myself get lost in it. The easy camaraderie. The familiar banter. The illusion of simplicity.

Soon, the Faire grounds were alive with people—families, couples, and groups of friends—wandering in with wide eyes, some in elaborate garb, taking in the sights and sounds. Excitement bubbled around us as visitors admired our costumes and asked about the cannon I was adjusting.

I leaned over the large prop, checking its placement, when I heard a familiar voice behind me. Deep. Commanding. But filled with emotions.

"Ivy."

My breath caught. My hands froze on the cold metal as I turned. Nolan.

But not the Nolan I knew.

Gone was the polished perfectionist in tailored suits and shiny shoes. This Nolan, standing before me in the dirt of the Faire, was untamed, like he had stepped out of a forgotten century and into my world. His white linen shirt was loose, sleeves rolled up to reveal the tan of his forearms. A dark, weathered vest cinched his frame, worn but fitted, as if it had seen battles at sea. A navy-blue coat, slightly tattered at the edges, hung open, shifting with his movements. His trousers, a rugged blend of breeches and modern pants, were tucked into sturdy, well-worn boots. A belt crossed his waist, a scabbard at his hip, a dagger's hilt just visible.

It was the details that wrecked me. The leather bracelets on his wrist, frayed at the edges. The simple silver pendant at his throat, catching the sunlight as he moved. His dark hair, usually sleeked back, now messy, like he had run frustrated hands through it one too many times. And the stubble on his jaw, a shadow of roughness that sent heat spiraling through me.

If the usual Nolan was hot, this Nolan was burning me alive.

His gaze locked onto mine, sharp but softened.

"Nolan?" I whispered, as if speaking his name would make him real.

A slow smirk curved his lips.

He reached into the ragged pouch at his belt and pulled something out, stepping closer. My guild, Cleo included, watched us with the intensity of an audience at a 19th-century live theater show, but I barely noticed.

He opened his palm. Dirt.

I blinked. "What's that?"

"Dirt from this ground. For your pendant. And my vial," he replied, his voice steady and sure. "This place, this part of your life, will now be as much a part of me, of us, as it is of you."

My fingers instinctively brushed my chest, reaching for the hidden vial pendant I wore around my neck.

"Nolan…"

He closed the space between us, placing a finger against my lips.

"Shut up and listen to me now," he murmured, before pulling his hand away. "I never expected you to be objectively perfect. When I said you were perfect, I meant you were perfect for me. You fill the gaps I have. You make me better. But you were right about one thing." His jaw tensed before he exhaled. "I had a motive when I offered you that stake in my company. It wasn't charity. It was selfishness. In my own twisted way, I was updating you to make you a little bit more like me. So you wouldn't see how uninteresting I am. So you wouldn't leave."

I sucked in a breath, but he continued.

"It's not you who should be afraid of being undeserving. It was me. I was always terrified that one day, you'd find me too mechanical, too boring, too corporate-y."

"That's absurd, Nolan."

"Is it?" He gestured around us. "Look at your world. Only someone confident enough, someone authentic and unrestrained, could belong here. I could never be, not when I met you. It was my insecurity, my envy, that made me lash out when we first met here."

I remembered Elena saying the exact same thing during our first conversation at the apartment.

"And ever since, I've been afraid I'd never fit in with you," Nolan added. "That you'd sit with your friends one day and they'd joke about how I dull your spirit, and you'd shrug it off, but deep down, you'd know they were right."

It broke my heart, knowing how scared he'd been this whole time.

"But I was wrong," he continued. "We can be as different as the earth and sky and still be into each other." A humorless chuckle escaped him. "We even had the same fears. Isn't that funny?" he added. "I have apologized to Trent, by the way. Also did some damage control for him."

I swallowed hard, my heart hammering. "That's... a lot to reflect and work on in such a short time."

He let out a dry laugh. "You know me. I don't quit until I get it. Literally *and* figuratively."

When I didn't respond, he continued.

"I've been cooped up in my room for days, thinking about this. Well, except yesterday, when Elena and I were running around San Diego, hunting for this damn garb." He glanced at himself, amused but exhausted. "I'm sorry, Ivy. For making you sign that contract, for fighting with you, for offering you that stake. For—"

It hit me then.

"Nolan, your meeting?"

His lips parted slightly, but instead of answering, he stepped closer. "Can we go somewhere else? Just for a little while. I don't want to steal you from the Faire, but everyone is staring."

I chuckled softly, my eyes still wet.

This man. His words. His efforts. His concern, even now.

I would walk through fire with him.

"Nolan," I said, stepping into him. "I volunteer to be stolen for life."

My words brought a sweet smile on his tired face.

"It was my fault too," I added. "I am sorry I let my own issues wreck what we had. I shouldn't—"

"Ssshhhh..." he interrupted me. "We've had enough apologies for one day. Let's not waste the time we now have."

I stood on my tiptoes and kissed him. Hard, pouring everything into it.

The Faire erupted around us.

Tankards clashed together, voices rang out in a chorus of Huzzah!, and somewhere, Cleo rang a heavy ship's bell.

But all I felt was Nolan, his hands gripping my waist, his mouth claiming mine like he had been waiting forever.

Like we had finally found our treasure.

WE DROVE TO THE NEAREST beach, the distant hum of the Faire fading into the roar of the ocean. The sun hung low, streaking the sky with magical light.

"Awesome garb," I told Nolan as we stepped out of the car. "Well thought out and researched."

Nolan adjusted the cuff of his dark coat, the silver buttons catching the light. "Thank you. I didn't want to go for the Jack Sparrow pirate. It was done too many times. I wanted it to be real."

I patted his bicep. "Good job."

We strolled toward the shore, the cool breeze tugging at my skirts. Nolan lowered himself onto the sand first, then reached for my hand, guiding me down beside him.

For a moment, I imagined how we must have looked to the scattered beachgoers around us. Two pirates, lovers perhaps, washed ashore from another time, searching for a new world, one kinder than the one we left behind.

"Ivy," he said, his voice thick with meaning, "I canceled my meeting."

My heart stuttered. "What? Why?"

"I don't want to sell this technology to the highest bidder." His fingers laced through mine, warm and vulnerable. "I want to run this company as a non-profit myself. I can hire doctors, coders, more staff. Reach out and get government grants. I can do this, Ivy. I've never been more confident about anything."

I took in a deep breath. The last, teensy bit of doubt I had about Nolan, his motives, his vision, melted away. He wasn't just brilliant;

he had integrity. He had a heart that most people never got to see, but I did.

"This is amazing! Of course, you can do it. You are Nolan Sterling." I smiled, squeezing his hand. "I am so proud of you."

His jaw tightened slightly, like he was absorbing my words, letting them settle into a place he rarely let people touch. Then he exhaled. "And please don't take this the wrong way," he said carefully, shifting to face me, "but I still want you to join me. Not because of a fear or a motive, but because I really need you. I need your Ivy touch." His gaze held mine. "With a non-profit, I'd need someone like you who will remind me why we are doing this. That is, only if you want to."

He hesitated for half a second. "I am..."

"I'd love to!"

Nolan stilled. "Really?"

"Really."

A sharp sigh left him before he moved. His hand cupped the back of my head as he pulled me to him, his lips crashing into mine. Then he kissed me all around my face, lingering a bit longer on my nose.

When he pulled away, his breath was warm against my skin, his thumb grazing my cheek. "Okay," he murmured, his voice a little rough. "Now let's go back to the Faire. I don't want to keep you."

I arched a brow. "You don't want to keep me?"

His smirk was pure Nolan. Cocky, knowing. "I do. Forever. But this is your day. So let's go."

"What about you?"

"After I drop you at the Faire, I'll be hanging with Elena for a bit," he said, leaning back on his elbows, looking completely at ease, as if he hadn't just wrecked my heart with his confessions. "And then this pirate will come to pick up his booty. Both kind." He winked.

A loud laugh erupted out of me, drowning the sound of the waves.

I traced a finger along the worn edge of his coat, admiring his rugged look again. "You really went all out."

Nolan maintained his smile, but his voice grew serious. "I had to. I had to prove to myself that I could meet you in your world, without trying to change you."

I kissed him again, just a quick brush of my lips against his, but his grin widened like he had won something.

"You're amazing," I whispered. "I don't want you to change either."

"I know," he murmured against my lips.

I rolled my eyes but couldn't help laughing as I stood up and brushed off my skirt. "Let's go."

Nolan didn't move at first. He just watched me, his gaze steady and intent, like he was memorizing the moment. Then, with quiet certainty, he scooped up a handful of sand and said,

"Let's."

EPILOGUE

The soft hum of conversation and the glow of string lights made our little backyard feel like something out of a dream. It had been a long time since I stood in a space like this, one that felt like home, like something I had built with my own hands. But here we were, Nolan and I, in a quaint house outside downtown, hosting a party to celebrate everything we had worked for in the past year.

Laughter echoed from the patio where Jay stood, his arm slung around his girlfriend, a bubbly brunette named Olivia who had the kind of effortless charm that made her instantly fit in. "So, when's the next big celebration?" she teased, nudging Nolan. "Because clearly, you two are unstoppable."

Nolan, standing beside me with a glass of whiskey in hand, gave a humble smile. "One thing at a time." His tone was smooth, but his fingers brushed against mine, lingering just a little too long.

I caught Elena watching us from across the yard. She raised a brow in amusement, swirling her wine before taking a slow sip. There was something different about her, lighter, freer, but still carrying a quiet weight, like someone slowly untangling knots one by one. She wasn't all the way through it yet, but she was there, in her hometown, living on her own terms.

"You nervous?" she asked, nodding toward the makeshift art display we had set up along the fence, where Cleo's and my paintings rested on wooden easels. The local studio had requested them for an upcoming exhibit, and while I was proud, that old whisper of doubt still curled in my chest.

"A little," I admitted, glancing at the bold strokes of color on my latest piece. "But I like this nervousness. It's the good kind."

Elena clicked her tongue. "And here I thought the Pirate Girl would say something poetic and brooding."

"Give me a second. I'm warming up."

She laughed, but before she could respond, Cleo approached us with a plate of food in her hand, having left her group—Mateo, Evan, Mira, and Liam—who were sharing funny anecdotes.

"Where's Adrian?" Cleo asked, scanning the crowd without looking at me, as if she expected him to be here.

Adrian was here celebrating with us, as happy and accepting of our relationship as ever. He and Nolan even had inside jokes now, and it was his small house model that inspired the home Nolan and I now shared.

He, however, was on his way to pick Amber and Oliver from the airport.

"You just missed him," I said to Cleo, watching her expression shift to something unreadable. She shrugged and took a bite of her food, as if it hadn't mattered at all.

The party stretched into the night, voices blending with the music from my playlist, Colors and Codes, a mix of my and Nolan's favorite songs.

Nolan was in his element, confident, assured, discussing the latest updates on his non-profit. He had secured an NIH grant, brought in a team of doctors, and expanded outreach programs. I'd never seen him so content and relaxed in his life.

And I was part of it.

It wasn't just his dream anymore. It was ours.

I was about to head inside to grab another drink when Nolan's voice cut through the night. "Ivy."

I turned, the hem of my light lemon dress swirling with me. For a moment, the party blurred around me. He stood bathed in the soft glow of the lights, watching me with an expression I couldn't quite place. Something deep, something secretive.

He took a step forward, then another, until he was close enough that I could feel the warmth of him. Without a word, he reached into his pocket and pulled out a small box.

The world stilled.

I stared at it, my breath catching in my throat.

"Relax, Ivy Delaney." He gave a goofy, teasing smile. "This time, I actually mean it."

My heart pounded.

"You know me, Ivy" he added, voice steady. "I don't do things unless I'm sure."

"And?"

His lips quirked, just slightly. "And I've never been more sure of anything in my life. You are my home planet, Ivy."

He flipped the box open, revealing a vintage, renaissance era ruby ring. It was insane how truly he knew my taste. Inside the ring, there was an engraving. A single word.

'Let's.'

A breath of laughter escaped me, unsteady, full of emotion.

Nolan smirked. "Well?"

I swallowed past the lump in my throat, looking up at him. The man who had once been my nemesis, my frustration, my impossible opposite, my chaos, now standing here, offering me forever with the same certainty he had about everything else in his life.

I didn't need to think.

I reached for his collar, pulling him down into a kiss that said everything words couldn't.

And when I finally pulled away, I whispered against his lips, "Let's."

ABOUT THE AUTHOR

LUNA VERNE is a dreamweaver who once shied away from romance, both in her life and in the pages of literature, because of its overwhelming power. Yet, when she gently cracked the walls around her, love slipped through the cracks, igniting a fire of inspiration that compelled her to weave tales of passion and connection. Now, clad in pajamas all day in her sun-kissed haven in San Diego, she crafts a bit of nerdy contemporary romances, inviting readers to journey with her into the enchanting world of vulnerable and heartfelt love stories.

WEBSITE: http://lunaverne.wordpress.com
TIKTOK: @luna.verne
(Sign up on the website for bonus content ☺)